Praise for the national bestselling
Book Collector Mysteries

The Wolfe Widow

"The books continue to delight with sharp humor, quick-witted characters, a tough but vulnerable heroine, and celebration of the classic mystery genre."   —*Kings River Life Magazine*

"Victoria Abbott once again thrills readers with humor, plenty of sleuthing and some very eccentric characters. A great addition to the series!"   —*Debbie's Book Bag*

"If you haven't discovered this series yet and love cozy mysteries with a book theme, I highly encourage you to do so. I haven't read a book in this series yet that wasn't fun and a thrill ride."   —*Girl Lost in a Book*

"I was delighted by the surprising and satisfying conclusion. Readers who read the prior two books in the series won't be disappointed, and fans of Erika Chase, Ellery Adams, or Rex Stout will want to put *The Wolfe Widow* on this fall's reading list."   —*Smitten by Books*

The Sayers Swindle

"*The Sayers Swindle* has everything you're looking for in a fantastic mystery—there was a great mystery that kept me guessing. Victoria Abbott swung a great twist that I never saw coming . . . I can't wait to see what golden-age author will be featured in the next novel."   —*Cozy Mystery Book Reviews*

continued . . .

"If you are a book lover of any kind, you will love this series. *The Sayers Swindle* is well thought-out and executed. The authors don't leave anything to chance, they provide a great whodunit, and some really good humor. This is one you definitely want to pick up."   —*Debbie's Book Bag*

"Another fun romp . . . Filled with black humor in the midst of tragedy."   —*Lesa's Book Critiques*

The Christie Curse

"Deftly plotted, with amusing one-liners, murder and a dash of mayhem. There's a cast of characters who'd be welcome on any Christie set."   —*Toronto Star*

"With a full inventory of suspects, a courageous heroine and a tribute to a famous writer of whodunits, *The Christie Curse* will tempt her legion of devotees. Even mystery lovers who have never read Christie—if any exist—will find a pleasing puzzle in Abbott's opener."   —*Richmond Times-Dispatch*

"The mystery was first class, the plotting flawless."
    —*Cozy Mystery Book Reviews*

Berkley Prime Crime titles by Victoria Abbott

THE CHRISTIE CURSE
THE SAYERS SWINDLE
THE WOLFE WIDOW
THE MARSH MADNESS

THE
MARSH
MADNESS

VICTORIA ABBOTT

BERKLEY PRIME CRIME, NEW YORK

BERKLEY
PRIME
CRIME

An imprint of Penguin Random House LLC
375 Hudson Street, New York, New York 10014

THE MARSH MADNESS

A Berkley Prime Crime Book / published by arrangement with the author

ISBN: 978-0-425-28034-8

PUBLISHING HISTORY
Berkley Prime Crime mass-market edition / September 2015

PRINTED IN THE UNITED STATES OF AMERICA

10 9 8 7 6 5 4 3 2 1

Cover illustration by Tony Mauro.
Cover design by Rita Frangie.

Penguin
Random
House

This book is dedicated to Linda Toledi Arno, whose big heart and many years of magical meals will live on in our memories.

ACKNOWLEDGMENTS

We are particularly indebted to Dame Ngaio Marsh for her body of work. Her wit and insights, descriptions, settings and theatricality continue to entertain. You still need good luck figuring out "who-dunnit."

We must thank Nancy Reid—a generous good friend, and committed mystery reader—for the gift of twenty-nine of the thirty-two Ngaio Marsh novels, allowing for many pleasant afternoons of relaxed reading—oops, we mean research—in the construction of *The Marsh Madness*.

We'd also like to give a nod to Jeff and Donna Coopman of The Usual Suspects and Peter Sellers of Sellers and Newel for help, information, hard-to-find volumes and a few laughs on the way.

Thanks to Larraine Gorman for her generous support of Ottawa Therapy Dogs. We're glad Larraine has joined Jordan's friends here between the covers. She makes a great addition to the Harrison Falls community.

Along the way, we learned a lot about the buzz and excitement of community theater from our good friend Judy Beltzner and the Isle in the River Theatre Company.

ACKNOWLEDGMENTS

No doubt if you sat down with any of our family members, they might have a tale of woe about the ups and downs of having mystery writers in the fold, what with plot issues, deadlines and all that goes with the territory. Naturally, we're grateful, especially to Giulio, who keeps the boat afloat no matter how stormy the sea. Irma Toledi Maffini and Linda Toledi Arno have laid the groundwork for Signora Panetone with their life-long wizardry in the kitchen. Peachy the Pug provides much entertainment as our real-life Walter.

We appreciate the fellowship of our friends at the Cozy Chicks Blog and Mystery Lovers Kitchen. Please join us regularly at www.cozychicksblog.com and www.mysteryloverskitchen.com to stay in touch with us in between books.

We owe special thanks to our wonderful friend and colleague Linda Wiken, aka Erika Chase, for her valuable and skilled insights into our manuscript and to John Merchant for turning his eagle eye to the pages, yet again.

Dustin Ryan deserves appreciation for his support, general cheerleading and willingness to order pizza in times of need. Thanks also to the delightful ladies of Mansfield's Shoes, Kyra, Marion, Linda, Charley and the incomparable Miss Vicky. You put us in good shoes and even better moods.

We'd be sunk without the support of our long-suffering and big-hearted editor Tom Colgan and the ever-cheerful Amanda Ng. We know we're lucky. We also know that our agent, Kim Lionetti, of BookEnds, always has our backs. We appreciate everything you do, Kim.

To our many readers: Thanks so much for getting in touch, for reading and enjoying the books, for getting the jokes, for spreading the word and even for asking why the next one won't be for a year. We're on the case!

CAST OF CHARACTERS

Jordan Kelly Bingham—assistant to wealthy book collector Vera Van Alst

Vera Van Alst—a reclusive bibliophile and collector

Chadwick Kauffman—heir to the Kauffman fortune and owner of the Country Club and Spa

Lisa Troy—his personal assistant

Lisa Hatton—office administrator at the Country Club and Spa

Miranda Schneider—receptionist at the Country Club and Spa

Thomas—a butler

Tyler "Smiley" Dekker—police officer, Harrison Falls Police

Sammy Vincovic—pricey but effective barracuda lawyer

Kevin Kelly (Uncle Kev)—handyman and groundskeeper at Van Alst House, among other things

Signora Fiammetta Panetone—cook and housekeeper at Van Alst House

Michael Kelly (Uncle Mick)—independent "entrepreneur"

Lucky Kelly (Uncle Lucky)—another independent "entrepreneur"

Cherie—Uncle Kev's special friend

Karen Smith—Jordan's friend and Uncle Lucky's new wife

Lance DeWitt—Harrison Falls's hottest reference librarian and Jordan's friend

Tiffany (Tiff) Tibeault—Jordan's usually absent best friend

Poppy Lockwood-Jones—artist friend of Lance's

Shelby Church—an actress

Detective Drea Castellano—new lead detective in Harrison Falls

Detective Rob Stoddard—her partner

Larraine Gorman—former actress, now teacher

Doug Gorman—her husband

Lucas Warden—an actor

Braydon—young employee at the Country Club and Spa

Mysterious dark-haired man

Various actors hamming it up

CHAPTER ONE

BE CAREFUL WHAT you wish for, as they say. Whoever "they" are, they've also been known to mutter that
the heart wants what it wants. I was desperate to visit Summerlea. That's what my heart wanted.

Wanted it bad.

When the first call came, I wondered if it was a mistake.
We had an invitation to a very special luncheon at Summerlea, a famous and usually inaccessible grand summer estate
that was nothing if not worthy of daydreams. This chance to
peek inside a robber baron's extravagant country home would
be a treat. And it would be a first for me aside from seeing
it in photo spreads in *Elle Decor* and *Vanity Fair*. I was
revved up about the invitation to the traditional getaway of
the Kauffman family. The family was down to the last member: Chadwick Kauffman, heir to whatever was left. Even if
the Kauffman name didn't conjure up what it once had, it
still screamed A-list in our part of the world. I was way
beyond intrigued, imagining the treasures, art, books and
antiquities. I hoped I'd manage to snoop around.

Full disclosure: The invitation was to Vera Van Alst, the curmudgeonly book collector and allegedly wealthy recluse I work for. I had merely handled the details with Chadwick Kauffman's staff.

Although Vera wouldn't admit this, an invitation of any sort was very good news. She continued to be the most hated woman in Harrison Falls, New York, and surrounding communities, although you'd think that people would be getting over that now. It definitely limited our collective social life.

Now Vera was invited to inspect and purchase a collection of Ngaio Marsh very fine first editions. I'd be there to assist her, while perusing and drooling over yet unknown items. I launched into my Web research immediately after the first call and learned that Summerlea was a massive and rambling building with groomed lawns that sloped down to a sparkling lake. This would be the kind of country home full of family retainers—and monograms on the ornate silverware. Would the Kennedys stop by? Would we have champagne? Probably not at noon. I wasn't really clear on the rules for that. Did I need a petticoat? I almost hoped so.

The deckle-edged invitation came in the third week of March. We were summoned for the beginning of April, the first slot that Chadwick Kauffman would have time for us. So there'd be no strawberries in the gardens and no stroll on manicured lawns through the leafy grounds. Not here in upstate New York anyway.

The big question: What to wear?

I'd popped over to Betty's Boutique, my favorite funky vintage shop in Harrison Falls, and scored a raspberry wool day dress, a perfectly preserved prize from nineteen sixty-three. That was one good reason to enjoy spring's slow arrival. Jackie O would have worn this little number with white gloves. I might not be able to resist wearing a pair. There weren't a lot of opportunities to sport those.

Summerlea was getting closer. I pictured the new spring grass, peppered with early blooming crocus.

Only two more sleeps to go.

I was interrupted in my happy thoughts by Vera, who rolled her wheelchair into our own grand foyer looking even grumpier than usual. Good Cat and Bad Cat (not their real names), her identical Siamese, sidled along beside her. I kept clear of Bad Cat, although it was always hard to know which one that was.

"Are you excited?" I chirped.

Vera had a voice like crunching gravel. "Miss Bingham, I expect that by now you would be aware that I do not get excited. And is it really necessary for you to sound quite so much like a budgie?"

Crunch. Crunch. Crunch.

I had been fully aware that Vera didn't get excited, but it had slipped my mind that no one else was supposed to either. I made a mental note never to chirp again. I lowered my voice a half octave. I also moved away from Bad Cat's outstretched claws and said, "But Summerlea is historic. It is magnificent. It's—"

She kept rolling, barreling down the endless corridors of Van Alst House, past the ballroom and the portrait gallery festooned with ugly oils of her relatives. Have I mentioned that all the Van Alsts seemed to have suffered from serious constipation and bad teeth? I always try to avert my eyes, as the overflow relatives are displayed all along that hallway. You can't miss them no matter how hard you try.

Vera muttered, "I have my own magnificent historic home, Miss Bingham. I do not have to seek others like an overeager tourist."

Maybe I won't wear the gloves, I decided, breaking into a canter to keep pace with her.

"Of course, Van Alst House is wonderful, Vera. I love it here. But you've been cooped up for months, if you don't count the Thanksgiving event and Uncle Lucky's wedding and . . ."

I decided not to mention the various murders that had

disrupted Vera's stay-at-home policy. "And Summerlea has quite a history too. They say that FDR and—"

The wheelchair stopped abruptly. "My grandfather entertained governors and visiting royalty here in Van Alst House. We have our own history. I don't need to leave here to feel part of that." Vera pivoted abruptly and headed into the study, one of my favorite rooms. I hustled after her.

True enough. Van Alst House had a rich past. But Summerlea had welcomed presidents and world leaders, society's finest and Hollywood legends. Where Van Alst House had been built from the profits of a shoe factory, Summerlea was made of steel money and rail money and manufacturing money. The Kauffman heritage was more like a collaboration of robber barons on steroids. Never mind that the Kauffman family had dwindled and shrunk in influence over the years. Summerlea remained.

I knew I was being ridiculous. But I loved the whole idea. Was it a Cinderella thing? I was, after all, the motherless girl who grew up in the rooms over her uncle's "antique" shop. I would have been better adding the cash for that raspberry wool dress to the savings that would one day fund my return to grad school. Never mind. Summerlea would be so much fun. And really, it wasn't like anything could go wrong.

Speaking of wrong, Vera had continued sputtering.

I said, "Of course you don't need to leave here. I couldn't agree more. However, you have been chosen and invited to another wonderful place and given first dibs at one of the finest Ngaio Marsh collections in the world. At a very reasonable price, may I add. I've done my homework on this one. This is a very rare collection."

We never admit out loud that money is a factor for Vera, but it is. Anyone with a sharp eye would notice that there is less sterling silver every year and that several key antiques are now making someone else happy. Sometimes I worried that the Aubusson rugs would vanish next.

Vera couldn't ever simply agree. It's not in her. "Humph. We need to knock back that dollar figure a bit. And cash only? Who ever heard of that? Maybe this Chadwick has squandered what's left of the family fortune."

I couldn't let Vera bring me down. "I got the impression the price was firm. Anyway, you love Ngaio Marsh. You've been trying to upgrade your Marsh collection as long as I've been here. You know how hard they are to find, especially those early ones."

"Be that as it may, what kind of man only collects one author?"

I shrugged. What did I know about the late Mr. Kauffman and his collecting habits? "I don't know why he collected only the one author. It's working for us though. We'll be lucky to get these books. All thirty-two in fine condition. It could take years to locate the same quality any other way. Count your blessings. If they'd been part of a bigger collection, the whole shebang might have been sold off. It's to our advantage that this was it."

Vera sneered. "Still can't imagine it."

"When I spoke to Lisa Troy, his assistant, she mentioned that Mr. Kauffman liked Ngaio Marsh because of her New Zealand connection. Apparently, he had a thing for the place."

"Then the man's a fool. Marsh is a giant of the Golden Age, but it's not because of New Zealand, even if she did hail from there. I think she's the best of the British writers of that era."

"Well," I said, calmly. "This should all make an interesting discussion when we have our luncheon at Summerlea."

Vera snorted. "I've met him more than once. Kauffman's no prize, if you ask me. Anyway, I've heard that the old coot is practically gaga. Collecting only one author is probably a symptom."

"Um, the old coot," I said as tactfully as I could, "is dead."

"Magnus Kauffman is dead?"

"As a doornail, apparently. That's why the invitation came from *Chadwick* Kauffman. He's the heir and the person we'll be meeting."

"So old Kauffman's dead, is he? When did this happen?"

"Late this past year, Miss Troy, the assistant, told me. In the fall."

She assumed her scowliest expression. "I thought I would have heard something."

For sure Magnus Kauffman's death would have made news, certainly the *New York Times*, but we'd been otherwise occupied.

"If you remember, we had a lot on our mind around Thanksgiving."

Vera's brow darkened. We never speak of the events of last November. I'll say for the record that the weeks before Thanksgiving brought bad times to Van Alst House and a close call for Vera and her entire collection, as well as for my job and the life we all love. But that, as they say, is a story for another day.

I kept going. "Mr. Kauffman left everything to his nephew, Chadwick, his only close relative."

"Really? You mean all those fine old families intermarrying are now reduced to one impoverished relative?"

"Um, hardly impoverished. I checked him out. He has a number of businesses, including the Country Club and Spa, an exclusive establishment over in Grandville. I'm pretty sure I've even seen coverage of his charity events in the *New York Times* Sunday Styles."

"I must have missed that, Miss Bingham." Vera glowered.

Silly of me. As if Vera—who took the *New York Times* every day for the crossword—would ever read the Sunday Styles section. What was I thinking?

I didn't try to explain that it had been a charity event at the Country Club that had been covered, with women in gorgeous gowns and men in formal wear. "The point is that

Chadwick has made a name for himself and he took an interest in the, um, elder Mr. Kauffman."

"I bet he did. I guess it paid off for him, then. But why is he selling off the Marshes?"

"Not sure. His interests lie elsewhere, as I said. Maybe he wants the collection to go to a good home, say, for instance, here."

"Maybe there's not much left of the estate and he's starting to sell it off. Anyway, not sure I want to meet him at all," she sniffed. "He sounds like a drip. What kind of man finds himself in the Styles section? I am sure he doesn't have any interest in us."

Oh no. It would be just like Vera to turn her back on this wonderful opportunity and cancel the lunch. After all, she couldn't care less about other people's historic houses, and she'd only wear one of her hideous and bedraggled beige sweaters to the event, possibly a cardigan that had been donated to the Goodwill by a retiring goat herder. I clung to my dream of wearing my raspberry dress to Summerlea.

"Chadwick Kauffman *is* interested in you, Vera—"

I hate it when she harrumphs. It's a sound that haunts my nightmares.

The only selling point was getting our mitts on the books. I stuck to that. "He specifically mentioned that *you* were chosen to have first dibs on his uncle's world-class collection."

I didn't mention that Vera's own collection of Marsh novels was barely adequate. She had twenty-three of the books— nice enough, mostly paperback reprints in decent but not pristine condition. If this new collection was as described— fine first editions, practically untouched—she would be over the moon when she took possession of it. Not that she'd admit that. I knew I'd be finding buyers for the books she had, and if I was patient and businesslike, we'd collect quite a bit to offset the cost of the "Kauffman Find," as I thought of it.

While I was at college, I'd discovered the Marsh books

one rainy weekend at my best friend Tiff's family cottage. I read quite a few during the summers. Now I wanted to get back on top of the series, as part of the whole Summerlea adventure. I would never dare try to read Vera's collection. I'd been hunting for cheaper secondhand copies for myself. Even with my nose for a bargain, I'd found that a challenge as many of the Marsh paperbacks were out of print.

Vera wasn't letting go of her reluctance. She's not the type to be enthusiastic about anything, except maybe bursting my bubble. "Why me?"

We'd been through this already, but I took a deep breath and recapped. "Miss Troy said—if you remember—that as you are a preeminent collector, Mr. Kauffman believes the books would be in good hands and this would honor his uncle's interests and memories." I may have put some words into the mouth of Chadwick Kauffman. I had never spoken to him directly. But it was all in the service of a greater good, and there was an excellent chance that this would turn out to be true. Plus I wanted to enjoy my bit of anticipation and, most likely, Vera wouldn't remember the details of what I'd claimed he'd said.

Even so, she shot me a suspicious glance.

I returned her glance with my most innocent expression, smoothing my hair to the side, a horrible tell, my uncle Mick would say. "I really love those books. I haven't read her in a few years. But I've found myself a few paperbacks." I tried to pretend that my interest was purely professional, but then that Roderick Alleyn was really delicious.

I have a weakness for fictional males, and Inspector Alleyn was as aristocratic and intelligent as Lord Peter Wimsey and as entertaining as Archie Goodwin, my two all-time heart-throbs. He was better looking than Wimsey, and I was sure Roderick Alleyn had never looked even slightly foolish. He was more elegant than Archie, although maybe not quite as good in a fight. But what I liked best was that he had a foot in two worlds: his upper-crust origins and the much grubbier world of policing. Welcome to my life, living large at Van Alst House. I totally understood that. I was the first person in my entire family to go straight. And hadn't the inspector and I both stumbled into more than our share of murders?

I thought he'd get me.

Vera made another face that didn't do her any favors. "You really should stop mooning around, Miss Bingham. It's all such a waste of energy. I don't see why we can't do the transaction by phone or e-mail."

I felt Summerlea and my great adventure slipping away. Without chirping, I said, "We've already accepted and they've welcomed us. We've already arranged with the bank to get the cash. You know that, Vera. We can't back out now. Think of your status in the community." Okay, that was a stretch. It would be hard to imagine anyone who cared less about the community than Vera. Or anyone whose status was more compromised.

"Miss Bingham! Please stop squandering my time. Weren't you supposed to be finding a new supply of acid-free boxes today?"

"It's done, Vera."

"What about reordering our white cotton gloves for handling my books?"

"Twelve dozen should arrive by Friday. But back to Summerlea. Would you like to come with me in the Saab? It could be fun." I love my vintage blue Saab. It runs like a dream even though long before it was mine, it belonged to my mother. No wonder I'm so attached to the nineteen sixties.

Fun is to Vera as a big box of snakes is to others. She barely suppressed a shudder as she turned into the study. "Fine, we will go, but not in that silly blue vehicle. We will all go in the Cadillac. Mr. Kelly will drive."

What was so silly about my car . . . Wait, what? Uncle Kev? Coming to Summerlea?

"Mr. Whoozit's assistant called and asked that we bring him to assist."

I'm afraid that I wailed. "But I'm the assistant. I will assist!"

"Miss Bingham. I do not comprehend why you are behaving like a petulant child. Mr. Kelly will do the heavy lifting."

I couldn't imagine that there'd be that much lifting. Uncle Kev was our official groundskeeper, maintenance guy, bouncer and court jester. He was also the relative most likely to make *Guinness World Records* as the planet's most adorable walking disaster. Maybe Kauffman's assistant had spotted him while checking out Vera Van Alst on Google and had been drawn to the man in the "WHERE'S THE BEEF?" T-shirt.

Wouldn't be the first time.

"But, I can lift a box or two. I schlep heavy items every day. I'm very—" Sometimes that heavy item is Kevin.

Vera raised her eyebrow, usually a declaration of war. "Mr. Kelly will come along. He certainly merits a special occasion."

What? And I didn't? This bit of Kev news gave me a shock. I couldn't imagine that there'd be anything for Kev to do. And when had Vera been talking to Lisa Troy?

I shouldn't have been surprised. Like most women, Vera had a weakness for Uncle Kev. Maybe it's the chiseled cheekbones, the brilliant blue eyes, the uninhibited smile and the fine head of red hair that my Kelly uncles owe to Olaf the Viking, who was a hot commodity around Dublin in the ninth century.

My mother had been a redheaded Kelly too. I have the dark hair of the Binghams. Good thing, I wouldn't want to clash with my dream dress. But I digress. My original point was that Vera and our cook, Signora Panetone, think the sun shines out of Kev's—

Vera reached her desk and whirled. "Why are you still hanging around, Miss Bingham? I have work to do. I believe that you do too, as I pay you enough for it."

"But don't you need Kev here to—?" I paused, trying to

think of something that would be improved by Kev's presence on the home front. It was a short list.

But what if something needed lighting on fire?

"Miss Bingham." Vera snapped open a file. I knew I was taking a chance, but I predicted a world of trouble if Kev came with us. Why couldn't Vera see that too? Of course, I'd always kept Kev's biggest disasters secret from her in order that he could stay on as live-in staff at Van Alst House. I couldn't fault her not understanding the degree of risk involved. At that point, I decided I wouldn't ride in the Caddy with them. I'd follow them in the Saab. I'd deal with any arguments if and when they arose at the time of departure.

Uncle Kev chose that moment to stop whatever crisis he'd been creating elsewhere and pop into our conversation. That's when the entire thing first took on its surreal appearance.

There he was: lovable, handsome and enthusiastic. You could cut fabric with those cheekbones. His blue eyes were mesmerizing. And he was kind. It wasn't his fault that so much went wrong so soon after he walked onto a scene. To my great surprise, he'd fit in quite well at Van Alst House. "Hey, Jordie. Did you hear? I'm going to . . . wherever it is that you're so excited about."

"Summerlea." I smiled tightly before my attention was caught by movement through the tall study window.

"Kev! What's that?" I pointed through the window to a wisp of mist, or was it smoke?

He whirled. His ginger eyebrows lifted. His chiseled cheekbones pointed. His blue eyes gleamed and his freckles added emphasis to his entire face. "What? Nothing! Nothing at all."

I turned back to confront him and stared at Kev's denim backside as he vanished through the door and presumably down the endless corridor toward the back door of Van Alst House.

"Miss Bingham," Vera said with a sniff. "You really should get a grip. You are entirely too high-strung today."

Actually, I was entirely too high-strung about the miniature mushroom cloud of smoke that I had spotted through that window. The puff had emanated from the wooded grove at the edge of the property. The evergreens, mostly spruce and cedar, provided a much needed pop of green where our majestic maple trees stood, still bare. I wanted them to remain standing.

"You're absolutely right," I said. "I'll go and calm down now."

In my family, we have an expression: "Where there's smoke, there's Kev."

I hurried along the corridor, stuck my feet in my glossy red Hunter rain boots and shot out the back door. I headed straight for that wooded grove. Kev, of course, had beaten me to it. He was emerging, radiating innocence, when I reached the edge of the grove.

"Beautiful evening, isn't it, Jordie?"

"No, it is not. It's a miserable end-of-winter day. And if it had been a beautiful evening, the sight of that trail of smoke would have been the end of it."

Kev took my arm and propelled me back toward Van Alst House. "Jordie, Jordie, Jordie. Don't let your imagination get away from you."

"First of all, that doesn't make sense, Kev, and second, I saw smoke and I want to know what that smoke was all about."

"It's a long story. Shall we have a snack in the conservatory and talk about what you thought you saw?"

"I didn't *think* I saw anything, Kev. I *did* see something and—"

"Oh, look. I think Vera wants you."

"She doesn't want me, and you are trying to deflect my attention away from—"

But Vera was there at the back door of Van Alst House gesticulating. A gesticulating Vera is never a good thing, just as a puff of smoke in the vicinity of Kev isn't.

"We'll sort this out later," I grumbled, stomping my way to the back door.

Vera, it turned out after all, had decided she was ready to plan our trip. She needed Kev in on the action, as he would be taking her in the Caddy. I wasn't sure what was worse: Kev in Summerlea or Kev left behind with whatever he had going on in the grove at the edge of the property. I really didn't want to return to find Van Alst House a charred and reeking ruin.

Never mind, we were heading off on an adventure. But Kev was a Grade A blabbermouth and, knowing him, he'd already been on the phone to his brothers with the news. As his brothers were also my uncles, I'd been expecting to hear from them.

My phone gave the unique ring assigned to Uncle Mick, probably my favorite person in the world. I answered and found a barrage of suggestions.

"When you're there at that Kauffman place, make sure you scope out the silver. The grandfather had a collection of Georgian sterling. Not what everyone keeps at their so-called summer home, but the rich are not like us, as they say."

"Sorry, Uncle Mick, I—"

"And watch the walls. I hear there's some good stuff by Ansel Adams, Georgia O'Keeffe and—"

My uncles all had an appreciation for the finer things. Helping them scope out potential plunder is not part of my plan to get away from the family "business." It doesn't matter how many times I mention that I am going straight; it never seems to sink in. I've learned to save my breath.

I said, "Sorry, Uncle Mick. You're breaking up."

"Ansel Adams and Georgia O'Keeffe. And I heard there might be a Colville," he bellowed.

"I don't know what's wrong with the signal. I'll call you later." I rang off. I imagined poor Uncle Mick standing there, baffled, lusting after that silver and those artworks. He'd be as appealing as ever with the gold chain glinting in his curly chest hair, the match to his eyebrows and full head of ginger hair. I loved him to bits, but I did not intend to facilitate any pillaging of the Kauffman holdings.

I hustled after Vera and Kev. I wanted to be part of the planning. That was pure self-preservation.

Vera turned back to me as she rolled down the hall toward the study, "By the way, a package came for you, Miss Bingham. I signed for it. It's at the front door."

"A package?"

"Yes, flowers. A delivery of flowers."

"Flowers?"

"I wish you wouldn't parrot, Miss Bingham. It's most annoying. It's even worse than chirping."

"What kind of flowers?"

"How would I know? It's a long white box. Go find out for yourself." Vera radiated irritation.

"Who would be sending me flowers?" I mused out loud. Flowers were a good thing, but I wasn't used to having them delivered.

"Go look at the card," she muttered. "Mr. Kelly and I can plan without you."

I hesitated about leaving them together alone. "I'll be right back," I said, hurrying toward the front door.

It was indeed a long white box, with a lovely red satin ribbon and a note.

Especially for you, Jordan.
Guess who?

They must have been from Tyler Dekker, the object of my affections, even if he was a police officer and that wasn't a such good fit with my family, given their "business." Who else would send flowers? Lance, my longtime friend and favorite librarian? Maybe. He likes flowers and loves a romantic gesture. But Lance would never miss the opportunity to observe their impact. So Tyler, for sure.

I was almost dizzy with anticipation as I removed the ribbon and flipped the top off the box. Roses. Deep-red roses with long stems. They were once beautiful, but now they were very dead. The cloying scent of must and old roses wafted up.

I stared at the desiccated blooms and then at the box. Someone had taken the trouble to arrange to deliver a dozen long-stemmed roses to me.

I turned the box over. No indication of who they'd come from. The box said Flora's Fanciful Flowers. Never heard of them.

Oh well. I headed toward the utility room to stash them in the box that would make its way to our compost when Kev got around to it. I figured the paper box would break down too.

Kev scurried up behind me. "All systems are go. I'll tune up the Caddy for tomorrow."

"Wear something respectable, Kev. No jeans, no Hooters T-shirts, no runners. Dress up."

"Will do."

"Make sure, Kev. It's important."

"I won't mess up, Jordie. This is going to be fun. You coming in the Caddy with us?"

Not a chance. "I'll ride solo." I figured I'd be calmer that way. I decided it would be great. More than great, wonderful. I couldn't wait.

In fact, if it hadn't been for the two-dozen dead long-stemmed roses, I would have had only one thing on my mind.

Summerlea.

CHAPTER TWO

"DEAD ROSES?" TYLER "Smiley" Dekker said, in a slightly strangled voice when I called him. I got him just coming off duty that evening "Well, no. I didn't send you dead roses. Why would you even think that?"

Tyler Dekker, despite being a police officer, was one of the kindest people in the world. I knew that. He also seemed to genuinely like me. You can bet that's caused me a world of grief, but not from him. I pretty much genuinely liked him right back.

In an attempt to gain Brownie points, since he'd been so unavailable during my last brush with murder, he'd been working hard to make sure I knew he cared. We'd had romantic dinners, long walks, longer talks and a promise to always be there for me. No flowers though, except for Valentine's Day and a shamrock on St. Paddy's.

I said soothingly, "Obviously, they were live roses that took the scenic route. I'm letting you know, so you can get a refund."

A silence drifted over the phone. Then Tyler said, "Is there some occasion this time of year that requires roses? The Ides of March?"

"The Ides of March? Not what I would consider a festive occasion. Anyway, that was two weeks ago."

"No special occasion at all? Not some anniversary I might not have been aware of. Our first ice cream cone or something?"

I had to laugh at that. "I thought you were being romantic."

"I do try to be . . ." He cleared his throat. "But, I really didn't send them."

"Well, no worries. Just so you know, you don't ever need to send me roses, alive or otherwise. And I won't spring silly and previously unmentioned anniversaries on you either."

"But who did send them?"

"I don't know."

"Was there a card?"

"Yes. It said *Guess who?*"

"Maybe they were intended for someone else."

"Well, they had my name. So that's weird."

He said, "Huh. That's expensive and usually implies, um, an intimate, um, involvement."

"There is no intimate involvement with anyone else, Tyler, even if it was implied."

"Well, I guess you'll figure it out. But it wasn't me and you can cross me off your suspect list. But I'm still sorry you got them."

I knew he'd been blushing to the top of his cute blond head. I felt like a heel. "Thanks," I said. "It's some sort of screw-up. I'm not the only Jordan in the world, and possibly they got the addresses mixed up at the florist." But that didn't wash, as the roses had clearly been addressed to Miss Jordan Bingham at the Van Alst House address, correct down to the zip code. Nobody had sent me flowers in all the time I'd lived in Harrison Falls. I'd been given some, but delivered? Never.

"The box is from Flora's Fanciful Flowers, but I'm not sure where they are. The label's smudged."

"Nobody would purposely send you dead roses, Jordon. You're absolutely sure I didn't miss some kind of special event?"

"Nope. You did a great job on Valentine's Day and St. Patrick's, and there's been nothing since."

"Want me to try and find out who they came from or who was supposed to get them? I can contact the florist. They'd remember a delivery to Van Alst House."

"I don't think there's much point." But I knew Smiley and I also knew he'd be on that case. I was pretty sure it would boil down to one of those weird things that happen.

I was lucky to be going out with Tyler, even if my uncles thought it was the worst idea ever for one of the family to be romantically linked to a cop. They'd much prefer that I was arrested.

"I'll call you," Tyler said. "When are you back from wherever you're going?"

"We're just there for lunch. And it's at Summerlea, that secluded estate on the far side of Harrison Falls, near Grandville."

"I don't know it."

"That's right. I keep forgetting you're new here. If you check a map, you follow County Road 36 and the property is not far from where the ravine cuts through that beautiful stretch of woods. The woods and ravine are all part of Summerlea. And there's even a lake, although I haven't seen that yet."

"Sounds pretty fancy. No wonder you're so excited. Not that Van Alst House isn't fancy."

"It's only for lunch and it is business for Vera. And I am not 'so excited.'" I was almost hovering in anticipation, of course, but it did sound goofy when he put it that way.

"My mistake." I could feel his cute smile through the phone. "Be careful. You know how you seem to attract trouble."

* * *

THERE WASN'T MUCH chance I could attract trouble, despite Tyler's teasing. All I was trying to do was catch up on my reading of Ngaio Marsh. No need to be careful there.

My friend Lance is a genius reference librarian. He's easy on the eyes too, as is evident by the crowd of patrons in the reference department on any given day. As usual there was an octogenarian contingent. They're protective of their moments with Lance, and I knew I'd have to take my place in the lineup. I could have texted or called, but I wanted not only to see him, but to look him straight in the eye.

"Beautiful lady—" Lance always talks like someone out of an old-fashioned romantic melodrama, but today I was having none of that.

"Before you say another word, did you by any chance think it would be *très amusant* to send me a bouquet of dead roses?"

He actually flinched. "What? Ew. Dead roses! That's horrible. *Why?*"

Well, that was an honest reaction.

"I'm ruling out suspects."

"Suspects? I can't believe you would even say that." Lance feigned injury and put his hand to his heart. He'd missed his calling.

"I didn't really think you were a suspect. I thought there might be something going on that I wasn't aware of. Something really hip or . . ."

"Nobody says 'hip' anymore, Jordan. And I have never heard of this trend."

Somehow the smell of his Burberry cologne made the fact I was no longer hip—or even allowed to say "hip"—a bit less painful.

"So, did someone actually send you dead roses?"

I nodded.

"Anonymously, I take it."

"Well, *Guess who?*"

"What do you think that means?"

I shrugged. I really had no idea.

"Maybe someone didn't realize they'd be dead when you got them. A secret admirer?"

"We promised not to keep secrets anymore." I winked.

Lance looked embarrassed. We're still getting over a certain secret from Thanksgiving, but this wasn't the occasion to revisit that.

"Can't imagine who," I said. "Or why. But if there's one thing I hate, it's an incompetent secret admirer."

"I get that."

It's always good to ask a librarian, and Lance was pleased to check out the Kauffman family background and a history of Summerlea too, before our trip. Vera had asked questions, and I wanted to know that everything about Chadwick was on the level. Although I'd been madly researching, Lance always uncovers so much more detail than I can online, and usually it's all vastly more interesting too. As an extra I got a couple of flirty cheek kisses and a serious hug from him.

As I sashayed out the door, feeling the dirty looks from his reference room posse, I had a big, silly grin on my face.

On my way back to Van Alst House, I couldn't resist driving to the farthest reaches of Harrison Falls and sailing along the tree-lined road and the ravine to pass the entrance to Summerlea. I was smiling all the way, cruising slowly. I gave a cheerful smile and wave to three gray-haired ladies who were ambling along the side of the road, before heading home.

They looked to be in their late seventies. The little one reminded me of my Grandmother Kelly. That meant you'd probably never want to get on her bad side.

AS I PULLED into the driveway at Van Alst House, my pocket sprang to life with a text from Tiff. In typical Tiff fashion, she had offered to fill in for a colleague as a nurse

on a cruise. This was what I loved about Tiff. You could count
on her to save the day if you, say, broke your ankle in an ill-
advised attempt at roller derby and needed someone to cover
your eleven-day shift. On the phone before she'd left for
Miami she was excited. Tiff collects adventures the way Vera
collects books, only with more passion and far less caution.
She'd never been on a cruise or to the Panama Canal. And
the pay was going to be decent, considering all her accom-
modations and food were covered. Although the sun was
starting to get stronger here in New York State, our late-
coming spring was a far cry from the balmy tropical breezes
Tiff would have tousling her hair. I felt a twinge of envy. My
pale Irish skin had reached an almost translucent level of
white over the long winter.

> Hey J!
> Getting on board now. Tiny room, but at least I don't
> have to share! ;) I guess once we get out to sea, texting
> gets pricey, so I will check in when we get to Aruba in
> two days. Be thinking of you as I work on my tan. LOL
> xo T

I replied in faux jealous rage.

> T,
> You are a horrible person. I hope a dolphin steals your
> wallet.
> ;) Have fun!

I WAS BACK barely in time to accompany Vera and Uncle
Kev to the bank to pick up the money for the exchange of the
Marsh collection. We'd arranged to have the cash on hand.
Vera must have had a stash of cash somewhere in Van Alst
House, because she was able to keep the withdrawal amount
under ten thousand, which is the point where transactions

attract all sorts of unwelcome attention from the IRS and other government bodies. I did wonder about the need for cash. I was beginning to think that Vera was right and maybe the Kauffman estate was shrinking. However, we were the buyers, not the sellers, and it was up to Chadwick to report any income. Once again, no need to worry. I might have been going straight, but it wasn't like I worked for the government.

From the moment we got out of the bank, scanned articles and links kept appearing from Lance on my iPhone. *Bing! Bing! Bing!*

Lance had found lots of new stuff. I loved that boy. Soon I'd be immersed in more than I could ever absorb about the Kauffmans and Summerlea.

A last text from Lance:

Found a lot of info about art, but nothing about books. Chat later.

AS SOON AS we got home, Vera zoomed to the study to take care of some hospital board work. Kev muttered something about cleanup around the property. That reminded me about those puffs of smoke. I'd been too distracted to follow up. "Whatever you're doing, Kev, make sure it's inside. Stay away from the woods and forget whatever project you have going there."

"Sure thing, Jordie. You know you can trust me."

Trust him? Not so much. I had to keep an eye on him.

My attic space is one of the best things about living in Van Alst House. I had an hour to spare before dinner, so I curled up on my bed to do a thorough reading of the material from Lance. The ornate iron bedstead might not have looked comfortable, but the feather bed sure was. I snuggled under the well-worn comforter with its pretty green sprigged pattern that matched my curtains. Good thing the pattern was small and delicate, because the faded cabbage roses on the ancient wall-paper could still flatten any competition. I loved them too.

A cat pounced on the bed. Luckily it was Good Cat. Bad Cat seemed to have declared a truce of sorts, but that could end with no notice. Maybe he was under the bed waiting until I put my ankles within reach.

I turned my attention to the background information Lance had sent and did my homework on the Kauffman family, skimming the articles and clicking the many links. I stroked the cat as I read.

Even though Summerlea was not that far away, the Kauff-mans had never really participated in the life of Harrison Falls. Magnus Kauffman had done his best to avoid attention. But despite this, the family had made it to the national news from time to time: weddings and funerals, mostly. It was fun reading up on the Kauffman family, even though I found no juicy scandals or investigations. The Kauffmans hadn't lent their name to a world-class university or concert halls. But there had been society weddings a few generations back, linking the Kauffmans with some of the really great Amer-ican families. There had been grand European tours and expeditions to exotic locations. And there continued to be charitable activities and stylish fund-raisers. Magnus Kauff-man had held the annual Summerlea Night's Dream as well as a fall jazz festival and a winter cotillion. He had apparently enjoyed having his name and image appear in the society pages. In recent years, Magnus grew more reclusive, and the society fund-raisers appeared to be managed by Chadwick Kauffman on the grounds of his Country Club and Spa. Chadwick wasn't one to seek the limelight, and while the big patrons and donors appeared grinning for the cameras, he rarely stuck his mug into the group shots.

Refreshing.

It didn't take long before I felt I knew all about the Kauff-mans. Chadwick was indeed the end of a scandal-free line.

That was good, because I wanted to like him. And I wanted our visit to Summerlea to be perfect.

"JORDAN?"

I was glad to hear Tyler's voice again. "I thought you were on duty."

"I was checking out Flora's Fanciful Flowers to find out who sent your dead roses."

"And?"

"And there doesn't seem to be a Flora's Fanciful Flowers in Harrison Falls or anywhere else in the world."

"Oh. But the label . . ."

"Trust me. There isn't one."

"A practical joke, then."

"Yeah. And a creepy one."

"Who would have done that?"

"I have no idea."

"Do you still have the box?"

"It's on its way to the compost. I could dig it out."

"Do that and hang on to it. I'll see if I can get any information from it."

"It was a joke. Thanks, but does it really merit a police investigation?"

"Humor me. You know I want to be a detective when I grow up."

"Never grow up, Tyler. I like you the way you are. Tell you what, I'll drop the box off the next chance I get."

"And I'll see what I turn up."

I FOUND THE box of dead flowers, fished it out and put it in a large plastic bag. The signora had been happy to provide the bag. The signora, small, black-clad and round, followed me. She kept clucking over the flowers, muttering in Italian and shaking her head.

"*Sfortunata.*"
Unlucky? No kidding.
"Thanks," I said, "I hate them too."

I REFUSED TO dwell on those flowers. Instead I focused
on Craigslist for our area. I'd been watching all my online
sources hunting Ngaio Marsh books for myself and also trying
to locate suitable titles for Vera's collection. I checked often.
In my line of work, you snooze, you lose.

Today, I was a winner.

A couple who were downsizing and moving to one of the
new riverside condos in the neighboring town of Grandville
had given up their walls of bookcases in their sprawling
suburban home. They were prepared to liberate boxes of
mass-market reprints from the seventies. "Pristine," they
said, except for small labels on the inside front first page of
each book. They posted photos of the covers and spines of
hundreds of mysteries including many of the Ngaio Marsh
titles I wanted.

Best of all, the ad hadn't been up long.

I happily drove to Grandville, glad to get there before
any book scouts descended. Not that I had anything against
other scouts; after all, I was one myself in a limited way.
And I counted on my contacts to keep Vera's collection
improving. Aside from that, I also made a bit on the books
I found in the church bazaars, secondhand stores, Goodwill,
garage sales and other rich sources. Several of the scouts
were also my customers.

Labeled boxes were stacked by the front door when I
arrived. Although the packing looked orderly, the place had
that forlorn feeling that houses get in a move. I was greeted
by a tall woman with shoulder-length wavy auburn hair and
a full, almost voluptuous figure. There was something familiar
about her. "I'm Larraine Gorman," she said, "and the noises
you hear from upstairs would be Doug. Ignore them and him."

Larraine looked like she would have been more at home on a Titian canvas than in this jumbled, box-laden foyer. My uncles would have been captivated by her.

She'd put aside the books I wanted, neatly packaged up in two boxes and labeled "NGAIO MARSH." I could tell that the owner was parting with them reluctantly. "No changing your mind," her husband had boomed from upstairs as she greeted me. "And see if she'll take some clothes while you're at it."

She rolled her eyes and called back, "How about some golf clubs? I could slip in a few of those."

I grinned. "It's not easy cutting back, is it?"

"It certainly isn't. This downsizing effort is killing me," she said. "I don't mind ditching the knickknacks, but it's hard to get rid of my books. I've read them all more than once and treasured each one."

I got that.

"If it's any consolation," I said, "they're going to a good home. My employer collects first editions. I can't afford that, but I have my own little collection. And every book in it gets treated like a fine first."

"That's a relief," she said with a wan smile.

I checked out the other boxes of books, in case there were volumes we needed or with good resale prospects. Nothing wrong with funding future projects with a quick flip. I found some likely candidates and put them aside, before I opened the two Marsh boxes to check the condition of the books. I may have purred with delight as I inspected each book. I loved how the covers reflected the style of the era. Many of the Fontana reprints even had a charming little inset with a painting of Inspector Alleyn on the back and some details about him. "Educated at Eton and moulded in the diplomatic service," I noted and in my opinion both environments had served him well.

I checked inside and, sure enough, several had maps and floor plans of the grand house in that book. I loved that. Most had the cast of characters before the first chapter. I'd appreciated those lists when I first discovered Marsh. The device hadn't lost its charm. I wished more authors would give their readers a break by doing this.

I chuckled over the names in the lists: Cressida and Cuthbert, Nigel, Peregrine and Sir Hubert, Chloris and Aubrey, Sebastian, Barnaby and Hamilton, Cedric, Desdemona and Millamant! I thought they were all delicious. A new batch of names in every book. Of course, there'd be crowds of butlers and footmen, cooks and maids. Some staff would rate a name, but not all.

I looked forward to meeting more of Marsh's characters. Some would die in the interests of the story. In most cases, the death would be grisly and possibly bloody, but it would get our attention and teach us that this was a murderer who meant business and would stop at nothing. Ruthlessness can keep us turning pages. Never fear, Roderick Alleyn would put things right again.

I was counting on it. I noticed Larraine grinning at me. "You seem to appreciate them. I hate to give them up. It's like letting go of friends. So I'm glad you've discovered Ngaio Marsh."

"Rediscovered." I couldn't resist telling her about our luncheon at Summerlea.

"That sounds amazing."

I grinned. "I'm lucky to be along for the ride. It's all between my employer and Chadwick Kauffman. But I can't wait to soak up that ambiance. It will be almost like stepping into one of the great estates in these books."

"I'm jealous."

"Don't get me wrong. It's work too. I'm one of the nameless servants on this character list."

Larraine said. "Did you say you collect first editions?"

"Yes." I was glad I'd left Vera out of the story, as she was generally loathed in our part of the world, and anyway, the Van Alst name might be enough to raise the prices.

"Oh well, have a look at some of Doug's books. You may find something you like." A wicked smile played around her full, bright lips.

I glanced up the stairs, where there was a certain amount of crashing about and huffing going on.

"Don't mind if I do."

A half hour later, I had another pair of boxes with hardbacks, including a few firsts in quite decent shape. A Hammett. A Chandler. Some John D. MacDonalds. Vera had all those, but I'd invest my own money and they'd make me a few pennies on the side.

I could hear Doug carrying on about finally getting rid of those dusty old Christmas decorations. But that wasn't enough for him. "And who needs four closets for their clothes?"

"Leave my closets alone. I'll take care of them!"

"At least can I pitch these theater souvenirs. It's bad enough you have seen every play on and off Broadway—no matter how short the run—but do you have to keep this junk? You never look at it."

She glanced up the stairs. I foresaw stormy weather coming for Doug. A small nerve flickered under Larraine's eye. "My playbills stay. End of discussion."

I decided it was time to make tracks. Larraine and I settled on a price for Doug's books, for the other mysteries I'd found and for the Marshes.

As I picked up the first box, she glanced sadly at the box and reached out. "I love the theatricality of the Inspector Alleyn novels. I did a lot of theater in college and that really appealed."

No wonder we'd hit it off. "Me too. I remember that. I read *Death in a White Tie* first and felt as if I was actually watching it play out on a stage. How people came and went within scenes, the way the dialogue propelled the story forward was three-dimensional. They're so much fun and now I'll get to read them all."

Larraine said, "Apparently, theater was Ngaio Marsh's

first love, and it showed in the way those characters and settings with a theatrical connection rose from the page."

"I was involved in theater too. Every year in college I worked on at least one production."

"Onstage?"

"Sometimes onstage, or behind the scenes with wardrobe or makeup or as a production assistant. I enjoyed everything about each production, from the first read-through to the feel of the costumes, the smell of the theater, the buzz of excitement when you step in front of the lights."

"Why didn't you pursue it?"

"If I hadn't been so in love with English literature, maybe I would have switched to a drama degree. What about you?"

"I did go that route. Never really succeeded, although I was in a number of productions and some of my friends went on to success. Now I'm here, teaching. It has its good points too. But you know . . ."

"I hear you. There are such great bonds in theater. Wonderful friendships." Lance and Tiff had been part of all the productions.

Tiff had been reluctant. In her own words: "So I won't be forced to listen to Jordan blab on endlessly about something I'm not involved in."

Not so for Lance. He was born for the stage. These days his performances were reserved for his permanent audience in the reference department or in a presentation to the library board for funding or service enhancements. Still, he'd been a big hit in some Harrison Falls Theater Guild's performances. People were still talking about his Stanley Kowalski.

"Some of those friends will break your heart. Until you end up happily ever after." She laughed and pointed upstairs where Doug was thundering about.

I said, "Only one of them broke my heart. He also cleaned out my bank account and maxed out my credit cards."

"Ouch. Hope you're over him."

"Yup. With lots of help." Lance and Tiff and a raft of

redheaded Kellys. And we move on, as my uncles had taught me early and well.

"I'm so glad to hear it." She beamed at me, and I knew where I'd seen her before.

"I just realized why you look familiar. Are you part of Harrison Falls Theater Guild? I saw you in *Steel Magnolias*. You were an awesome Truvy! That was one of our college productions. We could have used you."

"You should come and try out. I can let you know when there are auditions. Give me your number."

"Sure thing." I headed out with the box and thought about her offer. I loved the idea of auditioning for one of HFTG's productions too, but I always seemed to be knee-deep in murder when the call went out.

When I came back for the second box, Larraine was still in a mood to chat. "I think Marsh is brilliant. You'd better run before I change my mind."

From up the stairs a bellow from Doug: "Since we're getting rid of some of my books, who needs seventy-five pairs of shoes?"

Larraine chuckled. "I can't wait to get back to normal. Doug has already taken the TVs and radios to the new place. He claims they're too distracting here. I'll need a week of theater to get me back to normal. Oh, and by the way, I try to catch everything I can on and off Broadway. And off-off-off. As you could probably tell, Doug's not so keen on it. I often meet up with old friends to go. But I like you too. Maybe you and I could attend a couple of performances together."

"That would be great." I was still grinning as I drove away. It would be nice to stay in touch with her. But I realized that I'd paid cash and forgotten to give her my name or my number, even though we'd talked about getting together. And I didn't know where she was moving. Oh well. I could probably track her down through the Harrison Falls Theater Guild. An occasional trip to catch a live performance in the city sounded wonderful.

I took a couple of minutes to drop the long white florist's box (still containing the offending dead roses), with a note, at Tyler's neat little brick home. It was easier than chasing him around town on his shift, and I did have a key.

Now, I had a lot of reading to catch up on.

AT HOME, I lugged the boxes up to the third floor and set out the books on my Lucite coffee table. With their bright colors and similar styles, my new finds brought some extra life to the space. Of course, there wasn't much time to read before our lunch tomorrow at Summerlea, but I wanted to use what I had. I chose *A Man Lay Dead*, partly because it was the first and partly because it took place in a stately home. How much fun was that? Inspector Alleyn was a suave and elegant upper-class character. He practically reeked dignity and elegance, but right from the beginning he managed to avoid being stuffy or arrogant.

I sifted through the other books, with flickering memories of the ones I'd read seven or eight years earlier. I read quickly, so I figured I could whip through them again.

I hadn't wanted to put my foot in it at lunch, so I'd made sure to brush up a bit on Marsh's history too. What do people talk about at luncheon in places like Summerlea? I felt I could at least chat about the books and their author. It seemed that theater was indeed the grand dame's first love and crime fiction second. I thought that explained a lot. I could see characters coming and going almost as though on a stage. The image of the scene rose from the page. But best of all was the dialogue, sharp and astute. You got to hear the English dialects from the various settings. I remembered reading these bits out loud. More than once, I'd thought, I wish I'd said what she'd written.

You couldn't gloss over a character who wandered onto one of these pages. We readers were able to check them out as if they'd been under a particularly heartless microscope trained on their less attractive attributes. She didn't mind laying her characters bare. With the exception of Alleyn, of course, who remained the perfect gentleman, irritatingly aristocratic, brilliant and unflappable. It appeared he never failed to solve a crime, with his small coterie of helpers to follow along, speaking in accents that were far less elegant. Once again, I knew if I'd been in one of these dramas, it would have been as the perky little Irish maid, who was maybe a bit too uppity for her own good.

I hadn't found myself yet, no dark-haired twenty-something woman with blue eyes "put in with a sooty finger." But with thirty-two books, anything was possible. Maybe I'd show up as a Bridget or a Molly with a brogue that Marsh would capture phonetically.

With the other characters, I had decided that Sergeant Fox was my favorite, large, occasionally burly, ginger haired (a good thing), solid in a crisis, he was the right-hand man. He reminded me of Uncle Mick, although clearly on the other side of the law. At least one of the Kelly family was on those pages. I loved the running gag about Fox studying French, which the upper-class Alleyn spouted effortlessly. There were clownish types flitting through the pages too. I wondered what Ngaio Marsh would have made of Uncle Kev.

Smiling, I dressed for dinner.

WE DINE AT eight at a splendid Sheraton table in the formal dining room. Vera at one end, me at the other, Kev halfway between us. We are not late if we know what is good for us. I wore my knee-high boots to prevent Bad Cat from giving me some new scars. Tall boots were a wise choice, because Bad Cat's claws raked at my ankles from the moment I took my seat. Good Cat watched benignly from the black walnut sideboard. Whenever the signora left the room, Good Cat would join Vera.

Signora Panetone was ready for an army even though we

were only three. The signora never joins us. She's too busy serving, fussing and hovering. I've learned to accept this as the way it is and stay in my seat.

Tonight the signora had promised tiramisu for dessert, my favorite.

She began by serving homemade spinach fettuccine with a mild but savory tomato sauce and lots of fresh Parmesan. Kev and I each accepted a small mountain of it. Vera took a tablespoon, if that. The signora uttered her familiar bleats. "Eat, Vera! You need to eat."

Vera has selective hearing, and she never seemed to hear a word the signora said. Kev eased the situation by asking for seconds before I'd finished my first mouthful.

Conversation turned to Ngaio Marsh and her work.

Vera said, "Alleyn is the finest of all the detectives, in my opinion."

I was mindful of what happened not that long ago when I'd yanked Vera's chain over Archie Goodwin from the Nero Wolfe books. Suggesting they should have been the Archie Goodwin books had been painful.

"Mmmm," I said. "I thought Marsh glorified the upper classes. The totally perfect Inspector Roderick Alleyn is proof of that in book after book." I chose not to add that I thought he was a bit too upper class, too constrained, far too elegant, not to mention annoyingly calm. Of course, I liked Alleyn as a detective, but he didn't have enough flaws for me to fall for him.

Vera shot me a venomous look. "Absurd, even from you, Miss Bingham."

"I like his wife, the painter Agatha Troy, more." I ignored the dirty look. "She's a bit messy, compared to Inspector Perfection."

Vera scowled as I spoke. The signora edged closer to try to slide a bit more fettuccine onto the plate.

I kept going. "And I like his mother. Alleyn had a warm relationship with her. I was kind of happy that he had a mother. Not enough detectives have mothers. Imagine her dining with the Dowager Duchess of Denver."

Even from the length of the table, Vera's stare was chilly. "We read stories, Miss Bingham. We don't make them up."

"But the Dowager Duchess is Lord Peter Wimsey's mother and—"

Vera sighed dramatically. "I know who she is. Sometimes you are too fanciful, silly, even. It's all about Roderick Alleyn. He is the glue that holds the books together. I believe he was the love of her life."

"Even more than the theater? Do you think?"

I imagined Alleyn looking a bit like Cary Grant (my mother's favorite actor from back in the day): laid-back, elegant and intelligent. Not only was the gentleman detective soigné, he was very nice to his mother. It would be pretty easy to spend time with a sleuth like that. I could see an author being in love. But I couldn't resist teasing Vera a bit. You'd think I'd learn.

"I don't know. Sergeant Fox also won me over, especially with his brave attempts to master the French language. Imagine how frustrating it would be, struggling with a language that came effortlessly to Alleyn."

"For heaven's sake. Fox is an . . . afterthought."

"Oh, hardly."

"*Cela suffit*, Miss Bingham."

Maybe Vera thought that would do, but I couldn't resist another little verbal engagement. "Poor Fox. I feel his pain. But should we be jealous of Agatha Troy, Alleyn's wife? I think I might be, even if she's a bit untidy and—"

"I do not have emotions about fictional characters."

I was wise enough not to mention Nero Wolfe again.

The signora arrived with *pollo al limone* served with rice and peas. "Not too much, thanks, Signora. I'm saving room for the tiramisu."

She inhaled sharply.

The room went quiet.

"What?" I said.

"*Domani!*" she said. "*Tiramisu domani.*"

"But I saw it in the kitchen earlier. Why not tonight?"

Vera stared at Good Cat. Kev stared at his feet. The signora said, "You eat lotsa fettucine! Spinach. And chicken. Very good."

"Let me guess. Something happened to the tiramisu."

"No, no, no, no!" The signora did a mad little dance around.

Vera muttered, "Let it go, Miss Bingham."

Kev said, "It was an accident."

Of course.

"An accident? Did it fall on the floor?"

"Not exactly."

"Did you accidentally eat it all?"

He flashed his Kelly grin.

"These things happen, Miss Bingham," Vera said.

"More tomorrow night," the signora said, slapping several more pieces of chicken on my plate. "Tonight, cookies."

This all should prove my point about Kev.

AFTER DINNER, I returned to my Ngaio Marsh reading project on my cozy bed. The gently used paperbacks I'd located were not good enough for Vera, but perfect for me. I hoped that I'd get enough of a sense of the Roderick Alleyn stories to hold up my end of the conversation about the series at our coming luncheon. Someone would have to. Vera usually offered nothing more than a grunt for an entire meal, regardless of who she was dining with. Soon I was lost in *A Man Lay Dead*. Time flies when you're having fun.

I COULDN'T BELIEVE how late it was. I needed to get a good night's sleep. I cleaned my face and teeth, and I took a peek out the dormer window. This was one of my favorite things to do at bedtime when I was a child and watched the night sky with my uncles. From my little pink-and-white bedroom over Uncle Mick's shop (Michael Kelly's Fine Antiques), the stars were magical and powerful. Uncle Mick could weave stories about the constellations. Looking back, I now think my uncles wanted to keep me from having nightmares. After all, I was a small girl whose mother had vanished and I lived with my bachelor uncles who were adorable, although undeniably crooked. I didn't care. I loved it when Mick would point and have me do my five-year-old best to say Cassiopeia. The night might have been overcast with not a star in view, but I still had happy memories of watching the sky.

I did a double take. Was that a furtive movement in the direction of the woods? I wasn't sure. But at least it couldn't be Kev. I could see the light in his quarters over the garage and his shadow against the blind. Just a fox, I decided, happily hunting. But I needed to remember to check on those woods in the morning. In case.

CHAPTER THREE

I FOLLOWED VERA'S old Caddy up the long, long approach to Summerlea. With its high stone walls at the entrance and vast formal grounds on either side of the front driveway, it made Van Alst House look like a shack in the woods. It was impressively over-the-top. I love opulence. If it looked this attractive in the gray early light with only evergreens and a wide swath of crocus for color, I could only imagine how beautiful it would be in late spring, and how stunning the summer events had been here.

A silver classic Aston Martin was parked creatively in front of the house, next to it a vintage red Mercedes convertible, both with muddy plates. I figured the Mercedes was from the seventies or eighties. It was a bit battered and dusty, and not a candidate for any classic car parade, but had I not given my heart to the Saab, this might have been what I'd buy if I won the lottery.

As I didn't buy lottery tickets, that wouldn't happen. Uncle Kev used up all the Kelly luck long ago.

I was happy to see there was a ramp for Vera's wheelchair. I'd made it clear when Miss Troy and I discussed arrangements. I was still kind of tickled by the coincidence of Miss Troy's name.

As Kev pushed Vera up the ramp, I headed up the wide steps to the door and rang. It was opened by a large, stone-faced butler. How's that for over-the-top? I had never met a real butler before, although I'd always enjoyed the butlers in the novels of the Golden Age of Detection. Bunter was my favorite. I may have already mentioned that I had a serious crush on his employer, Lord Peter Wimsey, but I'd been able to move on, with the help of Archie Goodwin.

This time, I'd been so distracted by the grand entrance, I missed the butler's name. Maybe butlers weren't supposed to give their names.

How would I know? I came from simple, criminal stock, good-natured and totally devoid of servants. Maybe it was instinctive for me to note the impressive security setup at the front door. I'd be sure to mention that to Uncle Mick. More impressive though was this butler. Even Vera didn't have a butler. Attempts to dress up Uncle Kev and have him answer the door had not gone well, shall we say.

But back to the moment. I was expecting more of a stereotypical British butler, the type you might meet on *Masterpiece Theatre*. But this was upstate New York, not England. This butler's pear-shaped body stretched the fabric of his somber suit, and he could have used a good color-consultant before choosing that flat, black hair dye. One of the things I liked about Ngaio Marsh when she described characters was that she commented on their hands. Somehow it helped to bring those characters to life. I found myself checking hands too. In fact, the butler's ham-like appendages seemed more suited to tossing a javelin than serving tea, or whatever it is that butlers do. I figured he might have had a career as a wrestler before he discovered that the butler's life was his heart's desire. I was surprised that those hairy fingers hadn't kept him out of the game, not to mention the five-o'clock shadow at noon.

The nameless underling ushered us in, much to Kev's astonishment. He is used to being the underling. He nodded to the butler in his best version of a gentleman of leisure.

Miss Troy was waiting and she seemed delighted to see us. "Please, call me Lisa."

I don't know why I was surprised by her warm greeting. Why had I been expecting otherwise? As Vera's assistant, I would have been equally happy to meet guests who were going to help her out in some way.

The grave look of the butler had worried me. Or it could have been the significance of the Kauffman family and their mighty history. I reminded myself that we lived in a democracy where everyone had a value and it was supposed to be how you lived your life that mattered, not how much money you had. I tried not to gawk at the huge crystal chandelier illuminating the foyer.

After all, I was not the upstairs maid. I'd be at the table.

I was impressed by Miss Troy. She was tall and willowy, and that severely tailored black suit and crisp white shirt couldn't disguise that. Her soft brown hair was caught back in a perfect chignon, a style that flattered her. With her luminous skin, she could have been the face of any major beauty company. Really, she would have been quite unbearable except for her dark horn-rimmed glasses and the barest suggestion of an overbite. That overbite was kind of endearing. And of course, she was so welcoming. She seemed to be working at being cool and professional, but her smile kept surfacing. Even so, in this environment, I kept thinking of her as Miss Troy. It seemed right somehow. Maybe because of the Ngaio Marsh connection.

Kev looked like he could get used to being an honored guest. Of course, we'd only been there for minutes and he hadn't had time to mess up.

Miss Troy murmured delicately that if we wished to freshen

up after our trip, there were facilities around the corner. She gestured beautifully with her long, slim white hand. I couldn't help but admire her modern manicure with the short, smooth nails in deep, glossy burgundy. I was glad I'd done my own nails in palest nude. My hands are small and dexterous, perfect for using the traditional tools of my family. Have I mentioned I received a set of lock picks for my Sweet Sixteen? Despite this encouragement, I've stuck to the straight and narrow. Mostly.

Uncle Kev and I took advantage of her offer to freshen up. Vera never freshens up; if anything, she blands down.

As we passed through the foyer, I admired the glossy marble floors with their intricate inlaid designs and the spectacular curving mahogany stairs. Everything gleamed. The space smelled of lilies from the towering arrangement on a Chippendale table. Unlike Van Alst House, the money was obviously still here to keep Summerlea at its best. The ladies' room was opulent in cream paint and dark mahogany woodwork. The soap was Crabtree and Evelyn Citron, Honey & Coriander. The hand towels were pale linen. I thought we should consider upping our game at Van Alst House, but of course, Vera rarely had visitors unless they were trying to kill her.

Anyway, why spend scarce funds on soap and linen towels when there were still first editions to buy, would be her response. Still, I decided I'd start keeping an eye out for linen hand towels at the vintage shows. Maybe I'd find some embroidered with *V* for Van Alst, or even better, *B* for Bingham.

Of course, I couldn't spend the day admiring the facilities when luncheon awaited. I reluctantly left this little oasis of luxury and rejoined Miss Troy in the hallway.

She smiled sympathetically, and I wondered if she could sense the generations of grifter from me, one of whom had tagged along. The smile seemed pitying.

We found Uncle Kev in front of a small demilune table

with another arrangement of lilies. He was gazing at a petite marble nude carving and grinning innocently, always a bad sign. Had he just put that down when we reached him? What else had his eye spotted? His blazer didn't seem lumpy, so I didn't need to worry about lecturing him to return whatever he'd pilfered from the little boys' room. At the same time, I didn't let myself touch the flower arrangement to make sure those blooms were real. Of course they were. I didn't want to come across as gauche.

We were shepherded into a large sitting room for drinks. The butler—whatever his name was—looked like he'd be right at home mixing cocktails. Inside the splendidly appointed room stood the person who could only be Chadwick Barrymore Kauffman, last of the Kauffman clan. He leaned against the fireplace, waiting with a weary smile glued to his thin face. He was not what I'd expected. There was no sense of warmth or welcome. It was impossible to imagine him presiding over charity fund-raisers. My research told me he was forty-three, although he looked younger. He seemed to do a slight double take when he spotted Vera rolling in. I imagined it was the mud-brown acrylic cardigan she sported. How the pilling danced in the light. And it felt worse than it looked. She wouldn't go for the blue silk blouse I'd picked out for her. Usually, I can at least count on her to wear one of her brilliant diamond brooches for a social event. This time, she'd declined to do that too. "Don't want to look like we're doing too well," she'd said. There was little danger of that. If Vera had looked any worse, someone might have started a fund-raiser for her.

Chadwick paused, watching her through heavy-lidded eyes. He reminded me of a lizard, and not the cute one from the commercials.

For a split second, I thought we'd be escorted out. No Ngaio Marsh collection for this motley crew. Here's your hat. What's your hurry?

After a brief pause, Chadwick extended a slender, limp

hand to Vera. I was relieved she didn't bite it, but returned his handshake like a normal person. Not a fan of lizards. I barely refrained from a shiver. Chadwick offered a bored nod of acknowledgment to me and to Kev. We were, after all, the help and merited only the minimum attention. His cologne stung my eyes. It smelled like entitlement. I didn't care if we were just the help. We were included in the lunch, as was Miss Troy. I did feel Miss Troy was higher up the food chain than we were.

The butler's name was Thomas, it turned out, and he was there to serve. Thomas had a talent for mimosas. They were perfect and served, naturally, in sparkling crystal. Although the mimosas may have relaxed us slightly, they didn't lead to anything approaching merriment.

Summerlea might have been a getaway, but it had a somber, dignified air to it. The staircase may have been magnificent, but I couldn't image that solemn Chadwick had ever slid down that shiny banister shrieking with laughter. I bet he'd been an aloof and withdrawn child. He'd probably spent most of his childhood sunning himself on a warm rock.

Conversation sputtered along.

Chadwick asked Vera about her collection.

"It's not bad," Vera said. "Coming along." That was an understated way to describe the treasured volumes in the climate-controlled library with its security system, Aubusson carpets, rosewood furniture and bookshelves and wrought-iron circular staircase leading to the second floor. Of course, Vera was crying poor on the off chance, in the end, the price for the Ngaio Marsh collection could dip a bit in her favor.

Chadwick tilted his narrow head and gazed at her speculatively. I figured he had her number. Sometimes, playing games can actually cost you money. Vera wanted that collection the way she wanted to keep breathing.

"Tell us about the collection here at Summerlea," I said, being careful not to chirp.

He glanced at me briefly before saying, "What do you want to know?"

"What did your uncle collect? Fine firsts? Other mysteries?" Those were Vera's passions, and she favored the authors from the Golden Age of Detection. Of course, Ngaio Marsh had been one of the giants of that era.

I guessed that Chadwick didn't appreciate an interruption from one of the minions. He gave a tight smile that went nowhere near those hooded eyes. "He collected many things, including certain authors. Marsh was a favorite, although he leaned toward American classic mysteries. He had some Hammetts and Chandlers."

There had been nothing about Magnus Kauffman's reading habits in anything I'd read.

"Did he keep his books here in Summerlea?" I wondered about the climate-controlled conditions. My guess was that Summerlea wasn't open all year round and that we were the first through the door at the end of winter. Would it be damp? "Damp" was a four-letter word in our business.

He flicked an annoyed glance in my direction. "No. The books are at the residence in Manhattan. There is a special room for them for the time being. Some were singled out in the will for the New York Public Library, Rare Book Division. If *Miss Van Alst* would be interested in seeing the others sometime before they are on their way, we could certainly arrange for *her* to visit."

If Uncle Kev noticed that we were pointedly not invited to visit the city residence, he gave no indication. Instead, he held out his empty mimosa glass. Thomas refilled it, with his eyebrows raised. And here I'd thought butlers were supposed to keep their reactions under wraps.

"I don't travel," Vera was saying, dismissively. It must have been difficult for her to look so uninterested, because of course, she would want to see, and yes, touch, the Hammetts and the Chandlers. I was impressed that she'd managed not to drool. But she's nothing if not a good negotiator. Her first principle: You have to be prepared to walk away. They can sense that.

Chadwick pursed his thin lips and glanced at me once more past those thick eyelids, as if I were responsible for Vera's rudeness. I kept my mouth closed. Although I found myself disliking Chadwick more by the minute, I didn't want to ruin lunch. Instead, I smiled and said, "What a beautiful room. I love the light and the view. It must be lovely in the summer looking down the lawn to the water." I didn't say, "Holy crap, is that a real Andrew Wyeth?"

Miss Troy, who had continued watching Chadwick intensely, produced a warm smile that transformed her face. "Yes, it's wonderful, isn't it? What a shame this isn't later in the season."

Chadwick barely stifled a yawn and said to Vera, "Who knows? We may have more transactions in the future and you could enjoy a visit here in June."

Vera didn't even acknowledge this, but Miss Troy shot an odd look at Chadwick. His reaction—a subtle frown and almost imperceptible shake of his head—caused her to turn pale. Her hand went to her mouth. If it hadn't been for that splendid manicure, I would have bet she might have nibbled at her nails. What was that exchange of glances all about?

Not my problem, I decided. If Chadwick Kauffman made his assistant nervous and was a jackass to boot, I would be glad not to see him again. All I wanted was this one memorable luncheon in *his* house.

After we polished off our mimosas in the sitting room and the desultory conversation ground to an end, at last we headed for the dining room.

The dining room was also splendid and heavy on the mahogany, not what you'd expect in a "summer house." But then nothing in Summerlea was.

My raspberry dress was equal to the occasion.

The room was easily as formal as Vera's in Val Alst House, although in better repair. The centerpiece was eye-catching, and there was no tablecloth, but rather snowy white and crisp place mats, as the etiquette books suggested, and the five place settings of Wedgwood china, luncheon-sized, were perfect. Emily Post would have approved. The silverware tips were exactly (I didn't have to measure) one inch from the edge of the table, all of it looking as though it had been freshly polished. There was lots of gleaming silver around. They couldn't have done any better at Downton Abbey. I wondered if there was a hidden tweeny or a second footman or someone to do that job. Maybe poor old Thomas had been stuck with it. I couldn't resist a glance at his hands for telltale silverware polish residue, but all I saw was a few green stains. Did Chadwick have Thomas working in the garden as well as doing all the work for our luncheon? I doubted that the Kauffmans had to cut corners and get staff to multitask like we did.

Let's face it though, four generations earlier when Summerlea was in its heyday, I wouldn't have been the researcher in the hot vintage number; I would have been the hidden tweeny with aspirations to be an upstairs maid.

By some miracle, we reached a deal over the lunch. I loved the light cream soup served in bowls with handles, and the poached salmon and homemade mayonnaise, although Vera barely nudged her food. Chadwick showed almost no interest in his, and the willowy Miss Troy seemed to push hers around on the plate. I noticed a small tic under her eye. Perhaps there was a lot of stress dealing with Magnus Kauffman's estate. But as the meal was delectable, I concentrated on that. I managed not to disgrace myself and left one mouthful on my plate, but Uncle Kev ate as though he'd been fasting for days. Considering that he'd been coddled by the signora, that took some doing.

I was in no hurry for our visit to end, not because I liked the company, but because I loved Summerlea. However, the minute the last coffee cup was whisked away, we all stood up and headed back to the sitting room. I'd no sooner settled myself into a chintz-covered chair when the deal was done.

I didn't have much of a role to play in any of the dealings, although I thought Vera had done surprisingly well by getting the price negotiated before we came. My role was like that of Miss Troy, purely decorative, I supposed, with unseen duties and abilities not necessary for this gathering.

The minute the trunk containing the Ngaio Marsh books was produced, the pace picked up. Vera and I checked out each volume. All thirty-two of them were in great shape. Vera kept her enthusiasm in check. To someone who didn't know her, she would have seemed bored with the entire experience. But I recognized that little glint in her eye.

Vera had brought the amount agreed on in cash, and after the genteel and entirely unsuccessful tussle for the final price, she nodded to Uncle Kev, who handed over a large burgundy tooled leather pouch. I knew it contained the ten thousand. I hoped—as Kev had been in charge of the cash—that it still contained the right amount.

Chadwick glanced at his watch, and Miss Troy jumped to her feet, looking slightly panicked. Getting rid of the visitors once the deal was done fell to the minion. As a fellow minion, I was familiar with the process. Miss Troy nibbled her lip. But she didn't have to worry about the awkward moment. The party was over.

Vera nodded to Uncle Kev to close up and carry the small trunk. We murmured our thank-yous. Vera's was so mumbled it could have been anything. Uncle Kev gripped Miss Troy's delicate hand in both of his in a vigorous good-bye handshake. He followed that with a rule-busting, jaw-breaking hug. Vera had rolled forward toward the front foyer and missed the faux pas. Mind you, I doubt she would have cared.

Chadwick sneered in polite contempt without moving from his lounging position, but Thomas the butler stepped forward with a look of alarm. Uncle Kev gripped Thomas's hand and shook it too. "Thanks for everything, buddy. Really great lunch." Kev gave him a playful jab in the bicep to top it off.

It was painful to watch, but I couldn't look away.

I said, "Beautiful meal, lovely home, thank you so much. It was a pleasure doing business with you." Even as I spoke I realized that in the world of the Kauffmans, I had probably sinned as much as Kev. In Ngaio Marsh's culture and probably the Kauffmans, "one" didn't ever comment about the possessions of others. Mentioning business after a meal was probably a gaffe of some magnitude.

I hurried after the others, glad I got to experience Summerlea and almost as glad to get away from Chadwick et al. I suppose I imagined Chadwick's reptilian gaze on my back. It gave me a chill.

We exited the grand front entrance, Kev making sure Vera didn't build up too much speed on the wheelchair ramp and me racing to catch up.

I gave one last glance at the silver Aston Martin and the red Mercedes convertible before we left.

From the window of the Caddy, Vera said, "We did well out of that. Can't wait to get home." Kev smirked at me through the rearview mirror, making me wonder how much he had liberated from the pile of cash. He gunned the Caddy and rocketed away. I turned back to see Thomas, the butler, staring at us from the front door. I hopped into the Saab and raced to catch up with them. Kev, as usual, cut it a bit fine as he passed a dusty white-and-blue delivery truck moving into the long driveway. I'm sure the driver saw his life pass before his eyes. As Kev made a sharp right turn at the stone pillars at the entrance to the property, a familiar trio of older ladies leapt back to avoid being splattered.

I waved apologetically to them as I drove past. It seemed to be too little too late.

One of them actually shook her fist while the others

pointed at us. Surely not a middle finger? But soon we were all out of sight along the winding county road. I leaned back and exhaled.

We were headed home to normal life. I could relax.

I had some delicious memories of a lovely luncheon with some less-than-lovely people in a truly beautiful house. I'd added a great dress to my wardrobe. It was enough.

Even Vera would have to admit it had been a good day.

We had the Marsh collection; nothing had been broken at or stolen from Summerlea; and no one had been killed.

CHAPTER FOUR

I WAS BARELY out of bed the next morning when Lance
called. I glanced at the clock. Seven fifteen, early for Lance
to be on the phone and for me too.

"So what's up?" I said, making sure there was plenty of
yawn in my voice.

"Did you hear the news?" Lance likes to drag it out a bit.

"In our lifetime, Lance." Oh God, Vera was rubbing off
on me.

"I thought you'd be interested since that's where you
spent yesterday."

"I am very interested, but also hoping that I won't spend
my morning waiting for you to tell me what it is I'm interested in."

"Chadwick Kauffman. I set a Google Alert for his name
and got a lot of responses today."

"What about him? Did the Lizard King saunter into the
reference department, which is nearly three hours away from
opening, by the way."

"Better for him if he had."

"Come on, Lance."

"He's dead."

"What?"

"Dead."

"Chadwick?"

"None other."

"But he can't be."

"Oh, but he can."

"We saw him yesterday. He was alive and kicking and kind of a pain in the— I didn't like him much but he can't be dead."

"He died from a fall in his summer home."

A memory of Chadwick's cold-blooded smile flashed through my brain. My voice quivered a bit. I never really get used to being close to people who end up dead.

Lance said, "The housekeeper discovered his body at the foot of the staircase, apparently, at—"

"Summerlea," I breathed.

"Yup."

"Was he alone?" I thought for a minute of Miss Troy and her slightly shaky hands. Had she had a premonition? It seemed like she was fretting about something. Maybe he hadn't been well. "Was there a woman with him?"

Poor Miss Troy, so worried and sweet. So welcoming.

"He must have been alone. The report said that the housekeeper found him when she arrived to take care of her evening duties yesterday. They said the security system wasn't on."

I sat back on my bed and tried to get my head around this. I had taken an almost instant dislike to Chadwick Kauffman, but I didn't wish that kind of an end on him. I wondered how he could have fallen on those familiar stairs. For some reason I thought of the leather case.

Lance interrupted my thoughts. "What were the chances that he'd die right after you met him?"

I shivered. "I can't imagine Chadwick Kauffman racing on the stairs or even tripping. He was so . . . deliberate. He would find rushing gauche and beneath him. You know the type? Cold and controlled."

"I guess you weren't in love with him."

"I wouldn't have asked him to homecoming, but that's a horrible way to go. I wonder if he had time to realize what was happening." I shuddered. What if he hadn't died instantly?

"Sorry to start your day this way, but I thought you'd like to know."

"Yes. Mmm. The housekeeper found him. So I wonder where the butler was."

"Ha-ha. Maybe he did it."

"There are thousands of comedians out of work, Lance. Better keep your day job. Well, I guess I should get dressed and go tell Vera."

WHEN I FOUND Vera at breakfast in the conservatory, she merely nodded at the news and went back to her *New York Times* crossword. Chadwick Kauffman—dead or alive—was of no interest to her now that she had her collection of Marsh mysteries. She expressed no worries for Miss Troy or anyone else.

"Take that as a lesson, Miss Bingham. As you age, you must take extra precautions. You cannot go running up and down staircases like a wild animal. The books are quite pristine. We will have to move a few items on the shelves in the library to give them the appropriate space."

Well, there you go. Priorities.

Signora Panetone shot out of the kitchen with a tower of fluffy blueberry pancakes for us. Maple syrup scented the air.

Uncle Kev is always first to the table for any meal. Without taking his eye off the approaching pancakes, he said, "Not to be a jerk, Jordie, but that guy was kind of a cold fish."

I gave him the stink-eye, for all the good it did.

"I guess all that money's sitting there now. Yeah, thanks, Signora, I'll have four pancakes, please."

Maybe the pancakes would take my mind off it too.

"Did the butler do it?" Kev said. Or I think that's what he said. His mouth was full.

"I guess his housekeeper found him. Lance said it's on the Internet. He had set an alert for the name and—"

Vera glanced up. "No jabbering about the Internet here at breakfast, Miss Bingham. You know the rules."

"But Chadwick Kauffman is dead, Vera."

"Horrible little man. Nothing to do with us," Vera said. "Stop loading up with those things, Fiammetta. One pancake is more than enough for me."

Chadwick might have been dead, but things were back to normal at Van Alst House.

NORMAL DIDN'T LAST all that long. For one thing, Uncle Lucky and his fairly new wife, my friend Karen Smith, arrived without warning and with Walter the Pug. Apparently, they had pressing business elsewhere and no pet accommodation. Would I take him? That was fine. Walter is actually quite a soothing little guy. It's hard to remain glum in his presence. I patted his thick velvety fur and he scampered around, turning in circles and attempting to wag his curly nub of a tail.

The truth is, although he's Karen's beloved pooch, he was with me a lot and I would have been very happy to offer him a forever home.

I wasn't the only one who felt that way.

With the definite exception of Good Cat and Bad Cat, Walter is popular and welcome at Van Alst House. I'm sure I've seen Vera almost smile at the sight of him. The signora was always cooking up endless dishes of chicken livers for him. The fondness was reciprocated.

After breakfast, I headed back to my heavenly little attic rooms to do some research. Walter hotfooted it up the stairs ahead of me and with a snort made himself at home in the middle of the flower-sprigged quilt. A Siamese stalked off in a huff, promising revenge, but leaving a warm spot on the quilt for Walter to press his wrinkled mug into and inhale noisily.

Another Siamese raised a paw from under the bed and barely missed Walter's muzzle. He scrambled for safety on higher ground and settled on my pillow.

I got my legs out of reach and did a bit of searching, setting up a few new Google Alerts of my own. In a moment of weakness I actually browsed through the images, even though I knew that was morbid.

None of the images that showed up were of Chadwick though. He seemed quite reclusive compared to his famous uncle. It was an hour or so later when one of the pings produced a link to a television story. There wasn't much new, except that Chadwick's employees seemed really choked up by the news when interviewers kept sticking mics under their noses. I found that hard to believe and felt guilty for thinking it.

Something odd tickled the edge of my mind, and I rewatched the television interviews of the employees from the Country Club and Spa.

As I played the clip of a reporter hounding Chadwick's assistant and spokesperson identified as Lisa, I did a double take. I hadn't caught Lisa's last name, but this person, a red-eyed, red-nosed, choked-up woman, was definitely not Miss Troy. But I guess if you have bags of money, you might need a fleet of assistants and more than one Lisa.

I searched online for Lisa Troy and found a number of accomplished women but not the skittish creature who had helped host us. But what did that matter? Lisa was a popular name. Lots of people don't have much of an Internet presence. For instance, my relatives were very careful to avoid it, and the rest of us should be grateful for that.

Back to Chadwick. But there was something strange there too. When I searched for images of the dead heir, Chadwick's heavy-lidded image never came up. Not even once. I could understand how Lisa and my uncles could avoid the spotlight, but the heir of the famous Magnus Kauffman and the man behind the success of the Country Club and Spa should show up somewhere. He didn't seek media attention, but he had been running a business and he must have been caught on camera somewhere, at something. Another man, reddish-blond and stocky, appeared over and over, smiling shyly and never quite gazing at the camera. Must have been someone else with the same name. There were sure to be other Chadwick Kauffmans out there somewhere. Right now I had bigger issues to worry about.

I was sorry that Chadwick Kauffman died a horrible death, but we were done with the Kauffman family. If they'd had any more mint-condition mysteries up for grabs, that would be different, but there was only the Marsh collection. The books in the Manhattan residence were lost to Vera's library.

FROM THE TIME I was a child, police at the door has been a bad thing and beloved uncles would vanish like fog through cleverly disguised staircases or leap out of windows. I believe this attitude has left me with a furtive look when police show up, and that's something I am trying to deal with.

As the cars rolled down the long driveway to Van Alst House, Vera and I were sitting in the conservatory, about to eat lunch and having a surprisingly heated discussion over whether the Marsh collection might be displayed outside the library for a while to celebrate its arrival and show it off. It wasn't my collection of fine first editions. It wasn't my secure and environmentally appropriate library either.

Vera was winning. But mostly she was arguing with herself. I was doing my best not to get on the wrong side of either argument. I'd managed to move my head in a way that could have been a nod "yes" or a nod "no" after each of Vera's points.

"And what if there was a fire?" Vera growled. "Or moths?"

Speaking of moths, the signora fluttered in with a large plate of panini stuffed with prosciutto and provolone cheese.

"Who's this coming?" Vera said.

Kev glanced out the window and stood up, a panini in each hand. I passed him a couple of napkins, and he stepped out in the direction of the back door.

"Police?" As I've said many times, we're not much for the police in our family, if you leave out Officer Tyler "Smiley" Dekker. Of course, I was very much in favor of Smiley, even if the rest of the family was less than enthusiastic. But at Van Alst House, Vera still holds to the belief that the police are the good guys, there to help the solid citizens of Harrison Falls. So the arrival of this long black sedan and a cruiser sent my heart racing. There was no reason for it. I hadn't done anything wrong. I rarely do anything wrong, and if I do, it's because there's no other choice and someone's life is in danger. I'm just saying there are some gray areas.

"What do the police want?" Vera growled.

It takes a while to get used to Vera's gravelly voice, but I'd had time. "No idea," I said, calmly. I was proud of myself. All my recent interactions with the police were paying off. My heart might have been thumping, but my voice was steady and so were my hands, and that was what mattered. "I'll find out."

The signora put her plate of panini on the table and made the sign of the cross.

I am tasked with answering doors in Van Alst House. Vera rarely condescends to. The signora gets too worked up, and Kev, well, anything could happen. At any rate, as these were clearly police cars, Kev would probably be about ten miles away by the time I meandered to the end of the corridor.

I always make a point not to rush to the door if the cops are on the other side.

They were.

The cruiser was from Harrison Falls Police Department,

and Officer Tyler Dekker had been driving it, but the sedan was unmarked.

I must have blinked in surprise.

Two cars.

Uh-oh. Had Kev pinched something? My mind ran over the contents of the rooms we'd been in at Summerlea. No. He wouldn't do that to me. Or Vera.

Although sometimes Kev can't help himself.

Before we got to Summerlea, I'd been worried that he might have been unable to resist the temptation to skim a couple of bills from our transaction. He hadn't been given much opportunity.

So I doubted that was why the police were there. Anyway, I was pretty sure that Chadwick Kauffman intended our purchase to remain discreet, shall we say. The rich may have tons of money, but they can be pretty darn cheap. Cash transactions equal no tax.

It must have been Chadwick's death. Why else would they come?

I managed a smile as though they were here collecting for some local police charity. Tyler Dekker shuffled his feet and squinted in an imitation of a smile. Where was his toothy grin, with the little gap that I love so much?

My own smile may have dipped a bit when the woman with him produced her badge. "Jordan Bingham?" She was tall with near-ebony skin, close-cropped hair and a smart, edgy look.

"Yes."

"Lieutenant Drea Castellano. Harrison Falls Police Department."

I blinked again. So many surprises. So little time. Lieutenant? Whoa.

The man next to her said nothing, although he waved a badge languidly in my general direction.

She said with a bit of bite to her tone, "And this is Detective Sergeant Stoddard."

Stoddard gave the slightest suggestion of a shrug, as if

anything more would have been too much effort. They must have had quite a ride over together. I knew a bit about Stoddard from Smiley. The part I knew was "lazy" and "conceited." I figured Stoddard had expected he'd been a shoo-in for that lieutenant's job until she showed up, but that was mere speculation.

Smiley had failed to mention that the new lieutenant was a knockout.

I tried not to stare at her. "Yes?"

"And I understand you know Officer Dekker. May we come in?"

I hesitated. Old habits die hard. "Of course, but may I ask what it's about?"

"We'd like to talk to you and . . ."—she glanced down at a paper in her hand—". . . a Kevin Kelly and a Vera Van Alst."

A Vera Van Alst? As if there was more than one! It didn't bode well for our interview.

Smiley stared at his feet.

"I'll see if they're at home." I led them into the grand foyer, doing my best to look dignified and calm. There are no chairs in the foyer, so they'd have to stand and stew while I pretended to see if Vera and Kev were "at home."

I hotfooted like Walter down the endless corridor and arrived breathless at the conservatory.

"The police want to speak to you," I said.

She waved a dismissive hand. "Send them away."

"Um, it doesn't work that way, Vera."

"Well, what do they want? This isn't the time of day for visits." She glanced at her *New York Times* puzzle with resentment.

"I don't know. But we have to see them. They want to talk to you and me and Kevin."

Kev was probably tunneling under the St. Lawrence River to Canada by this point.

"Mr. Kelly had an errand," she said. "Not sure when he'll be back."

I sighed. "We'll have to do, then. Here?"

"Certainly not. This is private space. Take them to the study if you can't get rid of them."

MINUTES LATER, I escorted them into Vera's study. The dyspeptic Van Alst ancestors had glared at them during the longish walk. Vera was seated in her wheelchair behind the beautiful Edwardian desk.

She nodded gravely as they introduced themselves.

The woman officer glanced around at the ten-foot ceilings and the long, faded silk draperies on the Georgian-style windows. It was a room to remember. I love the study. It was here that I first convinced Vera to hire me as her researcher. She hadn't thought much of me or the idea, but that was then. She's gradually coming around.

I gestured to the pair of chairs in front of Vera's desk. I perched at the edge of the velvet fainting coach, faded to pale amethyst after all these years. I patted the seat beside me so that Tyler Dekker would also sit. For some reason he was sweating.

"Well," Vera growled. "What can I do for you?"

Lieutenant Castellano—apparently unaccustomed to being growled at by women in wheelchairs—flashed her a look. A dangerous little flash, that.

"We'd like to know your whereabouts yesterday."

Vera looked bored. "We had luncheon at a colleague's home."

Colleague? I loved that.

The detective nodded. "I'd like to discuss that with you."

"Discuss?" Vera said.

"Alone."

Vera raised an eyebrow. "Alone?"

"That's right."

"You mean without Miss Bingham?"

"Correct again."

"Miss Bingham, will you wait in the conservatory, please?"

The detective nodded. "I'll speak to you later, Miss Bingham, if you don't mind waiting." I didn't think she meant the "if you don't mind" bit.

I got shakily to my feet. It was all very polite and civilized, no doubt a result of Vera Van Alst's place in Harrison Falls society. But I didn't like the direction it was taking. Detective Castellano wanted to talk to Vera alone. Later she would talk to me alone. There was a reason for that. She wanted to make sure our stories matched. I headed for the door. Smiley got to his feet to follow me, but a minuscule shake of Detective Castellano's head caused him to sit down again. He was alone now on the fainting coach. Still sweating. I wondered if he was coming down with a fever.

The signora chose that moment to stick her head through the door and arrive with coffee, almond cookies and a plate of cheese. The aroma of Italian roast filled the room.

"Not now, Fiammetta," Vera snapped. "I don't believe this is a social call."

"Yes, yes, cookies. Eat, Vera. Eat, Jordan."

Cookies sounded good to me, and so did coffee, but I was being expelled.

The detective inclined her head toward her partner and he rose and said, "I'll wait with you. Wouldn't mind seeing this conservatory." I noticed he cast a backward glance at the coffee and cookies.

Great. Just what I needed. A cop sitting with me so I couldn't get any advice from my nearest and dearest about what to do in this situation. I smiled weakly and led the way past the disapproving ancestors to the conservatory. The leather soles of his shoes squeaked to fill the awkward silence. It was a long walk and Stoddard sauntered the whole way. I was relieved that at least Kev hadn't chosen to sneak back in thinking the coast was clear.

The detective was not inclined to talk. I think they take training in how to keep you off balance, even in your own home. I knew Tyler Dekker's ambitions. He had plans to become a detective. I hated the idea of his naturally pleasant and helpful personality being twisted by police training in tricking suspects.

We were certainly being treated like suspects. No question about it. I felt like consulting a lawyer, but I had absolutely no idea about what. Nothing looks guiltier than the rush to get a legal opinion, and yet, I also knew that even innocent people say and do unwise things without good advice. My last encounter with a lawyer had been Sammy Vincovic, a pricey, but effective, barracuda from Syracuse. It had resulted in some very useful information: Don't say anything you don't have to. If you have to say something, make it, "No comment."

I took my usual seat in the conservatory. Three sets of lunch plates and a platter of rapidly cooling paninis sat on the table.

"Someone else with you?" the detective said, pointing around.

"It's only the three of us," I said. "Vera, me and the signora."

The signora had pursued us along the corridor and into the conservatory. Her black eyes widened as I said this. "Guess we'll all have to make up for missing lunch later on, Signora. Sorry."

"Coffee! Cookies!" she said, skittering through the door to the kitchen. I knew there were probably a dozen *caffettieras* there and a bottomless source of cookies, so we wouldn't miss out on that.

"I'll give her a hand to clear up," I said. "She gets alarmed if our routine is altered." I gathered up the dishes. The detective picked up the ones on his side and said, "Let me help with the plates."

How sneaky was that? What was he after? Fingerprints? Evidence? Signs of Kev? Panini? I had no idea, and I didn't care for this turn of events.

"Signora Panetone hates anyone in her kitchen," I sputtered.

But it was too late. He had already followed me through the door to the signora's sanctum sanctorum. Luckily Kev wasn't hiding out here either.

"Go, go!" the signora said, shooing us back to the conservatory, where we sat facing each other warily until coffee arrived. Honestly, it seemed like hours, if not days.

He relaxed and filled up his cup with the fragrant brew. He also accepted a plate of almond cookies. The signora piled up a few extra for him. I sat there feeling grimly resentful, but not so much that I couldn't have a coffee and cookies. We have to keep our strength up when the police are on the scene. My uncles taught me that. They also taught me that you don't ever inadvertently give them a sample of your DNA or a chance to get your prints. I didn't see how that could happen here, with the signora ready to wash up at a moment's notice. A CSI's worst nightmare.

As the time ticked by slowly, I took stock of my company and noted that Detective Stoddard wore pale chinos, a burgundy button-down shirt and leather loafers. His brown hair had been cut by a good stylist, and he wore rimless glasses. He was young to be a detective and had probably been born full of himself. In line with that, he was in no hurry to grill me.

Finally, I cracked. "Exactly what brings you here today, Detective?" I said. I'm not that used to hanging around innocent people, but I did believe that most folks would be curious by this point.

I half expected him to say, "Wouldn't you like to know," but he only smiled and pointed at his mouth, indicating that it was full and he couldn't be expected to answer. There was a lot of that full-mouth thing happening.

I had nothing better to do than wait.

When he had finished three cookies and not answered my question, I said, "What brings you here?"

"You'd better ask *Lieutenant* Castellano when she interviews you." I heard the undertone of resentment when he said, "Lieutenant."

"Interviews me? But why do I need to be interviewed?"

Of course, he had another mouthful of cookies by then. He was almost as good as Kev.

As a technique, it was very useful. Make the suspects nervous, edgy, and they'll spill their guts. I hated feeling nervous and edgy when we hadn't done anything wrong, except for paying cash for the Marsh collection. I'd done nothing and therefore wouldn't be spilling my guts. If there was an issue about the money, that would have been Chadwick's tax-dodging transgression, not ours. Of course that was silly.

There was an obvious reason why they were there.

Chadwick was dead, and we had been among the last people to see him. Naturally, a senior investigator wanted to talk to us one by one.

CHAPTER FIVE

I DIDN'T GET a chance to compare notes with Vera or Tyler before I found myself being interviewed by the impressive Detective Castellano. Detective Castellano had sent Tyler Dekker to get me in the conservatory, where I was on my third cup of the signora's coffee. I'd lost count of the almond cookies. They had no tranquilizer benefits, as it turned out, so I was relying on the spine I inherited from the Kelly side of the family.

With Tyler following, I was escorted back to the study by Stoddard. I noticed he avoided looking at Vera's ancestors on the way.

A long, awkward walk was had by all.

Castellano was waiting for me. She was installed behind Vera's desk, fitting right in with her natural air of authority. Vera was nowhere in sight. She would have gone up in flames if she'd seen the detective installed in the seat of power, acting like she owned the joint (to quote my uncles' favorite phrase). Smiley seemed to have vanished too. Maybe his job was to lead them to me. Weasel.

I used every trick in the Kelly book to keep myself cool. But alarming questions kept firing in my brain. What if they searched my room?

Be calm, I answered myself. *There is nothing in your room.* That was true. My beloved Sweet Sixteen lock picks were hidden behind the baseboard in my old room at Uncle Mick's place. No worries there.

My possessions in my attic rooms at Van Alst House were limited and vintage. I might have cherished them, but they were not the kind of thing that anyone in their right mind would steal. So even though my conscience was clear, why I was more nervous than Bad Cat?

Senior detectives do not show up at your home without good reason. I was weirded out by Tyler Dekker's presence and aloof behavior. I had a feeling there were more backups in the driveway.

Obviously, they knew we'd been at Summerlea the same day that Chadwick died. But he'd been alive when we left. The butler was still there. Lisa Troy was still there. He must have been alive when they left or they would have called for help when he fell.

Could this visit be about something other than his death? Had something of great value been stolen from Summerlea? I was praying that Uncle Kev hadn't actually managed to liberate some tiny incredibly valuable artifact while my back was turned. Instead of letting anxiety take over my brain, I concentrated on the unnervingly attractive and slouchy Stoddard.

Castellano had actually smiled at me when I entered the study. I wasn't fooled for a minute by her inquiring face, or the soft caramel two-piece suit or the paisley wool scarf she had looped fashionably around her neck. She'd have to be very smart and very tough to get where she was. She looked totally at home in the job. And if Kev had done something to get us in trouble, she was the enemy.

She fingered her scarf. "Cold in here."

"It always is. You'll be glad you're wearing those boots." She'd left her cognac-colored, knee-high boots on too.

She smiled at me and said, "Everyone seems quite tense."

As if to reinforce her point, the signora skittered through the door as though pursued by wasps. She deposited some slices of ciabatta bread and cheese and fled. Bad Cat reached out again.

"Nothing to worry about, Miss Bingham," she said. I noticed her smile didn't reach her dark eyes.

"I'm sure you're right," I said, smiling back. "But it is unusual to be interviewed by the police without any explanation. Isn't it?"

"I get that," she said.

"I'm sure you do. And as we all have things to do today, can we get to the point? What is it you want to ask us about?"

"Chadwick Kauffman."

"Okay. What about him?"

"You've heard the news?"

"About Mr. Kauffman's accident?"

"His death, yes."

Was she implying it wasn't an accident?

"Yes, his death. That was a shock."

"I'm sure it was." She was one of those people who could say one thing and you knew that she meant the opposite. "How did you learn about it?"

My uncles always say, answer the question you want to. "Yes, it was a surprise and very sad. But I still don't know why you're here." It suddenly occurred to me that the "alerts" would definitely look fishy. They'd find my new alerts in a minute if they checked my phone, of course. Mental note: Clear history. Even if we'd had good reasons to check out Chadwick.

"Very sad?" Castellano said, smiling slightly.

I winced. "Well, not devastating. I only met him once. We had a meal with him in his home yesterday and he seemed like a—well, you don't expect something like that, do you?"

She shrugged as if she wouldn't be surprised if people dropped dead after meeting with me.

"Hmm, yes, especially immediately after you met with him."

It was hard to miss the insinuation in her voice.

"Wait. Immediately? How is that possible?"

"In fact, it was right after you were out of sight of Summerlea. Would you like to tell me about your return trip here?"

I blinked.

"But it couldn't have been right after."

"What do you mean?"

"He wasn't alone in the house. The others were still there when we left."

"What others?"

"Miss Troy and the butler, Thomas."

"Ah yes. Miss Van Alst tells the same story."

"It's not a story. It's what happened."

"You left with Miss Van Alst and Mr. Kelly?"

"No. I was behind the Cadillac with Vera and Unc, um, Mr. Kelly. When they drove away, I looked back. Both cars were still there. Thomas, the butler, saw us leave. He'll be able to confirm that we were on our way and Mr. Kauffman was still inside. Alive, it goes without saying. We would hardly have left if something had happened to him."

"Ah yes, the butler," she said with a tight little smile.

"Yes, that's correct."

"Uh-huh. And you say this butler was there?"

"I don't 'say' it. He was. He served luncheon and generally did things you might expect a butler to do. And more, I think. Not that I'm familiar with butlers outside of television."

"You mentioned the cars."

"Yes."

"Miss Van Alst didn't mention cars."

"She wouldn't. She couldn't care less about cars. She only cares about books, really."

"So I understand. What cars were there?"

"A silver Aston Martin. Totally glamorous, in an early James Bond kind of way. I assumed it was Mr. Kauffman's. You don't see them every day. And there was also an older Mercedes-Benz, red, that I figured belonged to his assistant, Miss Troy."

"You did, did you?"

She asked her questions with a knowing half smile, as though she'd caught you in a lie and you knew she'd caught you and now she was enjoying watching you squirm.

I didn't plan to squirm, because I hadn't been caught in a lie.

"I didn't think the car was the butler's, but that was only an assumption."

Again with the half smile. "So, you and Miss Van Alst and, um, let's see, Kevin Kelly, met with Chadwick yesterday?"

"That's right."

"And do you mind telling me how that came about?"

I blinked. "Chadwick Kauffman asked us, well, he invited Miss Van Alst, to join him for lunch at Summerlea."

"Did he?"

I wasn't sure what she meant by that tone. "Yes. He did. Okay, to be precise, his assistant asked."

"Did she?"

"Yes," I said, trying to keep irritation out of my voice. The questioning of everything could drive a person to shout. And that would be very bad. "Miss Lisa Troy called and made the arrangements to meet with Miss Van Alst. Miss Van Alst hates driving, so she insisted that Mr. Kelly drive her. And she asked that I come along too. So the luncheon invitation was expanded to include us."

Close enough.

She raised an eyebrow.

I added, "You've met Vera Van Alst. She gets what she

wants by sheer force of will." As the words were out of my mouth, I wanted to claw them back in. Had Vera mentioned the transaction with the Ngaio Marsh books? This is why they question people separately. The old divide-and-conquer strategy.

She said, "And then what happened when you arrived after this 'invitation'?"

I left out talk of money and books. "We were met at the door by the butler, Thomas, and brought in. Miss Troy came to greet us, and then Chadwick arrived."

"I see. And where was Chadwick arriving from?"

"He came down that grand staircase. And may I say, he didn't look like he might fall either. He was very much in control of his movements."

"Huh."

Really? Should a detective say "huh" so dismissively?

"After introductions, we had mimosas in the sitting room, I suppose it's a reception room, near the dining room, and then we had a beautiful luncheon."

"Did you?"

"Yes. We did," I said, exasperated. "Surely Vera must have told you the same thing."

"She didn't mention lunch."

"What? Oh, well, that's no big surprise. She doesn't care about food. But I love food and it was excellent." Uncle Kev does too, but the less said the better.

"And Mr. Kelly?"

I managed a chuckle. "Oh, he likes food. You can ask the signora. He's her favorite."

"But he's not here to back up your story, is he?"

"I don't understand what needs backing up."

"How about your reason to be in an exclusive neighborhood where a body is found?"

I paused and calmed myself. "But I'm telling you. The butler saw us leave. Miss Troy said good-bye. They know we left."

She leaned forward and flicked an invisible mote of dust

from her cognac boots. Behind her Bad Cat watched and planned.

"Would it surprise you, Miss Bingham, to learn that there is no butler at Summerlea?"

She got me there.

"What?"

She shook her head, amused at the game. "No butler."

"But there was a butler. We all saw him."

"We have only your word for that."

"Well, you have Vera's."

"She didn't mention a butler."

Of course she hadn't. It was Vera. All she cared about was the books. "There was one. His name was Thomas. Miss Van Alst, as you may have observed, is not really a people person. She probably didn't notice him. He'd be part of the background to her. But she must have mentioned Miss Troy."

The dark eyes gleamed. "Miss Troy also didn't rate a mention."

"Vera probably didn't mention the laws of gravity, but I'm pretty sure those still exist."

"Good one," she said with a throaty chuckle. "But obviously not good enough."

"Vera must have told you about Chadwick Kauffman."

"She did."

"At least. That's good."

"Is it? It puts you and Miss Van Alst and the mysteriously absent Mr. Kelly in the presence of the victim without a single witness. Do you really think that's good?"

"What do you mean 'victim'? Wasn't it an accident?"

"It appears not."

"Well, there were witnesses. Two of them. Maybe Thomas didn't bill himself as a butler. Maybe he was a valet or . . . some kind of personal assistant, but he was definitely there. Please get in touch with Miss Troy. She'll confirm what I'm saying."

She watched me with pleasant anticipation, her beautifully groomed eyebrows raised just a touch.

I sputtered, "All you need to do is ask her."

"Well, I would, of course, but there's only one problem with that."

I slumped in my seat. Why was this so unsettling? "What problem?"

"There is no Miss Troy."

"Don't be ridiculous. Of course there is. We saw her. We spoke to her. We shook her hand. She was nice, kind. Well organized." I heard my voice trail off.

"The housekeeper and the staff of Mr. Kauffman's business all confirm: no butler, no one named Thomas. No Miss Troy."

I stared at her.

"They *were* there," I said in a small voice. "She was very pretty."

"Instead," she went on, as if I'd said nothing, "you three were seen fleeing the property where Mr. Chadwick Kauffman was, apparently alone, right before his death."

"Fleeing from what? We were not fleeing. That's just the way, um, Mr. Kelly drives."

"How about this: You were fleeing because Mr. Kauffman did not die from a fall. It appears he was killed by a blow to the head before he went down the stairs."

"A blow to the head? Did he hit his head on something and then—?"

"Not much chance of that, is there?"

"I don't know. But otherwise it means . . ."

"That's right, Miss Bingham."

I hadn't finished. I couldn't quite bring myself to say he'd been murdered.

She added, "And that means someone killed him."

I shivered. "There must be a mistake."

"No mistake."

"Maybe he hit his head on a post and—"

"He didn't."

"But—"

"We have the weapon, and it wasn't the staircase."

I held up my hand. My stomach lurched. Murder? Murder and the people we believed were entertaining us turned out to be not real. Except they had been real. They'd been flesh and blood. They'd talked; they'd shaken hands. They had definitely been there.

"Murder?"

"Yes. Someone hit him hard enough to crack his skull."

"His skull was cracked?"

"That was enough to kill him."

"Well, we didn't do that."

"I believe I will find out otherwise."

"If there was no one at Summerlea—and Thomas and Lisa Troy were definitely there . . . Wait a minute, how did you even find out that we were at the house?" I said.

"The neighbors, a group of elderly women, were almost plowed down by your Mr. Kelly. They gave a description of your distinctive vehicle, although the plates weren't readable, and they had the presence of mind to jot down the license plate of the Cadillac."

Damn Uncle Kev and his love of *Grand Theft Auto*. Also, why wasn't that license plate covered in dust like every other one that the Kellys drove? It was early spring in upstate New York. Plenty of mud everywhere. Even the Aston Martin and the Mercedes parked in front of Summerlea had muddy plates.

I sighed. "Kevin Kelly's not much of a driver, but that doesn't mean he's a killer. He's very gentle."

"There's more, of course."

"More? Chadwick was murdered. You say that there is no Miss Lisa Troy in his life. You say he didn't have a butler. What else? Is the earth suddenly flat?" My heart was racing. Everything was so hard to grasp. So inexplicable. And so likely to get us charged with murder.

She pounced verbally. "Fingerprints."

Was that all?

I relaxed. "Oh well, we all have fingerprints and we were in the house. So that's not surprising." Nothing much to worry about there, as we hadn't done anything. Fingers crossed for Kev, of course.

Her dark eyes glittered. "Unusual as it may seem for visitors to such a grand home, your prints, of course, were in the system as a result of earlier interactions with the police."

"But not because I was accused of a crime! I've been a witness. My prints have been taken for purposes of elimination and, um, other reasons. I've never committed a crime. Never," I squeaked. So much for cool and calm. Get it together, Jordan.

She didn't even appear to notice. And my statement wasn't entirely true, but any mild transgressions had always been in the interests of justice and keeping people alive. About that, the less said, the better.

"And Mr. Kelly's too, of course."

"Um, Kevin was with me all the time. He'd never hurt anyone. He's gentle and . . ." Best not to mention unintentionally dangerous.

"Even Miss Van Alst's were there."

"Well, you can hardly believe that Vera would kill anyone. She's only interested in her collections, and there was no threat to any of them." I added hurriedly, "And if there had been, she would take action with a lawyer, not a weapon. A dead opponent would be no use to Vera."

Again with the throaty chuckle. "She told me that about herself. She only cares about books."

"I don't understand how Chadwick's death has anything to do with us or the books."

"That remains to be seen."

"Vera's the one with the passion for the books, and even if there had been some issue, which there wasn't, she couldn't hit a man with a blunt object hard enough to kill him let alone haul him up the staircase afterward."

"What about the elevator?"

"What elevator?"

"The one in Summerlea."

I stared. Elevator? "So what if there was? Vera didn't take the elevator. She was never out of my sight."

She tilted her head to one side and met my eyes. "So you say. And yet you and Mr. Kelly both left to 'freshen up,' as you put it."

I goggled. "Yes. We did. Before lunch. But Chadwick was alive and well. We were all there."

"Did you go to the same powder room as Mr. Kelly?"

"Of course not."

"Right."

"And you were out of sight of Miss Van Alst and Chadwick."

"The other two as well. Lisa and Thomas."

"I guess you're sticking to that story. It makes me wonder if you're all in it together."

All in it together? Had she been reading Vera's vintage mysteries? "You mean you think we conspired to kill Chadwick?"

She smiled and nodded.

"Why? Why would we do such a thing?"

"Theft is my guess."

My jaw dropped. "Theft? We are not thieves." Most of us weren't, anyway. Oh, Kev, Kev, Kev.

This woman was good. I knew that none of us had killed Chadwick. Absolutely knew it. I knew that Miss Troy and Thomas the butler had been there and that Chadwick had been alive and smirking when we left. Why then was she able to make me so very nervous?

I reminded myself that the police can lie and mislead to get you to incriminate yourself. That had been drummed into me as a child.

I said, "We aren't. And no matter what you say, nothing can change the fact that what I've told you is true." Okay, that was a bit of a circular argument, but I did feel panicky. "It's like you're out to get us."

"Or if the shoe fit and you ran away in it."

"We didn't run away. And you can't have any proof that any of us was upstairs and hit Chadwick—for whatever reason—and then pushed him. We weren't there. Vera didn't take the elevator. Kevin didn't go upstairs. I didn't."

"Did I say he was killed upstairs?"

Was she just trying to rattle me? "But I assumed since he fell down after the blow—"

"Maybe there was a dispute about the price of the books and then tempers flared. A statue was lifted and brought down hard and—"

"What statue?" I cast my mind back to remember a statue. Nothing came to mind.

"Oh, but there was."

I slumped. "Didn't you say that Chadwick had been thrown or pushed down the stairs?"

"Mmm. With some force."

"But, how would we have gotten him up there? I could hardly lift a man. Vera even less so. And Kevin—"

"From what I hear, your Mr. Kelly is very fit and used to manual labor."

"I don't know if I'd call moving a body manual labor. Anyway, Kev would throw up."

"I hardly think so."

"I know so and I also know he didn't do it. And he never went upstairs."

"Evidence says otherwise."

My patience was fraying. "It couldn't. You're trying to rattle me, and you're wasting your time. We didn't do it. You don't have any proof that we did, because there's no proof to be had. Simple as that."

"Oh really?"

"Yes. Really." I usually resist the Kelly temper that is half my heritage, but this time it was hard to.

"How then do you explain Mr. Kevin Kelly's fingerprints on the statue found by the head of the stairs in Summerlea?"

"What?"

"You heard me."

"But I can't explain it. Wait, there was a statue—marble, I think—on the small table outside the powder rooms. A nude kneeling figure. Is that the one? It's possible that Mr. Kelly picked it up to admire it. But it was still on the table when we returned to the sitting room, where Chadwick was very much alive. It wasn't very big. I can't imagine that could be a murder weapon."

Even as the words came out, I knew how foolish they sounded. That thing was made of marble. Of course it could have cracked a skull.

Castellano opened her mouth to speak, and I burst out, "And we were not separated, after that, until we left, when, as I've mentioned, Chadwick was not only alive but said good-bye to us."

"It was good-bye, all right. You're going to have to tell the truth or you will find yourself charged as an accessory to murder. If not conspiracy to commit murder."

Sammy Vincovic's face flashed through my mind. He was shouting, *No comment.*

I swallowed. "I want to speak to an attorney."

"Sounds like guilty talk to me."

"You know that I am entitled to legal counsel."

"Your choice, of course. It doesn't look good, you know, if you're stalling us. An innocent person would cooperate with the police."

"You wouldn't be denying me my right to an attorney, would you?"

"Why? You don't need one if you haven't done anything."

I didn't trust Castellano. "I want legal advice. I think you are trying to set us up."

She shrugged. "Why don't I arrest you? We'll head to the station and then you'll be one hundred percent entitled to a lawyer."

I frowned. I wasn't falling for the innocent person talk. There have been many, many innocent people filling jail cells and many, many guilty ones walking free. My uncles like to say, it's all in the way you play your cards. I didn't know what cards I had, let alone how to play them. I didn't really have a lawyer either. I'm a researcher for a book collector. I'm saving to get back to grad school. It wasn't like I needed legal counsel on retainer. Vera had lawyers, but they didn't practice criminal law.

The one time I'd really needed Sammy, my uncles had arranged it. They had footed the bill for his time without being asked. I couldn't let that happen this time. I'd hoped never to see him again. Now I needed him and I didn't even have his number. I had no idea how to reach him. My Uncle Mick, Uncle Lucky and Karen were in Manhattan (I thought) on some business that it was better I didn't know about. Kev was on the run.

"I need to make a phone call."

"All right, then," Castellano said. "You are volunteering to answer questions. If you want your rights and your phone calls and your lawyer, then we're going to have to head down to the station."

The office door squeaked open. Castellano turned and glared at the man who lumbered through it. Sammy Vincovic appeared, fastening the top button of his blue two-button suit jacket, which managed to be tight and rumpled at the same time. Had he slept in it? Still, at the sight of his blocklike body and wild black, wavy hair, I felt a huge surge of relief.

"Who the hell are you?" Castellano snapped. "This is a police interview."

He smoothed his random waves. "Sammy Vincovic. I'm Miss Bingham's lawyer, and I'll be sitting in on this interview."

Castellano glared at Stoddard. The glare said, "You idiot. You let her contact a lawyer?" No words were necessary to convey this. For a second, Stoddard lost his studied cool. He shook his head, meaning, "Not on my watch."

How, then? I wondered.

Castellano narrowed her eyes at Vincovic. She returned to her questions.

"So you were about to explain how Kevin Kelly's fingerprints ended up on the murder weapon."

I opened my mouth to repeat that they couldn't have been.

Sammy said, "My client has nothing to say."

She said, "Miss Bingham, you really should answer this question. Evading it could go badly for you."

"To repeat, my client has no comment. And I would like a word with her."

As I was not under arrest at that point, Castellano had no choice but to vacate the chair and leave the study. Stoddard slouched out, looking chastened. She cast an angry glance at him, and he shrugged languidly and shook his head. I heard him say, "She didn't call anyone. We had coffee."

Kellys do not cry, and as I was a Kelly, I had to keep my eyes dry. I must say I felt like sobbing and wailing, but that was, of course, out of the question.

As the door closed behind the two detectives, Sammy said, "Now you can fill me in." He glanced at the door and touched both of his small, neat ears. I got the message. Say nothing I didn't want them to hear. Say only what was on the record. I could do that. It took a while to get the whole story out. He wanted every detail about the invitation, the luncheon and our relationship with Chadwick Kauffman.

"We didn't have a relationship with him. We got the invitation out of the blue. It was purely business. A cash transaction," I whispered with a glance at the door.

"You never met him before?"

"Not him and not them. He wanted to sell some books to Vera, who was willing to give him an excellent price for them. Everyone would be ahead. It was a good thing. There was no reason at all for anyone to hurt him."

"Okay, now tell me what she asked you."

I did my best to repeat all the questions. "She's saying that Kevin's fingerprints are on a statue and that the statue is the murder weapon." I reached out and touched his beefy arm. "There's no way that's possible. Kevin wasn't upstairs. None of us were. We could see the staircase clearly from the foyer and the sitting room and we had no way to know there was an elevator. So even if we were capable of murder—which we aren't—I couldn't have killed him. Vera and Kev couldn't have either. Anyway, even if one of us had been upstairs—which we weren't—Chadwick was alive and smirking when we left."

Sammy gazed at me, waiting.

"You do know that the police don't have to be truthful with you during interviews, don't you?"

Oh. Well. Of course I knew that. "I don't think she was lying, but I knew she was wrong. Kev might have touched that little marble statue. But it was still there when we went back to the sitting room. The lieutenant seems like a decent person. Tough, but decent."

Sammy let out a booming belly laugh. "That's cute, kid. You can't go by what she looks like. She's a detective investigating a murder. Her job is to break down your resistance and get the answers she needs to solve the case. This guy was a big shot, and the murder is in the news. She'll be under pressure. But that's not our problem."

"No. But we do have a problem. The whole situation is a problem. I've been thinking about it. I told you Castellano said that Lisa Troy and the butler don't even exist—well, they do exist. But obviously they're not who they said they were."

"Yep. Got that."

"It's all so theatrical. I felt like I was in one of the Ngaio Marsh books that Vera bought."

"Theatrical?"

"Yes, everything about it felt staged. But who would stage it?"

Sammy leaned forward and his black eyes bored into mine.

I returned his gaze. "So there's only one thing it could be."

He nodded. "A setup."

CHAPTER SIX

I SUPPOSE IF you were a defense attorney, you'd prefer something a bit more concrete to keep your client out of jail. Yelling, "Setup!" only gets you so far.

Sammy sat thinking. At least he wasn't one to scowl.

I said, "Thank you for coming. I felt I was being ground down and fast. How do people survive hours and hours of questioning without accidentally implicating themselves?"

"Usually they don't. That's why you don't allow yourself to be interviewed without representation. They trip you up. They get you rattled. The next stage they'd be saying that Vera Van Alst or Kevin didn't back up your story and pointed the finger at you."

"I wouldn't fall for that," I said.

"Says the kid who didn't think the cops would lie to her. These people have training. You'd be surprised what they can get people to admit to, whether they're guilty or not."

"I don't see how she can have any proof. It was impossible for any of us to kill him. I kept telling her that, but she didn't believe me."

"Remember this: She's not paid to believe you."

"Speaking of paying, who called you? I am grateful that you're here, but was it Uncle Kev?" Of course, that was ridiculous because Kev never had enough money for a bus ticket.

He shook his head. "Not Kevin. And as I'm representing you, he'll need his own counsel."

"I guess they'll have to find him first."

Sammy said, "That's bad."

"How bad?"

"It's a murder investigation and he's disappeared. So pretty bad."

"Well, technically, he's out on an errand. He doesn't know what's going on."

"You sure about that?"

"Of course I am. Uncle Kev always does errands when the police come knocking. It's like an instinct for him. But he didn't hurt Chadwick. You have my word on that."

"I've learned one immutable fact in my career: Anything's possible where people are involved."

"Unless the laws of physics were temporarily suspended allowing time travel, Uncle Kev couldn't have killed Chadwick. But the two people who were in the house could have."

"You mean Lisa Troy, who doesn't exist, and the butler that no one has heard of?"

"Exactly."

He nodded. "I hear you, but that won't get you out of this. Never mind. With luck, they left some kind of evidence. Fingerprints. Whatever. Let's give Castellano something to think about." He straightened his collar and tie, brushed a bit of dust off his too-tight suit jacket and tugged at it.

I figured I wasn't the only person who'd thought that Castellano was pretty spectacular. I said, "Don't let yourself be seduced by that pretty package."

"I'm your lawyer. I don't get seduced, but she is . . ."

I waited.

". . . quite a woman."

"No kidding. And you still haven't told me who called you. Was it Uncle Mick and Uncle Lucky? How would they have found out?"

He shook his head. "Not your uncles."

"But who? Vera?"

Vera could probably pay his fee, although I would expect a bit more of the Francis I silverware to disappear.

"Not Vera."

Not uncles. Not Kev. Not Vera.

"Who? I think I have the right to know."

"A friend of yours."

"Really?"

"He asked me not to tell you."

My heart clenched. I hoped it wasn't Sal Tascone, the best-dressed and most dangerous man in town. I'd done my best to stay away from him, and I didn't want to fall into his clutches now. Sal had once done me a favor, but with two favors, I'd be really in his debt, and I wasn't prepared for that. I was going straight, not going straight to the mob.

"If it's Sal, I'm going to have to let you go."

Sammy gave a short bark of laughter. "No, not Tascone. I don't work for him. You think a lot of yourself, don't you, kid? And you're wise to steer clear."

"I don't get it, then. No one knows. Only Vera, Kev, you and me, the signora, I suppose, the cops and . . ."

He reacted to that. The corner of his left eye twitched, and he tugged at the collar of his wrinkled jacket.

I stopped. Stared. Tyler Dekker knew, and his face had reflected his misery at accompanying his colleagues to question me about a murder. He'd met Sammy Vincovic, and he was smart enough to figure out how to reach him in Syracuse.

Was Smiley my savior?

Vincovic wasn't saying. "There was only one condition, and that was that no one could know who called me."

"Seriously? You don't think I'm at a disadvantage not knowing who hired you to represent me?"

He smiled.

I tossed my verbal grenade. "Is this the first time you've been retained by a cop?"

Vincovic might have been a wily street fighter, but the look on his face told me I'd scored a direct hit.

"So that's why Tyler left me alone. He was calling you. I thought he'd abandoned me." Abandoned me *again*, I thought. It hadn't been that long ago when he'd left me on my own in one of the most dangerous situations of my life.

"I can't tell you who called me."

"Fair enough. But now I know, and I'm grateful that he got you here. I'm not sure how I can afford your fees, but I'll find a way." I figured putting off grad school for another couple of years was probably the way, and I might still need some help from my uncles. They'd do what they could. They think that legal representation is like food and water, one of life's necessities.

"Ready to face the big, bad detective again?" he said.

I stood up. He gestured for me to sit down. "Look relaxed. Remember that you've got friends. And 'no comment' is your only comment."

Castellano strode through the door almost the second that Sammy Vincovic opened it. He smiled at her. It was the smile of man who is very, very impressed by a woman. "Welcome back, Detective."

She pointedly ignored him and took the best seat in the house again. I must say, the desk suited her as much as her outfit did. Bad Cat reached out and took a swipe at the boots as she passed. I didn't blame him. Good Bad Cat.

Stoddard slouched into the room and leaned against the wall, with his hands in his pockets. I half expected him to whistle a carefree tune.

Good Cat—not such an able judge of character—jumped into Castellano's lap. The resulting shriek was very amusing for Stoddard. He had to turn his face away to get that grin under control. Castellano might have shot him otherwise.

Sammy, on the other hand, rushed forward to help and, one assumes, brush the cat hair from her skirt.

"Back off," she said.

Sammy raised his hands in mock surrender. Good Cat leapt away and settled on the fainting couch, his back now turned to Castellano.

Bad Cat took the opportunity to give it another try. He crept behind the desk. At the end of Castellano's high leather boots he found some quite expensive hose that went perfectly with the caramel suit. It was only a matter of time until Bad Cat hooked his claws into those. If Castellano was in a bad mood now, I could only imagine what she'd be like if her fifty-dollar stockings were ruined.

I said, out of complete self-interest, "The cat that jumped on your lap is the friendly cat. The other that's aiming for your leg now, and I mean right now, might scratch or bite. Better let me take care of him."

"You stay where you are. I'm not worried about any cat. That jumpy one took me by surprise, is all."

I figured she was in for more surprises, but hey.

Sammy said, "I'll keep an eye on the cats."

I reminded myself he was on my side, even if he did seem to be more impressed with Castellano by the second.

From the look on her face, Castellano did not think that Sammy Vincovic was any kind of heartthrob. More like some kind of bug she'd like to stamp on.

Sammy's smile widened as he watched her. It had definitely reached his wily black eyes.

"Stop grinning," she said.

It would have taken more than that.

"Detective Castellano, you're grasping at straws here," he said—much like I might have said, "Lemon blueberry cheesecake, two slices, please."

"I don't think so, Counselor." Her eyes hardened and she shot me a look.

I sat up straighter.

"Think again. My client has answered all your questions and given you a statement. She was in Summerlea. Her fingerprints will be there, as will dozens of others. I am assuming you are interrogating everyone. She and her employer agree on the circumstances. Chadwick Kauffman was alive when they left. There was no reason to kill him."

"She was seen leaving—"

"So was the guy with the delivery van. I assume you've got him in a room somewhere and you've taken his fingerprints and his statement and are still giving him a hard time."

"If there was a driver. None of you seem to have noticed the company name."

"There was a driver! We saw him."

"We have only your word for that."

"What about the people walking on the road?"

She lifted her shoulders in a bored shrug.

Sammy'd had enough. Or he was worried I'd go and blow it. He said, "Either charge my client or let her go about her day. We're through here."

I gave an involuntary gasp. Charge me? I didn't mind Sammy playing chicken with Detective Castellano, but really, *charge me*?

Castellano said, "We've applied for a warrant to search the house."

Sammy shrugged his meaty shoulders. "You want a warrant to search Vera Van Alst's home? Good luck with that."

Ooh. Vera might not have been the sunniest of characters, but, hated or not, she was still influential in Harrison Falls and she sat on the hospital board with at least one judge. Sammy was right. They'd have to make it good.

Castellano rose and stalked out the door. Stoddard slouched after her, looking very Tom Sawyerish. The door closed softly behind them.

Bad Cat took his disappointment out on the drapes.

I felt a rush of relief.

Sammy said, "She won't let this go. She's not the type. We

have to get our story airtight and do a bit of research while we're at it."

Just what I'd been thinking. But I was worried. What if I was wrong about Vera's influence? "I think they do have enough to get a search warrant. We were at the scene of a murder. Our story isn't backed up. Even though Vera's powerful in the community, a lot of people hate the Van Alsts. That probably includes some judges."

"Sure, they'll get it. No problem. You are innocent, remember? So we have to take certain stands."

"Right. General principles."

"And, speaking of, here's my card. Memorize my cell number. Call the minute something happens. If you get new information, if the police show up again after this. Doesn't matter what or when."

"It will take you more than a couple of minutes to get back from Syracuse," I said, staring at the card dubiously.

"There's no going back to Syracuse until we've got this under control."

I exhaled with relief. Sammy was a lawyer you could lean on.

Castellano stuck her head back in the door. "Don't leave town."

Sammy showed her his best dental work.

CHAPTER SEVEN

I DIDN'T NEED Sammy to tell me that they couldn't stop me from leaving town. The police like to say that, to get you rattled. Of course, I had no intention of leaving town. Where would I go? I wanted to relax and live my life without the threat of a murder or accessory to murder charge hanging over my head.

I went over everything that happened one more time with Sammy. I answered questions. I tried to make sense of the events at Summerlea. When Sammy headed out at last, I walked with him to the front door. We found Vera, glowering. Castellano and Stoddard had just left, and she was still angry about their visit. There was no sign of Tyler Dekker. I wanted to thank him for sending Sammy and for being there for me. Face it, I needed a hug.

The signora fluttered in and did her little anxiety dance, crossing herself a few times. She was making a second attempt at lunch because of interruptions.

"For heaven's sake, Fiammetta," Vera grumped. "We can't be eating all the time."

"Yes. You eat, Vera! *La polizia!* No, no, no! Must eat."
Apparently the cure for anxiety caused by police was food. I
got that.

I said, "I wouldn't mind a bite. Our lunch was interrupted
by the police and being questioned by cops always makes
me hungry. Sammy, will you join us?"

He shook his head and tapped his watch. Of course, he
didn't really know what he was missing. And it crossed my
mind he might want to trim his waist before any future
encounters with Castellano.

Vera grunted and I waved good-bye to Sammy.

I figured lunch would help me regain my emotional balance and give my serotonin a boost, after being considered
a murder suspect had pretty much depleted it. I'd be in better
shape if I figured out what I could do to help myself.

I tried calling Tyler Dekker, but his phone went right to
voice mail. Of course, he was on duty and, in fact, may have
been meeting up with Castellano and Stoddard. He wouldn't
be free to talk. I decided against leaving a message, as I
wanted to thank him face-to-face. And, you know, lip-to-lip.

The signora must have worked out her own anxiety by
preparing her very special huge meatballs with the light
tomato sauce made from her own harvest in the garden last
fall. These are like a secret weapon in the war against feeling bad about anything. The signora serves them all alone
on a plate with an artistic swirl of sauce around them.

Of course, there was soup first and crusty bread and a
lovely green salad, but the meatballs were worth the wait.

Kev's place was set. I asked the signora to take it away, as
Kev wouldn't be joining us. I didn't want Detectives Castellano and Stoddard to swan back in and accuse us of harboring
him. Of course, we almost certainly would harbor him. We
didn't have to, as he'd vanished.

I figured they hadn't bugged the place, so I felt free to
talk. Vera was focusing on her *Times* crossword and didn't
seem to be bothered in the least.

"Vera, what struck you about our luncheon at Summerlea?"

She glanced up, surprised. "Don't know what you mean, Miss Bingham."

"I mean, what impression did you have?"

She shrugged. "Standard old money."

"And the place?"

"Typical summer mausoleum."

I snorted. Van Alst House could answer to that description on a slightly lower level. And of course, it wasn't merely seasonal. "What about the people?"

"Didn't pay any attention to them."

"Okay, so did it surprise you to learn that Miss Troy and Thomas the butler were not who they said they were?"

"Weren't they?"

"Not according to Detective Castellano. She strikes me as the type who gets her facts straight."

Vera fixed me with a long gaze. "I think you're right there, Miss Bingham. She strikes me that way too." She turned her attention back to her puzzle. I no longer existed. The signora took advantage of this to slap a massive slice from one of her plum cakes in front of me.

"Eat!" Apparently she figured I was eating for two, one of whom was Uncle Kev. But being grilled can definitely make a girl hungry.

"So, Vera," I said, once I'd done justice to the plum cake. "They weren't who they said they were. Who do you think they were?"

"I have no idea, Miss Bingham. Is that important?"

I kept my cool. "It is if you don't want one of us to get arrested."

"Why would one of us get . . . ? Do you mean *you*, Miss Bingham?"

"Not necessarily. Did they not ask you if you went upstairs?"

"They did. I said no. That was absurd."

"Did they ask you if Kev or I went upstairs?"

"I said I wasn't paying attention to you."

"Oh. But we didn't go upstairs. You must have known that. The staircase was visible from the parlor."

"Was it?"

"Yes. You didn't notice us at all?"

"My mind was on getting the Marsh books."

I sighed. "Yes, I can see how it would be."

"Don't be flippant."

"I am not being flippant, Vera. This is very serious. The police say that Chadwick was murdered. Didn't Detective Castellano tell you that?"

She shrugged. "She may have mentioned it. But that's nothing to do with us, surely."

"They believe that one of us went to the second floor—possibly using the elevator we didn't know about—bashed Chadwick Kauffman over the head with a statue and then pushed him down the stairs."

Vera huffed, "Why on earth would we do that?"

"We had no reason to hit Chadwick over the head, but it's obvious that pushing him down the stairs after he was dead was a ploy to cover up the crime."

"To cover up the crime?"

Really, for someone who had read all those mysteries, she seemed deliberately obtuse. "To make it look like an accident."

Vera rolled her eyes. "There are these procedures called autopsies. Everyone knows that would be obvious to the pathologist."

"Right. Everyone with a working television set or anyone who'd read a couple of police procedurals, but that's not the point."

"What is the point, Miss Bingham?"

"They think we wanted it to look like he slipped and fell."

"That's ridiculous. Stupid."

"Yes. But didn't they ask you all these questions, Vera?"

"They did not."

"They don't think you did it, but they believe Kevin and I did—"

"What an outrage! Mr. Kelly would never do such a thing."

"Of course he wouldn't. And *neither* would I."

"They certainly have a nerve. I shall have to ensure that he has legal representation."

"Thank you, Vera. I appreciate that," I breathed. "If we can find him."

"The poor man must have been traumatized by the very suggestion of culpability."

"Um, indeed." I didn't bother to say that Kev was in the wind before any accusations had been made. Vera wasn't altogether informed about Kevin's history. And that was a good thing. Trust me.

"This is a bad situation," Vera muttered.

"That's an understatement. They say they found all of our fingerprints at Summerlea. And our prints are all on file."

"Well, of course, they found them. We were in the house."

"Listen to me, Vera. They also say they found Kev's prints on a statue that was used to kill Chadwick."

Vera's always pallid, but she paled more. "Nonsense."

"It could be nonsense. They are allowed to lie to suspects."

"I am not a suspect."

"But they didn't tell you. They told me."

"Are you telling me that you are a suspect?"

"I think so. They may even think that you and I are shielding Kevin."

"Preposterous."

"Exactly, because we don't know where he is." I was pretty sure that Vera would shield Kev even if she did know where he was. For sure, I would have. "But Kev didn't kill Chadwick and he didn't go upstairs."

"I see now why that question was important."

"Exactly. But you weren't paying attention, so you can't swear that we never went upstairs."

"I didn't realize the implications."

"Mmm. Were you paying attention, Vera?"

"Not in the least."

"Well, there you have it. It's only me, and as you know, Kevin is my uncle—" I wasn't a hundred percent sure that Vera did know this, as we'd been vague on that detail when Kev joined the household as gardener, handyman, trouble-maker.

"Yes, yes. Old news, Miss Bingham."

"So they have a very good reason to suspect that I would lie to protect him."

"Oh dear."

"And they may believe—and who could blame them—that I was also involved."

"I would never employ someone who would do such a vile and uncivilized thing."

Uncivilized? That was one way of describing cold-blooded murder.

"It gets worse."

"How could it be worse?"

"I think they believe there was a conspiracy to kill Chadwick. And that we were part of the conspiracy."

"What?"

"That's what they think."

"But this is dreadful."

"Yes, it is. And that's why we have to be careful that we don't implicate each other. That's what they're counting on."

"But why would we conspire to kill him? He wanted to sell some books. We wanted to buy them. Everyone was satisfied. What reason could there be?"

"I don't know. But once the police come up with a theory, we've got real trouble."

I WAS SURPRISED by a text from Tiff. I had known she was in port today, but still wasn't expecting a text, because there must have been a million more interesting things to do in Aruba.

> Wow, I was so happy to get to port today! They sure
> work us hard, but the crew are friendly, and all I've
> really had to deal with was a few sunburns and
> some seasickness. I'm off to enjoy a few hours of
> well-deserved R & R. Our next stop is Cartagena, in
> three days. Hope all is well in HF.

I sent Tiff a smiley face with sunglasses on in reply. It was all I could manage, and I wasn't going to dump any of the current nastiness on her. There was nothing she could do from Aruba.

Meanwhile, my life was hardly relaxing. I kept expecting a knock at the door and the reappearance of the two detectives waving a warrant for my arrest or to search the house.

Before the detectives returned, I needed to check something. I pulled on a heavy sweater and dug my red rain boots from the cupboard by the back door again. I could hear the wind howling, so I jammed a wool hat over my hair, covering my ears, and even picked up mittens. So much for spring. This was a curling-up-in-a-chair-to-read kind of day, and if it hadn't been for the police ruining the mood, I would have been catching up on those Ngaio Marsh books. But I was worried about Uncle Kev. It was one thing for him to hide under the bed in case the cops came, but he'd left in the middle of a meal and missed his regular snacks as well as the makeup lunch. That was out of character.

I clomped through the back garden, avoiding the stubborn lumps of blackened snow that had survived our long, cold winter. It was easy enough to follow the muddy path that Kev must have created. What could he have been doing there? Whatever it was, I hoped he was still hanging around doing it, because I needed to tell him what was going on with the police and what had happened to Chadwick Kauffman. And he really needed to know that the police were saying that his fingerprints were on the statue that had killed Chadwick.

I trudged around behind a tight row of trees that had been planted as a windbreak near the edge of the property. "Kev!" I yelled. There was nothing but the wailing of the wind.

Behind the trees was not Kev, but a collection of odd-looking objects. First, what looked like a primitive stone fireplace or stove. It seemed to be connected by pipes to a few barrels. Some gallon jugs stood around, empty, but ready for business. One barrel was shattered, the staves scattered widely. That explained the puffs of smoke.

I sighed heavily.

Kev had built a still on Vera's property, and the construction of this highly illegal system coincided with the arrival of the police, soon to be back with a search warrant, to start inspecting Van Alst House and probably stalking around the property as well. Kev, Kev, Kev. I knew when I got the chance to blast my darling uncle, he'd claim that I'd never cautioned him against building a still there.

That was true.

I just needed to remain calm.

I whirled when I heard a rustling behind me. Kev stood there with a sheepish grin on his face.

"What is this?" I shouted. So much for remaining calm.

"Gonna be a nice little moneymaker, Jordie, once I get a few bugs ironed out on the distribution side."

"Get rid of it."

"Jordie, I can't. How could I do that?"

"The cops will be all over the property within hours. I don't care how you get rid of it, but do it. Do you want to get the ATF on our case too?"

"The ATF? That would be the worst thing that could happen."

"Actually, the worst thing will be if you go to prison for life for killing Chadwick Kauffman."

"What?"

"Uncle Kev, the police said they have your fingerprints on the statue that killed him."

"What?"

I repeated myself and added, "I don't know if it's true, but that's what they're saying."

"But I thought he fell down the stairs."

"Yeah, well, the police said he was killed by a blow to the head. And then he 'fell' down the stairs."

"That doesn't make sense. Why would anyone do that?"

"To make it look like an accident. And the cops believe you did it."

"But I didn't do that! I wouldn't. You know me, Jordie. I couldn't do that."

I knew Kev hadn't killed Chadwick.

Kev was still talking. "Why would anyone do that to a person? 'Course, he was kind of nasty, so somebody probably hated him."

"The big problem is that little statue on the table outside the powder rooms—"

"Never touched it."

"You did, Kev."

His familiar sheepish look was back.

"The cops found your prints. But I need to know, did you go upstairs?"

"Upstairs? Why would I go upstairs? All right, I did touch the statue. I couldn't resist it."

Knowing Kev, he'd given a bit of thought to liberating it from Summerlea.

He decided this would be a good time to get on his high horse. "I didn't see a 'DO NOT TOUCH' sign, Jordie. That little thing was just sitting there on this little table. I'm surprised you didn't touch it yourself."

"Then the cops would have found both our fingerprints on the murder weapon, wouldn't they?"

"That was the murder weapon?"

"That's right."

"Maybe it would have been better if I had taken it, Jordie."

I tried not to sigh. It was getting to be a habit. And Kev is, in case you haven't worked this out, like the world's largest and most dangerous child. We all love him, but there's always a lot of sighing when he's in the vicinity.

Still, there was a big difference between Kev being typical Kev and Kev committing murder. And this thing with Kev's prints on a murder weapon was really bizarre. If the police were telling the truth about the weapon. A big "if."

"Wait a minute. Did anyone see you?"

"Nobody. Well, that butler, What's-his-name."

Ah. That probably explained why the statue wasn't residing in Kev's quarters above the garage as we spoke.

"Thomas. They said his name was Thomas. And then what happened?"

"He just touched his nose like this." Kev tapped the side of his nose.

"Uh-huh. Well, there's a few other things you need to know."

"Like what?"

"Well, there was no butler."

"Yes, there was."

"Apparently, there was not. No butler, but Chadwick had a housekeeper."

"But we saw that Thomas guy."

"We saw someone who wanted us to think he was the butler. And someone else who said she was Lisa Troy."

Kev nodded. "Pretty lady. Real nice too."

"Except that she wasn't Chadwick's assistant. We don't know who she really is, but she wasn't who she said she was."

A pained expression of confusion clouded Kevin's face. "I don't get it, Jordie."

"Join the club."

"Why would they fake it?"

"A really good question. I wish I knew the answer."

"They were nice to us. They invited us. They served us that awesome lunch."

"Yes."

"But they weren't who they said they were."

It always takes a while for things to sink in with Kev. He scratched his nose. "And we don't know why."

"That's right."

"Well, Chadwick must have known who they were."

"If they were conning us, then they must have found a way to con him too."

"Why? Right, you don't know. But, Jordie . . ."

"Yes, Kev." I needed him to get the still out of there, but with Kev, you have to wait until he gets his head around things.

"Well . . ."

"Out with it, Kev."

"Anyways, was Chadwick really Chadwick?"

"Of course, he was—"

I felt a wave of dizziness as the significance of Kev's question hit me. I grabbed a tree trunk to steady myself. It's bad when Kev introduces the one piece of information you need to make sense of what's going on.

"Jordie? Are you all right?"

Of course I wasn't. Why hadn't *I* thought to ask that most important question?

Was Chadwick really Chadwick?

CHAPTER EIGHT

I LEFT KEV reeling from my threats of dire consequences if the still wasn't gone within an hour. It's not easy to scold an older relative, but there was no choice. And I wasn't exaggerating. If the police found this mess, someone would be arrested for running an illegal still, and I hoped it wouldn't be me or Vera or the signora.

As I clomped back to the house, I could hear Kev bellowing into his cell phone to his friend, Cherie. That was good. Cherie could make things happen. For all I knew, this wouldn't be the first still she'd relocated. Not much would surprise me about her. She was a whiz with wiring, technology and computers, but she wasn't a lawyer. I hurried back to do two key things: Make sure Uncle Kev had legal counsel ready to roll and find out if Chadwick had really been Chadwick.

Uncle Mick returned my call as soon as I left the message. We'd recently agreed on the code phrase "Olaf in Dublin." It meant trouble, as I am sure it had for Dublin way back when.

"I hate to bother you when you're in Manhattan, Uncle Mick."

"No problem, we're in the middle of—"

"Sorry to cut you off, but Kev is in trouble, though it's mostly not his fault."

"What do you mean, mostly? Of course it's his fault."

"This time it really isn't, believe it or not. He did pick up a statue and he did get his prints on it, but he didn't steal the statue, because if he had, it wouldn't have ended up as a murder weapon. So I guess he's getting better."

"Murder weapon? Kev wouldn't kill anyone . . . on purpose. Sure, he could blow up a house, but he's never been violent. Kellys are peace-loving people. You have to explain Kev to them."

Good luck to me explaining Kev to the cops. I said, "It isn't because the police don't believe me. They think we conspired to kill—"

"Kill who?"

"Not entirely sure about that, Uncle Mick. His name was supposedly Chadwick Kauffman, the heir to the Kauffman fortune. But at this point, honestly, I have no clue. It's like an episode of *Scooby-Doo*. Now I'm wondering who's real and who's really dead."

"You have to talk sense, my girl."

"I'll fill you in when I know more, but the reason I called is that Uncle Kev will need a good lawyer. Vera offered to pay. But she doesn't know any defense lawyers. Yet."

"I'll call Sammy."

"Too late. Sammy's representing me."

"But—"

"Someone called him and retained him on my behalf, and he says he can't represent the two of us. And I don't think even if I fired him that he could represent Kev after that."

"Who's paying him?"

"Oops. I've got to go. Can you get on it? I think the police are working on a warrant. They'll probably be back soon to comb through Vera's looking for who-knows-what."

"What's Kevin said to them?"

You never knew when someone managed to get a wiretap authorized. No way was I messing up on Uncle Kev by saying I knew where he was. It would have brought us a lot of grief.

"They haven't found him yet. He's out on errands and we haven't seen him. He could be anywhere, and he doesn't know the police want to talk to him."

He did, of course, but we had to play the game in case the wrong ears were listening.

Mick grunted. "Leave it with me."

WHEN THE GOING gets tough, the tough get going. They also get dressed up, or at least I did. I pulled on my vintage merino wool boatneck sweater in thick cream and black horizontal stripes. It went well with my black cigarette pants and sensible black ballet flats. Kind of Hepburnish. I was good to go. You'd never know I'd been grilled by the police.

I raced to the Saab and drove to the library.

Lance's eyes widened when he saw me. He came straight around the reference desk, bypassing a line of his posse, each with their *question du jour.*

You could tell he was rattled. He didn't bother with "beautiful lady" or any other endearments. "Jordan, about Chadwick Kauffman. Now, they're saying he was murdered."

"He was, and the cops think we did it."

"What?"

I sighed. "All anybody seems to be able to say lately is, 'What?'"

Lance crossed his arms over his chest and pursed his lips. "It seemed right for the moment."

"I get that. So here's the thing: We were seen leaving in a hurry. The Caddy and my Saab. There were witnesses. The people we met in the house have vanished and, in fact, they don't seem to exist, except for Chadwick, who is dead, unless he wasn't really Chadwick. And it gets worse."

"How can it get worse?"

I explained about Kev's fingerprints and everything that had gone on between Castellano and me. I said I had a lawyer. I may not have mentioned that Tyler had made that arrangement.

"Well, this time, I'm there for you, beautiful lady. Do you need . . . What do you need?"

"Information. And photos. I need to see what Chadwick Kauffman really looked like. I've done image searches and I can't find a picture of the man we met."

It's hard to surprise Lance, but I'd managed. "You mean that someone might have been masquerading as Chadwick?" His eyes danced when he said "masquerading." Lance kind of enjoyed being drawn into an old-fashioned caper.

"Looks that way."

Lance lowered his voice and leaned closer. "And you think that's the guy who was murdered?"

"So far, there's no way to know if it was the real Chadwick or the imposter."

A tall seventy-something woman with great silver hair stepped forward, frowning. "Excuse me, but I was at the head of this line, young woman. You can't push yourself in like that."

Lance turned and touched her forearm lightly. He said soothingly, "Family emergency." He then returned his attention and the full wattage of his gaze to me. Lance and I will never be an item, but up close he can still make my knees go weak.

A round little lady in a hand-knit pink sweater said, "I'm in a hurry too! People have to take their turns." Everyone needed their Lance fix.

Lance ignored them and steered me over to the bay of shelves with the encyclopedias, where we'd probably be unpestered.

I said, "And we can't forget the other two."

"The other two?"

"His alleged assistant, a Miss Troy, and the butler, Thomas, have vanished, and according to the police, he never had a butler and his assistant was not called Miss Troy."

"Nothing's like it seems, like that old film, *Gaslight*."

"Exactly, and then Chadwick or someone else was murdered. He was alive when we left him with two witnesses, but now our witnesses do not appear to exist. So I need to know if the person who we met as Chadwick really was Chadwick. I cannot find this guy's image anywhere, but I understand that Chadwick doesn't seek the camera."

"I'm on it. What a weird setup."

"Yes, and I think that's exactly what it was. A setup for murder. But who set it up? And why would they have picked Vera as a target?"

"Did they seek her out? Or did Vera find out about the collection?" He stopped and stared. "Did you?"

"Chadwick Kauffman contacted us. Or at least his people did. Anyway, you can see how much I need your help."

"I sure can. Give me a bit of time and I'll find what you need. I may have to deal with the clamoring hordes first."

"I appreciate it, Lance."

"I'll send you links to whatever I find."

I headed out of the library, ignoring the dirty looks from the posse and hoping that the police wouldn't be through the door before I got away.

Thinking about the police reminded me that I hadn't yet thanked Tyler for his help. I tried to call him again. I wanted to hear his voice too. Again, straight to message.

I checked my own voice mails, but nothing from him.

My phone pinged again. Speak of the devil, Officer Dekker, texting.

Jordan, I think we need to step back from this
relationship. Between your work and mine, we're just
not compatible. I know if you really think about it you'll

feel the same way. You are beautiful inside and out. It's not you. It's the situation. Let's try to still be friends. xo Tyler

I had been so wrong about Smiley's reasons for getting me a lawyer. He wasn't looking after my wellbeing. He didn't want a guilty conscience about the woman he'd just dumped by *text*. Still be friends? My Aunt Fanny.

I stiffened my back and kept my lower lip from wobbling. I was, after all, half Kelly, and we hold ourselves together when the emotional weather gets stormy. From what little I knew about the Binghams, they were no pushovers either. I reminded myself that I'd been an idiot to let myself fall for Tyler Dekker. He was, first of all, a police officer, and that had been tempting fate. Still, I'd thought he was willing to work at things regardless of our differences. What a fool I'd been.

Now that I was being questioned by his colleagues, he had to put distance between the two of us. He was ambitious, and how would it look to be in a relationship with an accused killer?

And in the unlikely event that he ever attempted to get back together again after this, he'd be really sorry he tried. I was really going to miss his dog, Cobain. Good thing I had Walter on a semi-permanent basis.

I still had Tyler's house key in the pocket of my deep-orange purse. I liked the idea of flinging the key in his face. But that could wait.

"Who needs a cop hanging around ruining things, anyway," I muttered, and made a new plan. Time to get into and out of Van Alst House quickly.

PING! LANCE HAD done it again. Somehow he'd found photos of the late Chadwick Kauffman. I clicked on the attachments.

I got that old sinking feeling. Not one of the photos was of a lean, dark man with a gecko-like gaze. Instead, a stocky man with a shy smile and reddish-blond hair was the subject. I recognized him from my online search for Chadwick Kauffman. His face had shown up in many of the images. He was alone in each of the photos that Lance had sent, so no chance to see if one of the others was with him.

Lance confirmed the images. "I talked to people who've met him at cultural events and fund-raisers. My patrons came to the rescue."

I wasn't a fan of Lance's posse, but I had to admit they'd come in handy this time. A lot of thoughts whirled in my brain. The man who'd met us at Summerlea was not who he said he was.

The big question was: Which of them was dead?

How to find out?

Normally, I would have asked Smiley, but that wasn't going to happen.

I shot the images of the shy-looking man with the reddish-blond hair to Sammy.

"This isn't the man we met at Summerlea. But it seems he's the real Chadwick. Can you confirm and find out if this is the man who died?"

I called Lance instead of texting. I guess I wanted to hear his voice.

"Thanks, Lance."

"All part of the service."

"So, that's not the guy I met at Summerlea."

"I trust my sources."

"Oh, I'd never doubt you. Sammy will try to find out if the man in the pix was the victim."

"Who else would it be?"

"No idea. But no one at Summerlea was who they said they were, so who knows if the real Chadwick was involved with any of it."

"This just gets weirder and weirder."

"Yes."

"What can I do, beautiful lady?"

That saved me asking him for more help, and to be honest, I needed the flowery compliment too. "I appreciate it, Lance. Can you keep looking for any other photos of Chadwick?"

"He was pretty elusive. It took a while to unearth these. Most people are all over the Internet with no good reason, but not this guy, even though he's the heir to a fortune and a descendent of an influential family."

"Now we need you to look for a woman, light brown hair, tall, slender, nicely put together, with a slight overbite. She's the woman who met us at Summerlea, and I believe she's an accomplice. See if you can find anything that links her to Chadwick."

"Right. I'll hunt for photos of Chadwick with female associates. How old?"

"Somewhere in her late twenties, I think. She was supposed to be the assistant, Lisa Troy. And we really need to identify a tall man, around forty, give or take. Dark hair. Thin face. Cold eyes. Looks a bit like an iguana. That's the man who introduced himself as Chadwick."

"Got it."

"The third person was the so-called butler, Thomas. He was large, but pear-shaped, dark hair too. His hair was dyed black. He had heavy, hairy hands and a couple of chins. Five-o'clock shadow, even at noon."

"I'm on it."

I left Lance to his hunt, knowing he'd do whatever was possible.

I WAS FULLY installed back in my garret and having a really hard time distracting myself. I was so down I barely remembered eating although usually every bite makes such a happy impression. But tonight, there was no escaping reminders of the crummy things piling up around me. "Somebody That I

Used to Know" and "Rolling in the Deep" crept onto my random playlist, as if to taunt my heart. Usually a bit of music could lift my mood, but it only led to further wallowing. Dumped, again, by a cop, and by text, no less. "Fool me once, shame on you. Fool me twice, shame on me," Mick would say. And I sure didn't need to hear that right now. I'd finally let my walls down for Tyler, and I guess he didn't like what he saw back there. I was hurt. And angry at both of us.

Tiff was unreachable. Usually, she'd be my go-to for this kind of thing. She was always able to find the right words or vintage wine to ease the pain. I didn't really want to get into relationship stuff with Lance, because . . . well . . . just plain awkward. Pulling out my earbuds, I opted for a bit of mindless TV but found *Law & Order*, a *Cops* marathon, *The Bachelor* and *The War of the Roses*. Sometimes it's like the universe is pointing and laughing. Why, I'd almost forgotten the dead flowers I'd received and their sickly scent. Who hated me enough to go to that effort? On the plus side, though, if I went to jail for murder, I'd probably be safe from the wacko who sent them. Off with the television.

Walter sighed heavily, sensing this was a rough time for me. He ground his soft, furry face into my side in a show of commiseration and support.

"Let's go to bed with a book, Walter." I helped him into my fluffy feather bed and cuddled up with another Marsh, as I'd already whipped through *A Man Lay Dead*. This time I picked *Final Curtain*, another setup in a grand house with a bit of theater and a large group of suspects who weren't quite what they seemed. Sleep did not come quickly.

YOU CAN PICK your friends, they say, but you can't pick your relatives. My relatives proved a challenge on a daily basis, but the good news was that the skills I learned from them came in handy this morning.

I didn't have much from the Kelly gene pool, aside from

what I like to think is a strategic mind. No ginger hair, no red cheeks, no fifth-generation-removed Irish blarney. But I did have the family knack with changing one's appearance on occasions when being oneself might prove awkward, mostly if the police were watching. In this case, I figured they would be.

A second benefit of my relatives was wheels. My uncles maintain an ever-changing fleet of anonymous-looking older compact cars, Civics, Fiestas, Accords, that kind of thing. The cars were always in beige, burgundy or dulled silver. Never in what Tyler used to call "Arrest Me Red." I knew the registrations would be in order as would the insurance. The vehicles would be part of the rolling stock of shell companies within shell companies within . . . well, you get the idea. I would be listed as an occasional driver on all of them. I'd needed these vehicles before, but I'd always hoped I'd never need one again.

Oh well, when life gives you lemons, time to slap on a wig and drive off.

I left Van Alst House wearing highly noticeable clothing, a great swirling vintage cape in crimson being the center-piece of that outfit. I was accompanied by Walter in a fetch-ing little plaid jacket. Walter kept a much better pace when he was dressed. I guess my love of fashion was rubbing off on him. He pranced around proudly as we headed for the car.

I popped Walter into the passenger seat and then got behind the wheel of the Saab with what I hoped was a flour-ish and not a nervous twitch and spun down the long drive-way. I waved to the police officer who was keeping an eye on the house. The drive to Michael Kelly's Fine Antiques is only about ten minutes, but it takes you from the bucolic country setting of Van Alst House to the center of Harrison Falls. I pulled up in front of the family business and parked the Saab in the most conspicuous spot possible. There wasn't too much going on in that little part of the downtown, as Uncle Mick and Uncle Lucky seemed to have bought up most of the adjoining properties, using some convenient corporation. Better I didn't know how or why.

A dark Crown Victoria, obviously an unmarked police car, pulled in behind me and waited, idling.

Not surprising, but not good either.

Walter and I stepped up to the shop briskly, and I used my keys to open the door. Michael Kelly's Fine Antiques (By Appointment Only) is run by Uncle Mick, when he's in the mood. Lately that hadn't been all that often. Uncle Lucky had always been there, but only in spirit. I grew up in the rooms behind and above the shop. Some of my happiest memories were of the shop: the dim lights, the wide, dark plank floors, the full shelves and, of course, the dusty smell that hinted at other people's fascinating stories. I'd loved the glow and glimmer of possible treasures of glass, brass or silver set up by Uncle Mick. The gleam of the locked glass cases near the cash registers always made me happy. So many treasures so close to my old home.

I rummaged through the excellent supply of wigs that resided in a large drawer, marked "WIGS—NEVER WORN." Uncle Mick seemed to have an unending source. They were undeniably useful for certain activities. I had purchased several of the wigs myself for fun, for costumes, for emergencies. This was an emergency.

There wasn't a lot I could do about my blue eyes, dark brows and eyelashes, but I could ditch my dark hair. If, as my uncles claim, the Kelly legacy is from Olaf the Viking, then I must owe mine to some Spanish sailor who washed ashore half alive when the Armada had that awkwardness with the English fleet. Whoever he was, he and others like him left a genetic legacy around rocky coasts. Black Irish, some people say.

Changing my hair was the easiest thing to prepare for my bit of reconnaissance. People can gauge your age by your build, posture, ways of moving. It's very hard to disguise. But hair color makes a huge difference. My favorite bright red wig was familiar to many in the police department after last fall, but it wasn't the only game in town. I searched for and found an amazing little short and tightly curled honey blond number. It added at least fifteen years to my age and subtracted any cool factor whatsoever. Excellent. Next, I hunted for a pair of glasses in the jumbled glasses section. Mixed in with the vintage and collectible frames was a pair of horn-rimmed specs with clear glass lenses. All I needed was a severe suit and a briefcase and I'd be in business.

Upstairs in my old closet I found the perfect suit, a charcoal worsted vintage jacket and skirt, bought for a funeral a few years back, but too somber for anything else. My plan was perfect. Under my swirly cape, I had on a crisp white blouse, which looked exceptionally uptight under the suit. Back in the shop, I topped it all off with some supersized pearls—necklace and clip-on earrings—and a black leather briefcase. I was going to cover the *KRR* monogram using a washable black marker but decided not to. Usually, I'd wonder who KRR had been, that he had a gold monogram, but no time for fanciful imaginings today. Today, I would make use of it.

In front of the shop mirror, I thickened up my eyebrows and added an unflattering shade of coral lipstick, and I was ready to go.

In the apartment, I left the lights on and turned on the television set.

Next I found the newly added recess behind the kitchen cupboard and fished out a burner phone. I left my iPhone on the kitchen table and pocketed the burner. I didn't have a plan for it, but I was well aware that it's often advisable to make an untraceable call. That's part of being careful and planning to avoid trouble.

I trotted upstairs again to check myself in the only decent full-length mirror. I turned and twirled. The shoes were wrong, but I had no choice. I would have to do.

Walter looked at me with worry in his huge googly eyes.

"Don't worry, Walter," I said. "You'll be taken care of. Too bad you don't have Cobain for company, but it can't be helped."

Back in the kitchen with the bare wall as a backdrop, I managed an excellent selfie with my iPhone and uploaded the image. With Uncle Mick's first-rate equipment, printer and lamination machine, I soon had myself a driver's license and a very good ID tag for a well-known firm of auditors: Jackson and Dogherty.

I thought I looked like everyone's stereotype of an auditor. Stereotypes are our friends when we need disguises. I'd learned that from the best.

I took ten more minutes to look up a few phrases used by auditors, memorized ten of them and was ready to depart. First, I needed to give Walter the few little treats he expects if I am leaving without him. We definitely didn't want to have any separation anxiety.

I tossed the treats, and Walter scampered after them. My departure was no longer a concern.

Kathryn Risley Rolland was on her way, with her monogrammed leather briefcase and a plan.

Minutes later I was out the back door heading for my ride of the day. To my surprise, I found a shiny black Infiniti parked in Uncle Mick's spare garage two doors down. I could have taken the dreary old Civic or that washed out Mazda6, but this looked so much better. It was about three years old and exactly the kind of car Kathryn Risley Rolland would drive. I hoped that my uncles didn't have big plans for it that day and made a phone call from the burner to check.

With all systems go, I slipped behind the wheel and exited. Without an apparent glance and with chin held high, I drove past my Saab, which was patiently parked in front of Michael Kelly's Fine Antiques. I didn't acknowledge the officer in the unmarked police car, who was obviously tasked with keeping an eye on me.

CHAPTER NINE

THE COUNTRY CLUB and Spa was worth the drive. I sped along the access road, noting the number of Beamers, Mercedes and glossy Caddies parked near the entrance. The Infiniti fit in.

I used my most businesslike stride to arrive at the front door. A fresh-faced teenage boy was stationed at the door for security. His sandy hair had natural highlights from the sun, and he stood well over six feet with a build that indicated time in the gym. He was pretty enough for any movie screen. In fact, I wouldn't have been surprised to learn he was discovered here one of these days. If I read his tag correctly, his name was Braydon. I approached him for what I assumed was an entirely normal and appropriate member's ID check. I resisted straightening my tightly curled blond wig—which would only draw attention to it—and donned the look I remember from my third grade teacher, Miss Dagenham. It could stop your blood cold and could not be withstood.

He stepped back a bit. I held up my hand to stop any requests for ID.

"Kathryn Risley Rolland, auditor. Jackson and Dogherty," I said, crisply. "The police are aware that I'm here. I need to visit your corporate office, please."

He blinked. He also blushed. So cute. Of course, this was a country club and spa, so he probably didn't know there was a corporate office.

"The person in charge," I said. "Lisa."

"Oh right. Lisa Hatton."

I wasn't sure why he was blushing quite so much, until I noticed a cluster of women arriving right after me. He glanced their way and then back to me, a slightly hunted expression on his handsome face. They looked to be in their late thirties, expensively dressed, and they were all giggling as they took the stairs. I hoped they weren't laughing at my shoes, but I suspected they were acting like high school girls because of Young Mr. Handsome and Blushing. Ladies, your hormones are showing.

I made sure I still had his attention. "Do you accompany me, young man, or shall I go on my own?"

"Oh. I'm supposed to stay here. You can go over on your own, ma'am. If you don't mind."

"Not at all." I stepped confidently through the front door. I experienced a small frisson of excitement. Yes, I was going straight and I genuinely planned to live my life on the up-and-up, but this gaining entry while wearing a disguise, while technically totally illegal, was a bit of a rush. I reminded myself that I wasn't going to be making a habit of it and that it seemed to be the only way to start trying to figure out who was trying to frame us for murder.

Of course, the offices were near the front of the establishment, but I wasn't quite ready for that yet. First, the ladies' room. I knew that would be a good spot to overhear gossip.

I was followed through the door by the giggling clump of women. As far as I could tell they were speculating about Braydon in ways that could have him blushing to death. Poor thing.

The conversation changed as two gray-haired women entered, both talking about Chadwick. Yes!

"Can't believe it, really," the shorter one said.

"Neither can I. It's terrible. I mean, he looked so well the other day."

While reapplying my hideous shade of coral lipstick in the vast gilt-framed mirror, I noticed the taller woman blink at her friend's comment. Chadwick had, after all, been murdered, which didn't really reflect on his state of well-being before that violent act.

The gigglers stopped and looked appropriately subdued.

"Which is more than you can say for poor Lisa," the shorter one said, fluffing her pale reddish curls and frowning at her wrinkles. "She's certainly having trouble holding things together."

I noticed the gigglers making eye contact. One managed to let a loud snicker escape. Both older women fixed her with looks that could easily have killed. With a swirl of their expensive curly blowouts, the younger crowd departed.

Hmm.

"Well," said the taller woman, "I hope she manages a bit better. The members are very upset, and people need reassurance. I thought Lisa had more spine, to tell the truth. What do we pay her for if not to be professional?"

Her friend was more sympathetic. "I always thought she carried a torch for Chadwick. Not that he ever seemed to reciprocate, but still, it must be heartbreaking for her." I suspected she'd carried a torch or two in her own life.

"She's flipping out, is what I heard," her friend said, applying a thick layer of Dior lipstick, with hardly a glance in the mirror. "They say she's unable to hold it together even in public."

"People should be kinder. It will be devastating for the club if she leaves after this. I think she is the one who actually kept things going. Chadwick wasn't much for the business side. Really."

"Well, why would he be, with all that money coming to him? He just had to wait."

Fat lot of good waiting did him, I thought. I managed to fuss with my frumpy blond hair, visit the dark mahogany stall, emerge, wash my hands again and straighten my suit, fiddling until all the women left the ladies' room.

I headed off to see Poor Lisa, hoping she could hold things together long enough for me to get some information out of her.

THE PALE AND very pretty young woman with the halo of strawberry-blond curls tried everything to keep me from Lisa Hatton in the administration office. Her round china-blue eyes stared at me as she used her body to block the entrance to the office.

"Not sure if you understand, *perfectly*," I said, narrowing my eyes grimly at her. "It's a matter of complying with the letter of the law." I was blowing hot air. "We cannot let this wait. If"—I glanced at my notepad—"Lisa Hatton is not available, I will need to see the chair of the board. This is a legal requirement, as I have already said and as I am sure you are aware."

She stared at me, completely unaware of this—or any—legal requirement. That wasn't a surprise to me, as I had made it up that second.

"It's all right, Miranda," a raspy voice said.

Miranda turned and squeaked.

Lisa Hatton had dark shoulder-length hair, cut in soft layers. I figured she was about thirty-five and quite curvy. Her navy suit was about a size too small, and the fuchsia satin blouse she wore was unbuttoned far enough to show a bit of cleavage. I couldn't tell if that was the way she always dressed or if she was too rattled to do up the third button from the collar. On a good day, the flashing dark eyes, the heart-shaped face and the wide mouth would have made her very attractive. I was betting there was always a hint of cleavage.

But now, with her swollen eyes, crimson nose and tear-tracked cheeks, this was looking like the worst day of her life. Angry splotches covered her face and neck. Some women were not made for weeping. Lisa was one of those.

"Kathryn Risley—" I started.

She shrugged. "Yes, yes. Come in and tell me what you want and why it can't wait."

Miranda bit her lip as I passed by.

"Spot audit," I said as I sailed into the room, stiff curls high. But now I felt pretty low taking advantage of her misery to ferret around in the late Chadwick's life and affairs. Inside her office the wall was covered with large photographs, each in distinctive sage-and-gold frames, apparently celebrating special moments for the Country Club and Spa. A few more on the dark wood console looked personal, during happier times for Poor Lisa.

I turned to her and said, "I understand that there has been a tragedy, and I am sorry to be here now. Would you like to take a couple of minutes to . . . ?" Platitudinous, yes. But I meant it. I was wishing I'd found a less emotionally intrusive way to get in here. But it's funny how your moral compass can shift when you're being framed for murder. Lisa was collateral damage. I was a jerk.

She nodded and seemed to choke back a sob.

"Take your time," I said with what I hoped was an understanding smile.

She stared at me warily.

"I'll wait here with Miranda," I added, in case that was what she was worried about.

Miranda's startlingly blue eyes grew wider. I guess I made her nervous.

Lisa nodded. "You can get our guest a cappuccino or

some jasmine tea, Miranda. Or fruit juice. We have mango nectar. Whatever she wants. I'll be right back." She left the room, wobbling unsteadily on her three-inch heels.

I smiled at Miranda. She in turn avoided my eyes and pretended to pay attention to her work. I pretended to glance at the photos with all the fake interest of a person who could not care less. "Hot tea would be lovely. Thank you, Miranda."

She hesitated.

"Plain hot tea," I added firmly. "Very hot." That should take a few minutes. I wanted a bit of time alone in the office.

The man I now knew to be Chadwick presided over the events captured by most of the photos. But I wasn't looking for him or for Lisa, Miranda or Braydon. I was looking for a glimpse of the dark and arrogant person who had presented himself as Chadwick. I was looking for the slender, pretty image of Lisa Troy. Or even the false butler, Thomas.

There appeared to be group photos of every tournament and awards ceremony in living memory. Lisa Hatton smiled out joyously in most of them, always Chadwick-adjacent. Sometimes, her hand seemed to reach out for him and stop short of his sleeve.

The other wall was given over to glamorous guests at the famous garden parties. Two new framed photos lay on the surface of the filing cabinet ready to be added to the available space on the wall. A small hammer and hooks were ready for the job. I spotted something in the second row of photos, when the door opened again and Lisa Hatton said, "Let's get this over with."

I turned and joined her by the desk. I would have done anything to slow down time, because I was pretty sure that I'd seen a glimpse of Lisa Troy in one of the group shots of a garden party.

I needed to buy some time.

"Before we start, I'll need to see your hospitality expenditures for the past seven years."

Lisa stared at me. "That's not possible."

"Nevertheless."

"Some are stored off-site."

"Start with the records you have here and make arrangements." I was feeling lower by the second, making this grieving woman chase her tail. At this rate, soon I'd be lower than a snake.

Miranda appeared in the doorway, carrying a cup of tea that—unless I was wrong—had been steeped in resentment.

In my best auditor imitation, I said, "Perhaps your assistant, Miranda, would help you bring them." Deep down I was feeling this was about to blow up in my face.

Lisa stared and then nodded. My karma "bill" was going to be through the roof this month. Miranda put the jasmine tea down slowly and followed Lisa from the room, her strawberry-blond curls bobbing with annoyance. I raced to the wall and checked. Sure enough, that was Lisa Troy in the first picture, on the second row of frames. I lifted the photo off the wall and substituted one from the filing cabinet. I opened my briefcase and dropped in the framed photo. I hurried to the door.

"Please tell Miss Hatton that I have been called back to the office unexpectedly," I said to the first person I saw. "Tell her that the audit has been postponed indefinitely." No point in letting the poor woman suffer any more.

I moved as quickly as I could toward the front door. I spotted Lisa and Miranda conferring with a man with a suit. He looked like security. There was quite a bit of gesturing and hand waving on Lisa's part and a lot of nodding and curl bobbing from Miranda. I had a feeling "the jig was up," as my uncles like to say. Even at that distance, I could see Lisa blowing her nose vigorously. Pivoting on my heel, I speed-walked down a corridor and into what turned out to be a huge kitchen. My uncles had always warned me never to break into a run until you had no choice.

"Spot check. Health department," I said, pointing to the far corner. "Do I see droppings? I'll be back with my citation tablet." I believe I said that as if it were a real thing.

The startled kitchen staff turned to look at the nonexistent droppings, and I barreled through the door to the outside. I skirted the building and stuck my head around the corner to check for anyone who might recognize Kathryn Risley Rolland. I whipped off the stiff blond wig and stuffed it in the briefcase. I folded the jacket and squeezed that in too, followed by the glasses. With the photo, these new additions tested the hinges on the briefcase, but it held. I found an elastic in my pocket and pulled my hair back. With the dark ponytail and without the jacket and glasses, I headed for the parking lot, hoping no one would recognize me or "Kathryn." My adrenaline was pumping. It wouldn't do me any good to be caught here, for sure. What had I been thinking? I was a suspect, and I'd pulled a stunt at the workplace of the victim, unsettling his obviously grieving co-workers. Lisa was devastated, and I had made her life worse. Even though I'd found a useful line on Lisa Troy, I felt like a rat. A rat that needed a bath.

But before my ratty self could reach the Infiniti and drive off, I caught sight of something and ducked back behind the yew hedge by the side of the building. Detective Drea Castellano and Detective Stoddard were making their way up the front stairs. She was all business; he was languid as usual.

I would have some explaining to do, if either one of them discovered me at the Country Club and Spa when I was technically under police watch in the apartment at Michael Kelly's Fine Antiques.

Logically, I'd be better off taking my chances with the Country Club and Spa staff or garden workers than with the detectives.

I leaned against the wall and whipped off the elastic band. I retrieved the suit jacket and the wig, plus, of course, the glasses. I had to balance the briefcase on my knee to wrestle on the wig. I slithered back into the jacket, which had not been improved by being squished in the briefcase. Still, it was the best I could do. I put the dark-framed glasses on and legged it across the lawn.

I thought I heard Miranda shout something, but I kept going. Young Braydon was headed my way too. I was prepared to knock him over if I couldn't intimidate him. Out of the corner of my eye I noticed a Harrison Falls police car at the entrance of the parking lot. I practically dove into the Infiniti and peeled on out of the lot, spraying gravel. Once I was on the road, I pulled into the first driveway I saw and caught my breath.

"I will never, ever put on another disguise," I said out loud. "I am cured of that habit." My bad angel gave me the thumbs-up and whispered, *But you got away with it.*

My good angel tapped my other shoulder. *And did you notice who was driving that police car?*

The answer, of course, was Tyler "No Longer Smiley" Dekker. My former number one guy.

Had Tyler recognized me? Did he see me duck behind the yew hedge and emerge as a different person who then high-tailed it to her car and took off like one of the Dukes of Hazzard?

That would have been even stickier than running into Castellano. He had contacted Sammy on my behalf, but I knew that he'd draw the line at aiding and abetting my foray to the Country Club and Spa.

What if he followed me? I found myself fighting panic and glanced in the rearview mirror. Sure enough, the Harrison Falls police cruiser zoomed past and continued on down the highway. That meant I was in the clear.

I caught myself in the mirror: My wig was crooked and my glasses were fogged up. I reassured myself that he hadn't seen me getting into the Infiniti, as it had been far enough away. Plus he'd never take me for an Infiniti type.

I wondered if he'd decide to check out either Van Alst

House or Uncle Mick's. Would he wait for me and then arrest me? And maybe break up with me again, for good measure? If he saw me driving the Infiniti, would he recognize me? If so, what would he do? Call for backup? Castellano's face came to mind. I glanced around in a panic. Had Smiley recognized me and also seen me put on the tight blond wig? If—and it was a big if—he hadn't spotted the car, I might be able to get out of this sticky situation. On the backseat was Uncle Mick's favorite Panama hat. In the glove compartment, a pair of sunglasses. Wig off, hair tucked under, sunglasses on, I reversed out of the driveway at top speed and headed along the highway. I was looking for the first opportunity to get past Tyler, without getting pulled over and ticketed.

Luckily for me, Tyler pulled over, shortly after. It looked like he was making a phone call, as I shot past, looking straight ahead.

BACK IN HARRISON Falls, I parked the Infiniti in the garage two doors down and raced along the alley and through the back door to Uncle Mick's. I'd left the briefcase with the wig and other evidence back in the car. The photo came with me. I careened through the door and clattered upstairs. I wiped off the unflattering coral lipstick and didn't make a substitute. I grabbed my old pink, daisy-printed flannel pajamas from the drawer and tousled my hair. A flop on the bed to cuddle Walter was next.

"You could have warned me, Walter, that I was about to make a very big mistake."

But you have the photo, Jordan. Walter tilted his head to the side.

Well, he didn't say that, actually, but I did have the photo, and I took that moment to tuck it into the mattress. No one should be surprised that at Uncle Mick's house, all the mattresses have hollow bits to hide things.

The front door bell rang, and there was a banging that

corresponded with it. Walter yipped. We practically tumbled down the stairs to answer.

I was rubbing sleep out of my eyes, which I thought was creative, and Walter was doing a little circular dance of joy.

"This is definitely not good news, Walter," I said as I opened the door.

"We don't need any," I said to Tyler.

"Oh," he said. "You're here."

"And where else would I be?"

"Nowhere," he said, glancing at my pajamas. The flannel pj's weren't doing me any favors.

"As long as that's settled, then, I'm behind on my sleep due to certain horrible things that have happened. I'm sure you can figure out what they are. So I'd like to go back and finish my nap. Unless you have some police harassment you'd like to engage in."

"That's not fair. I don't engage in police harassment. You know that." The red flush that I used to love rose from his collar to the tips of his ears and rushed toward his hairline.

"Not fair? Not fair? I'll tell you what's not fair. A police spy is not fair, watching everything I do." I pointed to the officer who had been in the unmarked car, but who was now standing behind Tyler.

"You aren't being watched," Tyler said, running his hands through his blond hair.

His colleague said, "Yeah, she was. That reminds me, you here to take over?"

"What? No. I just need to talk to, um, the suspect."

"Sure thing. Anyway, she didn't get up to anything this afternoon. Couldn't be more boring." The other officer yawned, scratched in the vicinity of his armpit and sauntered back toward his car.

"Boring is good," Tyler said.

"Is there a point to your visit, Officer Dekker?" I said. "I was in the middle of a much-needed nap when you so rudely interrupted."

"Were you?" he said, with narrowed eyes. Narrowed eyes did not look good on him. He had a wide-open cheerful face. His eyes were round and blue. Suspicion wasn't one of his usual accessories. "Are you sure you didn't leave the premises?"

Tyler is, after all, a police officer, and at times he talks like one. I should have realized much earlier that would be evidence of a serious incompatibility between us. It bothered me that he'd caught on to the fact we were an impossible match, while I was thinking I'd fallen in love with him. It just goes to show you.

"Sure, I left the premises. I was out and about in my pajamas and your fellow officer didn't notice, even when I did doughnuts with the Saab right in front of his very obvious police car."

"It's unmarked," Tyler said before he could stop himself.

The other officer stopped and turned around. "No one gets away on my watch."

Pride goeth before a fall and all that. I grinned at that officer, not at Tyler, and shrugged. "Of course I didn't leave the premises. I came here to calm down, and now I want to rest. It's been pretty rough."

He glanced at his colleague, who now seemed to have decided to pay attention to whatever it was that was going on. I wasn't entirely sure I knew what that was. I hated being mad at Tyler, but he had brought that on himself. I wasn't about to forgive that crime, but if I hadn't known better, I would have sworn he was trying to tell me something. He has the kind of face that can't keep a secret. He probably thought he'd spotted me at the Country Club and Spa, but he couldn't be sure of it.

And what could he do if he was sure of it?

Arrest me?

CHAPTER TEN

I CLOSED THE door in Officer Tyler Dekker's face. Our relationship was at an end. He was a police officer, the traditional enemy of the Kellys and the Binghams. He had figured out before I had that these things can't work.

But I'd been hurt before, and what doesn't kill you makes you stronger.

Not for the first time, I felt a strange gratitude to my cheating hound of an ex, the one who maxed out my credit cards, hoovered up my college fund and left me alone and heartbroken. If it hadn't been for Lucas Warden being a scumbag, I would never have limped home to my uncles in Harrison Falls and my pink-and-white girlhood bedroom with all those My Little Ponies. I would never have needed to find a job that got me out from under their watch. I would never have lived surrounded by polished mahogany and priceless antiques at Van Alst House. I wouldn't be comfortable in that huge historic home, with the signora's wonderful food and my own attic apartment. I wouldn't be on the lookout for first editions to augment an amazing collection in a climate-controlled room with rosewood shelves, leather chairs and an Aubusson on the floor. Yes, I know, it all came with Vera, of course, and she took a lot of getting used to, but it was still the best job in the world, and I wouldn't have any of it if I hadn't been betrayed by Lucas.

"Thank you," I whispered, to the guy who wasn't there. "Although wherever you are, I hope you're getting what's coming to you." I hadn't seen Lucas in more than two years and hoped never to set eyes on him again. Still, I knew if I'd gotten through that awful, humiliating experience that cost me so much figuratively and literally, I could weather this thing with Tyler.

Back upstairs, still in my pajamas, I whisked out the photo from the hiding place in the mattress. I felt a little bit disappointed that there was nothing else hidden in the cavity.

The photo was, if you can imagine it, the Spring Soirée from the previous May, according to the small plaque at the bottom of the frame. Against the backdrop of the sweeping green lawns of the Country Club and Spa, the young women were stunning in their long, swirly gowns. Shiny hair gleamed, and there were enough white teeth to blind a person. The men were in formal wear too, all looking dapper and Ivy-Leaguish. I have never been to a soirée, but I loved the look of it. Of course, it was only a photo, but still, I could almost smell the money in the air. If I remembered my research, the Spring Soirée was a benefit for a local women's shelter, a cause that was supposed to be dear to the late Chadwick's charitable heart.

In the front row, Lisa Hatton leaned slightly toward Chadwick, her arm actually touching his. Her voluptuous figure strained at her plum satin dress. Her red lips were curved in a satisfied smile. Chadwick's own smile looked perfunctory and formal. But he didn't lean away from Lisa. Not at all.

So that was interesting.

But more than interesting was the blond beauty in the

second-to-last row, third from the left. There was no sign of the light brown hair she'd had when I met her. In this shot, bare shouldered and elegant, Lisa Troy smiled off to the side, seeming to ignore the camera, her face tilted just so, to flatter her. Her asymmetrical updo looked natural, yet I figured it had cost a small fortune. Whoever Lisa was in real life, she had some cash to dispose of. The guy at her side was not the man who had presented himself as Chadwick Kauffman. He was a conventionally handsome fellow, tall, dark and well put together, but not all that interesting. Who was she smiling at off camera? Not the real Kauffman, who was at the end of the first row.

My heart was beating fast. I had found Lisa. And if I had found her picture, I should be able to find the woman herself. Sure, there had been a scam at work at Summerlea, but among the beautiful people at this glittering event, the chances were very good that someone would recognize her.

I was so caught up that I hadn't noticed loud pounding at the door. But I couldn't miss the thundering of feet on the stairs. I stood up as Tyler Dekker called out my name. There was no time to return the pilfered photo with its distinctive sage-and-gold frame to the mattress hiding place. I whipped it behind my back, as Tyler loomed in my bedroom door. My face was flaming, more from anxiety than embarrassment. Visions of police cells flashed in my brain. Orange is not really my best color. I plunked down on the photo to hide it.

"What are you doing here?" I said, hoping as I snapped out the words that the glass in the photo wouldn't crack under my weight. It was not designed for someone who'd enjoyed so many of the signora's meals.

"Just checking," he said, averting his eyes.

"Checking what? Do you think I have a dead body over there?" I pointed to the far end of the room, where my Smurf collection had a place of pride on top of the white bookcase.

I suppose it was instinctive, and as Tyler turned to look,

I stood up and flipped the blanket over the photo. Luckily, no shards of glass were stuck in the seat of my pajamas.

I folded my arms and glared at him. The effect might have been more intimidating if it hadn't been for all those daisies on the faded pink flannel.

"I wanted to make sure you were still here."

"Where else would I be?" I've been taught by the best. Believe the lie. Look them in the eye.

He wavered. He wanted to believe me. For some reason, I was sure of that. "Investigating."

I snorted.

"You know what you're like, Jordan. You have to go and find things out. Sometimes you play fast and loose with—"

I said, "I don't—" at the same moment he shouted, "You know you—"

A second thundering on the stairs caused us both to whirl, stuck mid-sentence.

"Everything all right?" The other officer blocked the door, staring at us.

"Well, you are both here without a warrant as far as I can tell. Aside from that and the fact I don't seem to be able to have a nap without the SWAT team, everything's peachy."

"Peachy?" the other cop said. "Really?"

"Very funny." Tyler gave me a glare. "Stop messing around. You're caught up in a dangerous situation."

"I'm glad you pointed that out. The murder itself and the fact we are somehow implicated in it wasn't enough for me to catch on."

Something flickered across his face. Anger? Regret? Some mysterious cop emotion that the rest of the world doesn't get?

"Stay out of it."

He glanced around the room, squinting. I'd never been exactly open with Tyler about my uncles and their . . . enterprises, but I knew he had a pretty good idea. Up until this point, I'd thought he believed in me, believed I was an honest person, going straight, despite the odds. Now I wasn't sure what to think. Our relationship was toast. Served me right for imagining I could be happy with a cop.

The other cop scratched his head. "You want to take her in?"

"No grounds."

I said, "And let me repeat, no warrant. Shall I walk you to the door?"

"What?" Scratchy said.

I ignored that and watched the two of them leave. The staircase echoed with their boots. I heard the door from the kitchen to the shop close. I made my way to the front window, and I could see them actually get into their vehicles. Tyler Dekker made a U-turn. He slowed his cruiser. He opened his window. He glanced up, and our eyes met as I stared down at him.

The other police officer was settled in behind the steering wheel of his obvious but unmarked car. I assumed he was scratching. I rescued the photo from under the blanket. I tucked it into a cushion and headed down to Uncle Mick's scanner, conveniently located out of sight of the officer. I'd been lucky that the photo hadn't been ruined when I'd sat on it.

I carefully ejected the photo from the frame and laid it on the scanner. I scanned the photo and saved it to my laptop and a memory stick. Next I forwarded the image to Lance from one of Uncle Mick's lesser known e-mail addresses. I reinserted the original into the frame and stuck it back in the cushion.

I used my burner phone to call Lance to give him a heads-up.

"Hi, Lance."

"Beautiful lady," he purred.

"I need a big favor."

"Anything," he said.

"I've sent you a photo, and I need to identify a woman in the second-to-last row. Third from left."

"Um, okay."

"It's a formal shot taken at the Spring Soirée at the Country Club and Spa, last year."

Lance made choking noises.

"You are the best, Lance."

"I am, but I'm not sure how to . . . Never mind. Send it over and leave it with me and I'll do what I can."

I smiled happily. "You should already have it."

"Don't count on anything though."

"No pressure," I said, knowing that Lance wouldn't be able to relax until he found the elusive woman. "But if you can't identify her, maybe you can find out who some of the other people are. Don't bother with the staff members on the side, including the late Chadwick, and the still-alive Lisa Hatton.. They're in the first row on the right side of the photo."

"Why her?" he asked.

"That's the woman who called herself Lisa Troy at Summerlea. I knew she had a connection with Chadwick somehow. We are getting closer to figuring out who is behind the death of Chadwick Kauffman."

"But Chadwick was murdered. Maybe you shouldn't be poking around in that. Maybe you should leave it to the police."

"But we do know that *this* Lisa is involved, and the police don't believe us about the people at Summerlea. Once we identify her, I'll have something to take to them."

"Even though it's fun to help you sleuth, maybe you should take the photo directly to the police."

"I didn't come by that photo, um, legally. Anyway, I'm going to need something solid about who this Lisa is before I go whispering in Detective Castellano's ear."

"Why do I feel like this is going to turn out to be dangerous?"

"It already turned out to be really dangerous for Chadwick. We can't let someone get away with murder and with trying to pin the blame on one of us. It was an obvious setup, in retrospect."

"So please be careful."

"I will be. And don't leave any information for me on my cell. In case the cops bug it."

"Now you're being paranoid."

"I don't think so. They wouldn't put a trace on your phone in the reference department, but you can bet they'll get warrants for my phone and electronic records. That's why I called you from a burner."

"Where are you now?"

"I'm about to head back to Van Alst House. I want to check and see how Vera's doing, although she wasn't really too broken up over Chadwick and she doesn't really think we'll get arrested. But she hates disruption. So the cops hanging around are bound to be getting her down, and I wouldn't put it past her to get on her high horse with them. Plus, you know, there's always something wonderful for dinner. Thanks for helping, Lance. I owe you."

"I have an idea that might work. Give me a bit of time."

"I'll be in touch."

I GOT BACK into my regular clothes, swirled my terrific crimson cape, dropped my iPhone into my pocket, leashed Walter and picked up his lovely little bed. We ambled to the Saab. Walter was so excited that he snorted and circled. I didn't snort or circle, but I did give a jaunty little wave to the police officer who was stuck with the boring job of watching me. I walked over to his car.

I said, "I'm heading for Van Alst House for dinner. I'll drive slowly if you'd like."

He looked at me and scratched his nose. As I settled myself and Walter settled in the Saab, he was fairly obviously on his radio communicating this information. What would he be saying? *Suspect on the move?*

Not my problem.

I was starving, and I imagined that Walter was too.

As I turned to pull into the Van Alst driveway, Cherie's cable van careened out the gate and rocketed down the road and away from Harrison Falls. I crossed my fingers she'd come through for me. I hoped that Uncle Kev was with her, out of sight and out of trouble.

I was still being tailed. I hoped that my dozy watcher hadn't taken note of the cable truck. I glanced in the rear-view mirror once again. The bored officer didn't appear to be passing this information on to anyone. I downshifted the Saab and drove onto the pea gravel drive, taking my time winding around to the back, so I could make sure he followed me. He did.

My plan was simple. Take the dog for a walk. It's not that I didn't trust Cherie to do everything I asked. I wanted to double-check. Knowing Uncle Kev, he was entirely capable of helping Cherie clean up all evidence of the still and then spray-painting *Kevin Kelly was here making moonshine. For more information please call Jordan Bingham 555-1234* in red on the nearest tree.

First, we made our way to the kitchen. I told the signora that there was a poor, hungry policeman in the car outside. She didn't react by racing out the door with some food for him, as I'd expected. It seemed that the signora was annoyed by the police. If I understood her rapid speech and even more rapid hand movements, she didn't like the idea of them interrogating us and upsetting Vera's routine. She'd served coffee and almond cookies and where did that get us?

"*Disgraziati!*" she muttered to finish off.

After nearly two years around the signora, I'd learned that she meant the two detectives were scoundrels or good-for-nothings. I was fine with that, but I needed her help.

"For sure, Signora, but the detectives have left. The officer in the car is here to help us, I think. To make sure we're safe." I widened my eyes.

She shook her head.

"Okay, well, I need him to be distracted for a few minutes.

He is not very smart. If you give him a snack, I can do what I have to. Will you help me?"

She mumbled something that I thought was "*pan di Spagna*" and bustled about the kitchen, slicing sponge cake and arranging it on a plate. There was enough for five dozy officers, but I said nothing. "You take," she said.

"Will you do it, please? And maybe the officer needs a glass of milk. I need to walk Walter before he has an accident."

The signora is not a fan of dog accidents, so Walter and I slipped out the door along with her. She approached the car with the cake. From over her black-clad shoulder I said to the officer, "The dog needs a walk." His eyes, after a disbelieving glance at the signora, were on that pile of cake slices. He took the cake plate with one hand and the glass of milk with the other.

Walter and I sashayed down the driveway, our steps crunching on the pea gravel, but I held my breath after we stepped onto the grass and until we got to the edge of the property. After making a big production of stopping at every second bush, we scurried toward the clearing behind the cluster of trees where Kev had set up shop.

As soon as we arrived at the spot, I could see Cherie had done what she'd promised. There wasn't even a twig of evidence from the still. The only way I knew she'd been here were the stiletto-heeled boot marks peppered around the forest floor, and the slightest hint of Mariah Carey perfume in the air. Thank goodness I could still count on someone to do what they said they would.

Walter sniffed at the familiar scents, making the sweetest agreeable snorts.

"Were Kev and Cherie here, Walter?" Something about that little dog always makes me smile. No matter how bad things get, a snub-nosed pooch can make you feel a bit better.

Mmm-hmmm, he answered as his wild whiskers flicked at the ground.

"Well, they're gone now." I only hoped it was far away and nowhere that the police would think of looking. We needed a lawyer for Kev first.

The longer Cherie could keep Uncle Kev out of sight, the better.

Walter and I sauntered back toward the house, waved to the munching policeman and headed inside. The little pug skipped and skidded through the door. He felt very at home in Van Alst House.

The signora sprang out from the kitchen to greet us.

"Any chance of cake for me and not only the cops?" I said.

Walter spun in a giddy circle. He likes cake too. A paw protruded from the kitchen door and aimed for his hindquarters. But Walter was onto Bad Cat's little tricks, and he danced out of the way.

"Cake!" the signora intoned, drawing Walter's attention. "You want soup? Bread? Coffee?"

I resisted the urge to say yes to all of that. "Anything. I'm starving."

"*Sì, sì. La casa degli zii.*" She nodded meaningfully. My Italian was getting better, and I knew that meant "the uncles' house." She also implied that there would be nothing there but Kraft Macaroni and Cheese, canned beans and maybe some presliced baloney. This was true enough.

Still, I didn't want to denigrate Uncle Mick's kitchen. I said, "Too busy to eat today, Signora. That's all."

I gave her a big smile. I did know what was good for me, but I needed to go hide that memory stick.

In spite of that urgency, I found myself seated in the conservatory with a steaming bowl of *ravioli in brodo*, some fresh rustic bread and a small plate with a puddle of extra virgin olive oil, with a few herbs and a swirl of balsamic vinegar in the puddle.

The coffee would arrive when I was finished, but I could hear the *caffettiera* thumping from the kitchen.

No doubt there would be dessert too. I fell upon the food

like a starving wolf. I was lost in a world of taste and silky
texture, paying no attention to my surroundings, when I
heard someone clear their throat.

Vera.

"Miss Bingham."

I kept eating. It didn't seem to require a response. What
would I have said? *Yes, I am Miss Bingham? No, I've decided
it's too dangerous to be Miss Bingham?* I could hardly deny
it. I did raise an eyebrow to indicate that I was willing to
engage in whatever it was she wanted to engage in.

"You have been out."

Two more spoonfuls of the *brodo*. I managed to nod and eat.

She said, "The police have been nosing around."

I swallowed and said, "I know."

"What do they want *now*?"

"Right this minute, there's an officer watching the house
to make sure I don't disappear. I assume that Detectives
Castellano and Stoddard want to find proof that you or I or
Uncle Kev killed Chadwick Kauffman. They'll be off doing
their best to figure out if we did it alone or as a conspiracy."

"The fools."

"No argument here. But 'the fools,' as you call them,
have it in for us, and they'll need to close this case. It's high
profile, because of Chadwick's prominent status and your
own. It's been making the news, and they'll be under pressure."

"And where have you been?"

Uh-oh. The less Vera knew about my activities, the better. "I needed to get away from things. I went to my uncles'
place to try and think straight."

"Are you thinking straight now?"

"I believe I am."

"But you seem to be stuffing your face, Miss Bingham."

"Stuffing my face has always helped me to think straight.
And it keeps up my strength."

The signora beamed approval. "Eat, Jordan!"

"Humph. And where is Mr. Kelly? Keeping up his strength somewhere else?"

"So he's not here, then?"

"No, he's not where I pay him to be."

"He'll find pressing business elsewhere until the police come to their senses."

"If they do."

"Let hope that happens, because if not, one of us will be tried for murder and the others will be tried as accomplices."

The signora crossed herself.

Vera said, "Not you, Fiammetta, but the rest of us."

It seemed only right that the next sound after "*O dio!*" was ringing at the front door. This was followed by loud knocking and raised voices. That would be the police with all the right warrants.

"Gosh. Listen to them. Do you mind answering the door, Signora? I want to fix my makeup first." Okay, that was very lame, but no one seemed to notice.

"No, police, no, no, no!"

"Signora, please get the door!" I called out as I took the stairs to the attic two at a time. I knew I should have taken the time to hide that memory stick and my burner phone earlier, instead of letting my taste buds rule my brain.

I could hear Vera yelling, "Stop fussing, Fiammetta. The police won't kill you. Somebody get the door. Miss Bingham!"

As I reached the third floor, the muffled strains of her rant wafted up the narrow wooden staircase. I resisted the urge to go downstairs and protect Vera and the signora. But I had the memory stick with the scan of the stolen photo, and I didn't want them to find any evidence that I'd had an exceptional interest in Chadwick. Warrants or no warrants, seasoned house searchers or not, these police would never have encountered a rabbit warren like the upper levels and servants' quarters of Van Alst House. As spectacular as the hiding places were in my uncles' home, they were nothing compared to the hollows in walls, loose boards, hidden rooms and miscellaneous rafters in this old place. In short order I had slipped a pair of socks over my shoes, ducked into the rear entrance into the box room, clambered over some old boards and trunks and deposited the stick out of sight. I made sure the burner phone was off—and not on vibrate—and shoved it in too. Not convenient, but effective. I gave them both a push so that I'd have a challenge to retrieve them. I retreated to my room. I slipped off the socks and opened the window. I looked out and saw no one. I gave the socks a shake and dropped them in the hamper.

I changed into a pair of dark-wash skinny jeans and a casual gray knit V-neck sweater, my latest bargain find at the end of the winter season. I twisted my hair into a ponytail and took a swipe with my lipstick. It would have to do. I was putting on my little red lace-ups when there was a knock on the door.

"One min—" I said. The door opened, and Castellano and a pair of uniformed officers stalked in. Well, Castellano stalked. I took pleasure out of the fact she was a bit breathless. The male uniformed officer was red in the face, either from the stairs or from barging into someone's bedroom. The extremely young female officer was cool and collected. She looked at me as though I was something she'd remembered seeing under the microscope in biology class. When she grew up she'd probably be like Castellano. Heaven help us.

I stared at the three of them, my jaw dropping enough to reinforce the surprise, but not so slack as to look ugly and stupid.

"We have a warrant," Castellano said.

I bit back the retort, *Well, aren't we special?* I didn't want to find myself at the police station if I could avoid it.

Instead, I shrugged. "Knock yourselves out. Not sure what you'll find, but I lost my library card. Let me know if it turns up."

"Very funny." Castellano stared around. I hated the fact that she was there contaminating my oasis of tranquility.

I finished the double knot on the laces and stood up. "What should I do? Stay here?"

"Stay here. We may have questions." She nodded to the officers, who snapped on gloves. "Get at it."

She glanced at the stack of Ngaio Marsh books by the side of the iron bedstead, bent and read the spines. "Were these the ones you got from Kauffman?"

I blinked. "What?"

"Are these the books you obtained from Chadwick Kauffman?"

"Oh. No. These are just paperbacks. They're not valuable."

"Really?"

Despite myself, I found my enthusiasm for the project rebounding. "The ones Vera bought are first editions. They're quite rare. That's why we went to Summerlea. It was such a great offer. Almost too good to be . . ."

Of course, it had been too good to be true.

"Or so you'd like us to believe."

"That's what happened. We were thrilled, and maybe we should have realized that something was up."

"Something other than you robbing and killing your host, you mean?"

"That's not what happened, and I'm pretty sure you know that. We had nothing to do with it, except for being set up, of course. Vera Van Alst would never be involved in anything criminal or violent. She's a respectable member of this community."

"Oh, well then, that settles it. I can't imagine a respectable member of any community doing anything wrong. Please accept my apologies."

I laughed out loud despite myself. "Put like that, I suppose that leaves out a lot of embezzlers and—"

"And violent abusers and worse, in case you've never run into people like that among the elite."

"Point taken. I know that people aren't always what they

seem. But I think there are usually indications of . . . criminality. With Vera, you'd find nothing. She doesn't care about anything but books. She acquires them honestly, and if she needs to, she sells off some antique treasure that her great-grandfather owned or bit of family jewelry to get the funds."

"Money's a problem, then?" she said with a touch of a sneer. That sneer was almost as unflattering as duckface. It didn't do her beautiful features any favors.

"It's not a problem. There's tons of stuff here that Vera can sell if she wants or needs to. Her collection isn't secret. It's all above board, and you can—if you haven't already—go see it in the library. She's proud of it. You can turn this house upside down searching. There will be nothing that implicates Vera in any kind of dishonest or illegal behavior. I'd bet my life on it."

She flashed a grin at her co-workers. The female officer stopped tossing my bras and panties out of my underwear drawer. The male paused in flipping the mattress to study her carefully. Both of them were scared to death of the good detective.

"You hear that? She'd bet her life on it." She chuckled—a warm, rich sound that gave me goose bumps. "Miss Jordan Bingham was raised by common criminals. Did you know that?"

CHAPTER ELEVEN

THE TWO COPS gawked at me.

"Not true," I said, drawing myself up in outrage. "My uncles are not criminals."

"Oh really?" she said. "Mick Kelly and Lucky Kelly— not criminals? That's a laugh."

"They have no criminal records. They've never even been charged with a crime. Does your definition of criminal extend to every citizen in our community whether they've ever been charged with an offense or not? That's a big net you've got there, Detective."

Her eyes glittered. She was a dangerous adversary, and I was challenging her in front of two subordinates. Of course, the subordinates were trashing my home on her orders, so you can figure out what got my back up.

"They are known to the police."

"Who isn't? You are known to the police, being a serving officer, but that doesn't make you a criminal. Or, at least, I assume that."

I was pushing my luck. But I am half Kelly, and sometimes we are luck pushers. I said, "I am not a criminal nor have I ever been."

"You've certainly been under suspicion."

"Being under suspicion doesn't mean a thing. You know that. And this was a violent attack." I heard my voice catch. My uncles would tell me to man up at this point. Of course they weren't here, were they?

"And Kevin Kelly? You're telling me he's innocent too?"

Kev had been on the wrong side of the law, meaning he'd served a bit of time because of youthful indiscretions and less-than-brilliant legal help. I said, "He was a kid. He's a changed man now."

"Right. And if you have a bit of Florida swampland for sale, I'd like to take it off your hands. Can I give you my credit card number?"

I ignored her sarcastic tone. "He has a good job here at Van Alst House. He makes a contribution. He's valued and appreciated and helpful. He'll do anything for anybody, and he didn't kill Chadwick Kauffman." My voice went up in a girlish way. I told myself to get that under control, because if the cops know you really care about something, they try to use that against you.

I was spared any further slurs against my family when Tyler Dekker stumbled up the stairs and into my room. Another young officer was right behind him. "Something you should see, ma'am."

"What?" Castellano and I said in unison.

"It's outside, Detective Castellano," he said with emphasis. I noticed he couldn't make eye contact with me. He did look around the room. I was positive he spotted the randomly tossed bras and panties on my flower-sprigged comforter. I took some pleasure in the fact that his blush had already started. It was very bright. Tomato-like, even.

Of course, I was also blushing. What a pair. Too bad we were barely speaking.

Castellano turned to the other two and said, "Don't miss anything."

I said, "Yes, make yourselves at home. I think I'll head downstairs for a snack if I'm not needed." I was pretty sure they'd never turn up the burner phone or the memory stick, but even with that confidence I was glad that my lock picks were safely stowed far from Van Alst House.

"Evidence of something in the trees by the edge of the property, ma'am," the second officer said with barely concealed excitement. He'd have to learn to keep his thoughts to himself if he wanted to rise in the force. Castellano kept her own thoughts hidden, although she did nod. Tyler Dekker's blush was beginning to subside. Of course his career trajectory meant nothing to me, but if all it took was an underwear drawer to get that flush, he'd be a patrol officer for the rest of his life.

Castellano nodded and everyone trooped downstairs and the police delegation trooped outside. The signora was spinning with distress. Vera had rolled off in a temper.

I picked up my iPhone and called Sammy. At the same time I asked the signora for a snack. I did everything to keep my thoughts off the search and not to imagine what they might find. Maybe a snack would reduce stress. Of course, the possibility of forgotten evidence of illegal liquor production was at the front of my mind. I'd been clear that Cherie and Kev needed to clear up the still, but I'd never asked Uncle Kev if he had any more stills around the property. In retrospect, that was an oversight.

I was distracted by the signora. She stopped the panicky little dance and headed for the kitchen to create some magic with food. Yes, it had only been about half an hour since I had last eaten, and dinner would be at eight, but coffee and cookies seemed like a good idea. If we weren't off the hook soon, I'd need a whole wardrobe in a new size. Still, I planned to enjoy my snack and read a bit to take my mind off what I couldn't fix.

Stoddard came to get me soon enough. He slouched through the door, and I followed him outside to an area off the pea gravel drive. It had been cordoned off with police tape. Stoddard lifted the fluttering yellow-and-black tape.

"Festive," I said.

Police with gloves were milling around. Stoddard stood back, looking bored, his hands in his pockets. Smiley hung around the fringe, not smiling even a bit. I was getting used to him not making eye contact with me. It would become a way of life. A police photographer had recorded the scene. I figured even Kev wouldn't have set up a still so close to the driveway, so what were they looking so smug about?

Castellano looked down her nose at me. I noticed she had a bit of mud on the beautiful cognac-colored knee-high boots, so that wasn't helping her disposition any. Of course, I hadn't asked her to tromp over the soggy post-winter lawn.

"Recognize anything?" she said, pointing to some objects on the ground, behind a decorative dwarf pine.

"Should I?"

"You tell me."

I leaned forward and squinted. What was this? Monogrammed silverware?

I glanced at her. "It looks like someone's sterling silver."

"That's right. Guess who has silverware exactly like this?"

"They had it at Summerlea."

"And this stuff has prints all over it." She pointed to a tech heading away from the site. "We'll wait for results, but I imagine we'll find yours and Kevin Kelly's."

"You can't seriously believe that we would steal traceable items from Summerlea and then leave them lying around in plain sight for two days."

"And yet, here they are."

"That doesn't strike you as strange? Or stupid?"

"If the shoe fits." She smirked.

"That shoe doesn't fit. If we wanted to hide stolen merchandise, we could have done a lot better than that, especially as you made such a big deal about returning with a warrant."

"Have you ever heard of the Darwin Awards?"

I glared at her. "Of course I have. We are not criminals and we are not fools." Kev, mind you, was remarkably foolish and a prime candidate for a Darwin, but never mind. "None of us stole these items, and if we had, you wouldn't have found them here. You know that and so do I." I didn't mention that the sterling would have been already melted down if anyone in my family had a hand in it.

"Mr. Kelly has disappeared," she said.

"I'm sure he'll be back. You'll notice he didn't disappear with any of this." I pointed to the so-called evidence. "Lieutenant Castellano, you should be asking yourself who wants to frame us."

"Give it a rest," she said. "You haven't been framed. Don't think for one minute any of us here will fall for that. One of you slipped up, and we're going to keep on this until we've made sure there's nothing else. But I'm betting there will be."

I managed to look unfazed.

But I did realize somewhat late in the game that I'd forgotten all about "no comment" as a means of communication with the police.

What would Sammy say?

But Sammy wasn't there and Castellano was.

She must have had royalty somewhere in her DNA. How else could she stand there with such unassailable dignity and power looking down at me, the Irish peasant accused of poaching? Of course, the heels on those boots added to her visual impact, even if they had a bit of mud on them now, but the woman was born to power, I swear. Maybe being a detective was the route to world domination or something.

"*Cui bono?*" I said, tossing in a bit of college Latin in an attempt to balance things.

She raised a beautifully sculpted eyebrow.

I added, "It means—"

"To whose benefit? I know what it means. But what do you mean by it?"

"Well, I mean to ask who benefits from this whole situation." I was babbling. I reminded myself to chant one of the many Kelly mantras: *You're as good as anyone, Jordan, probably better.* My uncles had sent me off to school with those words in my ear, and they'd helped.

But Castellano wasn't a school yard bully out to make the new kid miserable. She was a detective who could practically taste victory. Wild-goose chases would not be her thing.

She said, "Get to the point."

"Well, none of us would benefit from Chadwick Kauffman's death. Not at all. Vera wanted the collection for sure, but Vera buys things. She doesn't steal them. And she still has enough money to do that. You can dig around until you retire, but you won't find anything to indicate she has ever stolen an object or even done something dishonest. You're barking up the wrong tree, Detective."

"Not a dog. Not barking. You're out of time. We've found the evidence we need."

"Wait." I tried not to squeak. "This whole Summerlea thing has brought us nothing but trouble. We certainly don't benefit. My point is that Kauffman was an incredibly wealthy man. So follow the money. I say where there's a will, there may have been a way."

She rolled her eyes. "Is it National Bad Pun Day already? Even if it is, we've found the equivalent to the money. Right here."

"We'd have to be fools to leave that there. From the look of it, this stash had everything but a treasure map with an X to mark the spot. Do you not see that we're being framed? Who benefits from that? Relatives! Heirs! Surely they are suspects too. Isn't that a more logical approach—?"

"Don't question my logic. It is impeccable, and as for your 'where there's a will there's a way' idea, that was one of the first possibilities we checked out."

I inhaled.

She stared at me.

"And?" I said finally. "Close relatives?"

"No. There were second cousins, but he didn't have much to do with them."

"Friends?"

"No."

"Lovers?"

"No. Chadwick Kauffman did not have any relatives closer than second cousins. He didn't leave anything to them, except for some family jewelry, a coin collection and a stamp collection, more sentimental than valuable."

"But—"

She raised an elegant, long-fingered, scarlet-nailed hand to silence me. It worked.

"He didn't seem to have friends outside of work. And no romantic partners turned up."

"They could have been discreet. What about Lisa Hatton? She was crazy about him."

"Whatever. They were discreetly left out of the will, then. Chadwick left everything to several charities."

"What charities?"

"United Way, Second Chance Foundation for Homeless Families, the Sierra Club, UNICEF and the endowment fund at his alma mater, Yale. He left Summerlea to the Historical Society of Harrison Falls."

"No individuals?"

"No, and none of the employees of these charities are likely to have hit him over the head and pushed him down the stairs. Unless you think the president of Yale did it."

I gulped. "Everything?"

"Small stipends, here and there, hardly enough to kill him. He left a few trinkets to staff at the Country Club and Spa, such as Lisa Hatton. He also funded her retirement fund outside the will. Quite generous, but hardly enough motive to kill him as she'd get that anyway."

One phrase really got to me. "What do you mean, hardly enough motive to kill him? You've been suggesting we did it for a few bits of antique silver and—"

She continued as if she hadn't heard me. "He'd set up a college fund for the children of the housekeeper and the groundskeeper-gardener, and there were generous retirement funds for them and other long-term staff at his residences, but those arrangements were established as savings funds in their names. The arrangements were made outside the will and wouldn't be affected one way or the other by his death. Except their jobs would probably end, so they'd most likely prefer to keep him alive. His social life seemed to have involved other very wealthy people. If he had a love interest, she or he never worked their way into the will."

"But maybe his second cousins will contest the will."

She shrugged. "Move on."

"Maybe they didn't know and thought—"

"Everyone named in the will was formally notified through the lawyer well in advance. It seemed to be ironclad, and according to his lawyers, if they wanted to squander their own resources going after more, good luck to them. Waste of time. As is this."

I felt disappointment seeping into my spirit. I'd been counting on those faceless cousins to be the villains with some connection to Lisa Troy.

"There must have been other people who wanted him dead."

"Apparently, everyone loved him." From the look on Castellano's face, she doubted this.

"Everyone has some enemies."

"Maybe. But there's no sign that Kauffman had any. We've pretty much ruled inheritance out as a motive. We're sticking to our main theory: You and your uncle, who, unlike Vera, do have a history of criminal behavior—"

"Your theory is wrong."

"We're closing in. Everyone else we've had any reason

to think about has an airtight alibi, from the housekeeper and her family to the staff at that country club. But you were there. The evidence connects you, and it sure looks like the murder was planned and premeditated. It's only a matter of time until the noose tightens, as they say."

I rubbed my neck. We no longer execute people by hanging in this country, and no one has been executed in New York State since the sixties, but it was still a very scary moment. "What evidence do you think you have?"

Castellano shot me one of her incandescent smiles. "You'll find out soon enough."

Sammy arrived while they were still mucking around outside. Then we got "no comment," all right. Castellano was furious, but Sammy pointed out she'd better charge me or let me go about my business. I wasn't crazy about him playing chicken with her again.

She signaled to Smiley, gave me a poisonous look and headed back into the house.

I wasn't entirely sure why they let me go back inside, but they did. I noticed she didn't wipe her boots as she entered the back hallway. This sent the signora into a fit of mopping. *No more coffee and cookies for you, Lootenent*, I thought. But the visit wasn't a good thing. Castellano demanded to see Vera. Vera didn't have a lawyer yet.

Vera was in the library, the signora finally admitted, looking Italianate daggers at Castellano. I wondered how the detective would ward off that evil eye.

"You stay here," the lieutenant said to me.

"But—"

"'But' all you want. Stay here."

Sammy stepped forward. She shot him a glance. "Do you represent them both, Counselor?"

"No."

"Then you can stay here too."

Smiley looked pale as he followed Castellano's clicking heels along the endless corridor to the study. He was lugging two boxes, taped with evidence tape. "VAN ALST" was written in black marker. Stoddard stood inside, lazily observing us. I barely stopped myself from asking him to help the signora clean up after his colleague, if he had nothing to do but lounge around. But she'd already done the mopping.

My iPhone pinged. A text from Tiff.

Haven't seen the sun since we left Aruba. I am the only nurse, and I'm pretty sure we are about to have a norovirus outbreak. :(Ship satellite keeps going out. I think I've made a huge mistake. :(:(:(

Here I was imagining Tiff enjoying herself on the high seas, but it was more like *Clutch of Constables*, only with less murder and even more irritated Americans than Ngaio Marsh had included. I think Tiff and I were both wishing she was back in Harrison Falls right now.

Five minutes later, Smiley returned, still carrying the two boxes. Vera wheeled after him, her face contorted. "Spitting mad" came to mind.

"Miss Bingham," she said when he'd left. "That young man took my Marsh books. Every single one of them. I think you're right about that lawyer. Let me know when you get him lined up."

I stood outside and watched while Castellano and Stoddard left, Stoddard at the wheel of a black Chevy Tahoe. Smiley brought up the rear in his clearly marked cruiser, following the other officers in theirs.

Our regular guy stayed behind, to keep an eye, I guess.

When I came back in, Vera had rolled off in a rage. I didn't blame her.

Would they be back to sift through every molecule of our possessions again or arrest us?

I asked Sammy, "What will they do with the books?"

"Forensics will check them for . . . evidence."

"Why did they wait until now to collect them?"

"Who knows? Maybe they have a plan to rattle you one by one."

"This has definitely rattled Vera. But what should we do?"

"You have to wait and see what they come up with. Don't go running off."

"That would never have occurred to me," I fibbed.

"You didn't make any statements about the stuff they found? Did you stick to 'no comment'?"

"I may have said a few things. This stuff was obviously planted. It was in such a stupid place. No self-respecting thief would leave it there. I'm sure they would sell or melt it down, not leave it under a bush."

Sammy huffed. "Tell me you didn't say 'melt it down.'"

"I didn't."

He said, "I should have been here. You call me the first sight of them the next time. 'No comment.' That's what you say. It's easy. And that way you don't say something you can't unsay. It's too late for this time, but remember from now on, because they'll be trying to trip you up."

I hated the idea of "next time" and "after this." "I did call you as soon as they said they found something."

"You call me when they get here or when you know they're coming."

"Lesson learned, but we knew the police were getting warrants. Why would any one of us leave that stuff there? How could they believe that?"

"I deal with stupid criminals all the time, Jordan. You're not stupid and you're not a criminal, so I know you wouldn't. But they will have seen stranger and more self-incriminating things. Trust me."

"But if they have so much evidence and they're convinced we're guilty, why haven't they arrested any of us?"

"They probably like Kevin for it. They've got his prints on the weapon. They're waiting until one of you can't take it anymore and makes contact with him, in person or on the phone. That's probably why you're at home instead of in an interrogation room. They always have a reason."

"We have no idea where he is. Or why."

"Keep it that way."

I snorted. "We don't have much choice. Kev's in the wind."

"They'll be hunting for him everywhere."

"Someone is aware of that, Sammy. Someone who knows us and knows about us is behind it."

"You have to forget about that. Concentrate on living normally."

"Are you serious?"

"Eat your meals. Go about your daily tasks."

"We're worried."

"So be worried. I don't blame you. But keep your mouth shut and steer clear of Kevin."

"You think they'll have our phones under surveillance?"

"Is the grass green?"

"But what can I do? I can try to find out more about Chadwick or—"

"You"—Sammy poked my arms with his stubby finger—"do nothing. I'm the one who has to look into this guy Chadwick."

"And are you looking into him?"

"For sure. What? You think I'm at the track all day?"

That hadn't occurred to me until that very moment. "Have you found anything?"

Sammy's information confirmed Castellano's. "No girl-friends that anyone knows about. No close friends. No relatives. Nobody that anyone knows of."

"But the people at the spa really liked him."

"Employees. Yup. They were paid to like him, and I hear they all got along fine."

"I believe that, um, I heard somewhere that his assistant, Lisa Hatton, had a crush on him."

"Yes. We learned that too. She had it bad according to some of the other staff."

"And he—?"

"Was kind to her, from what I heard. He needed her to keep things running."

"Poor Lisa. You have to admit she'd make a great suspect."

"For sure. Too bad she didn't do it."

I squeaked, "How do you know that?"

"She was representing the Country Club and Spa at the Community Service Awards Luncheon.

"She wasn't at Summerlea, but that doesn't mean she wasn't involved in some way."

Sammy squinted at me. "Let it be. You have to stay here, looking like everything's normal. Remember? No chasing around trying to find out who's setting you up. No looking into Lisa Hatton."

"No comment."

AS PART OF the pretense of being normal, Vera and I ate a distracted dinner in the dining room. Vera could barely manage a grunt. I wondered if she'd ever get over what she called "the theft of my books." The signora was feeling the stress too. The muddy floor was probably part of it. She forgot to bring Parmesan cheese for the pasta and was really rattled when I offered to get it.

"Let things be," Vera growled, the only words she spoke all through dinner.

That should have prepared me for the discovery that the signora had forgotten to make the tiramisu.

Things went from bad to worse. Good Cat and Bad Cat prowled, both restless and unpredictable. Bad Cat managed to nick one of my knees. And I may have even heard a muffled ouch from Vera.

Walter was the only cheerful one of the bunch. Unlike us, he wasn't waiting for the police to show up and arrest Vera and me. He was waiting for tidbits to fall in his vicinity.

In the meantime, in case we weren't planning to stay

home and forget about everything, Castellano hadn't taken any chances.

There was a fresh new officer in a parked cruiser outside the front of Van Alst House. They'd stopped trying to fool us with unmarked police vehicles. I didn't know this guy, and as I'd spent altogether too much time with the police, I wasn't crazy about getting to know him, but I was pressed into service. The signora—once she decided that he was only a victim of circumstance—had sent me on several forays with thermoses of very good coffee, buckets of almond cookies and, on my last errand, a large and very smelly sandwich of Genoa salami and Asiago cheese on ciabatta. I knew she'd be wringing her hands and dancing her little dance while she waited for me at the back door. She seemed to have a mandate to feed the world.

I didn't need to distract the police, but it seemed like a good idea to keep on this guy's good side. It took a while to wear down his initial truculence—we were under surveillance, after all—but he mellowed as the evening wore on. I kind of felt sorry for him. We'd invited him to wait inside a couple of times. I suggested he'd have a better chance of making sure we didn't leg it. But apparently protocol meant he had to freeze in his vehicle, even though nothing really prevented me from skulking out the back door, then dashing through the trees and over the fields. In the resulting confusion, Vera and the signora could have vanished in the Cadillac.

I paced around, restless. My special place still bore the signs of the invasion of the snoopy police. It took quite a while to get it back to normal, as much as anything could be normal. I decided I'd have to wash my police-tossed unmentionables and made a trip down to the first-floor utility area with my laundry basket. On my return I plunked on the love seat and put my feet on the Lucite table. I picked up and put down three separate Ngaio Marsh books. I couldn't concentrate on any of them, no matter how many rambling and remote estates the author dangled in front of me. At the moment, our own circumstances were every bit as mysterious.

Inspector Alleyn wasn't one to make lengthy notes about cases or even write that much down. He had Sergeant Fox for that. But I was on my own and Foxless. Notes always work for me. I found a sheet of paper and a pen and started to work things out, beginning with the heading. Paper and pen can help me think. I scrawled thoughts, words and ideas randomly on the page, making a "mind map." In the end, sorting it all out, pulling things together, I ended up with this.

THE CRIME: What do we know?
First I wrote: *Setup—elaborate!*
Under that: *Targeted*
Knew Chadwick
Knew Summerlea

There was so much that bothered me. The setup. The whole charade of the luncheon. The food, the place settings, the invitation itself. It had all been so very intricate, so perfectly staged. Elaborate also meant *premeditated.* The scam had been premeditated. Had the murder been premeditated as well? Was it intended all along that Chadwick be killed and that we would take the fall for it? Or had he turned up at the wrong time, in the middle of the scam, and been killed?

That led me to my next observation:

Targeted
Knew about Vera's collection
Risky

We had definitely been identified and targeted. It would have taken time, planning and energy to reel Vera in to buy the Ngaio Marsh books. Whoever did it knew about Vera and her collection. And to what advantage? As Uncle Mick had pointed out, there were valuable paintings, silver and other goodies. Why go to the trouble to sell us the books, even if there had been a transfer of ten thousand dollars? That wasn't such a huge amount of money. Why not just simply clean out Summerlea, fence what was taken and be gone, without anyone seeing your face? That would have had a higher rate of return, with far less risk of being identified. Unless the purpose was really to kill Chadwick and frame us.

Naturally, I wrote:

Why us?

Certainly Vera was still the most hated woman in Harrison Falls and surrounding communities. No news there. But were lingering resentments against the lone survivor of the haughty Van Alsts and the daughter of the man who closed the Van Alst factory and brought the town to its knees enough to do something like this? I imagined Uncle Lucky saying, "Why not run her over?"

Why not indeed?

Was the motivation jealousy? Vera still had the home, the books, the antiques and her staff, a life of comfort and privilege. In this era of *Keeping Up with the Kardashians*, who kills a frumpy old lady because she has lots of old stuff?

It lacked something.

I turned my mind to the next question.

Why Chadwick?

There was no doubt in my mind that the perpetrators were familiar with Chadwick and Summerlea. They'd needed the code for that impressive security system. I was pretty sure the back and side doors and the windows would all have been alarmed. The housekeeper had noted that system wasn't set. The police hadn't mentioned a break-in, so it was likely our friends also had a key. If they had a key and the code, did they also have a motive for murder?

Finally, I wrote: *Who were they?*

Even with the photo of "Lisa," what were the chances that Vera, Kev or I would find a way to identify the other people at Summerlea? Still, with all those nosy neighbors, maybe one of them had seen our fake Chadwick and his team. They had taken a chance. But why?

Time passed, and I continued to analyze my paper. I was now up to three sheets of paper, all with arrows, sticky notes, squiggles and crossed-out words.

I rewrote my list and read over the analysis.

But now I knew we had to figure out how the plotters had gotten the key and the codes. I could think of only three possibilities.

Chadwick had given the code or he'd been there to let them in or someone who was close to Chadwick had access to the key and code. I knew one employee who could have done that. The heartbroken Lisa Hatton.

CHAPTER TWELVE

AT ELEVEN, SIGNORA Panetone staggered up the stairs with a large mug of delicious hot chocolate and a couple of biscotti. Why would I resist? We were trying to behave normally, and that means saying yes to the signora. Given the hour, it seemed unlikely that I'd be called out to help Uncle Kev in any way or that Castellano and Stoddard would pound on the door with a warrant for my arrest and that I'd be hauled off to be grilled by "the rubber hose brigade," another "uncle-ism." For the record and in case you're worried, none of my uncles has ever ended up on the wrong side of a rubber hose, but you'd never know it to hear them talk.

The day with all its events had gotten to me, and the biscotti and cocoa seemed necessary. I mean, there wasn't only the worry about Uncle Kev and the possibility of any or all of us getting arrested, nor was it the violation of our lives and property. Chadwick Kauffman had been murdered in a horrible way and we were—for a reason we didn't know—deeply involved.

"Vera is not sleeping," the signora said darkly and with a bit of worry on her puckered face. "No good."

I nodded. I knew why Vera wasn't sleeping. The signora, herself, never appeared to close an eye, so there wasn't much point in urging that she go to bed.

I took my mug of chocolate and wandered downstairs to check on my laundry. I hung my delicate items up to air-dry and then went to the library, wondering if I'd find Vera there or if she was upstairs in her own suite, stewing. But I located her in the study, with a fire in the fireplace. She was wrapped in an ancient tartan dressing gown. It was probably pure wool, something you'd need in the study on a cold night, and from the look of it, that garment may have belonged to her father. I looked closer and, sure enough, there was the monogram *LVA*. Leonard Van Alst. She glanced up from her much-interrupted *New York Times* crossword and gave me a bleak look.

"Are the police still there?"

"One bored and cold but well-fed officer is still sitting in his vehicle. They're obviously not taking chances that we'll run off."

She snorted. "As if that would stop any of us. At least the other two haven't come to arrest us yet."

"In case anything happens, Vera, and I'm not within earshot . . ."

She fixed me with a glare. "You'd better be, Miss Bingham. I pay you to be within earshot."

I decided to keep on her good side and not mention the books that had been carted off. "But, say, in a worst-case scenario—"

She huffed loudly. "You know I hate that expression."

"Fair enough, I'll try to avoid it in future. But what I want to say is that I have Sammy Vincovic if I get arrested. Who can we call for you if you're taken in?"

"I? Why should I be taken in? I've already answered all their incredibly annoying questions."

"Well, because you and I and Uncle Kev are implicated in Kauffman's murder."

"Absurd."

"But we are. I've been thinking about it. The entire thing was a setup. I'm sure of it now. The stage was set to deceive us."

"Well, we were in the wrong place at the wrong time. That could have happened to anyone."

I sighed. "Hardly, Vera. We were part of a plan. They lured you with the books. They knew about you. They had to realize that you would want those books and that you would be willing to travel to . . ."

"They could have come here."

"Right. But they didn't. They got us to go to Summerlea. They staged an elaborate lunch. Why was that?"

"I don't know, Miss Bingham. What are you suggesting?"

"I don't know what I'm suggesting. But there must have been some reason for using Summerlea and for enticing *us* over there."

"To get their mitts on *my* money."

"That might have been part of it. If they'd stolen the books and brought them to you here and taken the cash from you, that would have been easier."

"Part of it! Isn't that enough?"

"They didn't come here, which would have avoided that elaborate charade. No, we were lured to Summerlea. And now the police think we planned the entire thing and then lied about it."

"But why would we?"

"Excellent question," I said. "And I intend to find out. I think it has as much to do with us as it does Chadwick Kauffman."

"I don't see how it could."

"Is there anything I should know about your relationship with the Kauffmans, either one of them? Or any of their relatives?"

It's hard to take Vera by surprise, but apparently, I'd done it.

"Nothing I can think of."

"No old grudge or . . . ?"

"I met the uncle a million years ago at some tedious gala, but I don't think he'd have remembered. Aside from that, I was never at Summerlea or anywhere else where I came face-to-face with a Kauffman. I don't know any of their relatives or even if they have any. I can't imagine what the connection could be."

I said, "So back to my point: You should have legal representation. And you'll need someone very good. Sammy can't represent both of us or even Uncle Kev if he's taking my case. I can ask him to recommend someone or ask, um, my uncles if they may know someone else, but we should do something."

"Do what you must, Miss Bingham. Not that fool Dwight Jenkins."

"No chance of that. And that brings me to another issue," I said, stiffening my spine.

"Out with it, then, and in my lifetime, please."

"Yes, well. We are in a very tough spot, and I am going to do my best to keep us out of the police station and jail, not to mention avoiding trials."

"Would it ever come to that?" Vera actually took her eyes off the puzzle.

I said. "It could. And finding out what's going on may involve incurring some expenses." I was starting to talk like a blend of Vera and one of Ngaio Marsh's characters.

"It's already been said, Miss Bingham."

It had been said? I blinked. "Oh, you mean, 'Do what I must'?"

"Try to keep up." She went back to her puzzle.

"I'll pass on the bills," I said, with an attempt to maintain my dignity.

She ignored me. Fine. It was bedtime, and my response was to yawn widely.

"Good night, Miss Bingham," Vera said, absently, glancing up briefly.

"Time for me to hit the hay," I said, channeling my Uncle Billy, who had apparently spent a lot of time sleeping in barns.

I left her with her fire and her puzzle and the understanding that I'd find out what the connection was, although so far, I hadn't been winning any prizes for that.

I'D HIT A wall with my theorizing, and there was a police officer in the driveway keeping me in my place. I decided to focus my mind and escape into the world of Ngaio Marsh's *Death at the Dolphin*, yet another theatrical mystery. I'd see if I found some useful connection while I was reading or sleeping or worrying.

I burrowed down under the comforter, luxuriating in the historic theater—the Dolphin of the title—and all the over-the-top characters from the play about Shakespeare and a glove that belonged to his young son, Hamnet. This was the play that would revive the theater and make the name of the young playwright and the players. The stakes were high. I felt a little shiver as I compared the situation with the one we found ourselves in.

As I read on, I chuckled over the relationships, betrayals, alliances, ego and deceits in the fictional production. I had loved being involved with productions. Marsh captured it so perfectly. It all took me back to college. I'd spent a bit of time on the stage and considerably more behind the scenes. My talents ran to costumes and props and less to emoting onstage. I don't mind saying I'd made a wonderful Mrs. Drudge in *The Real Inspector Hound*, but that had not been the route to more glamorous parts. Uncle Mick's antique shop with its bits of everything and my entire family's familiarity with disguise came in handy. I had been in demand, if not as an actress. It had even led to romance, but that was not such a happy ending. Lance had helped me deal with all that. Good old Lance. You could always count on him.

I sat bolt upright and actually banged my head on the

iron bedstead. Lance! I had hidden my burner phone after insisting that he use that to stay in touch. I made my way to my hiding place and retrieved the phone.

I had a pretty firm idea that Lance might be hopping mad around now. I did hope—smart boy that he was—that he would figure out I had good reasons for not responding.

My reasons were that I'd been distracted by police and searches and planted evidence and lawyers and the threat of arrest. Still, I felt like a giant pink goofball. How could I have forgotten Lance?

Uh-oh.

Fifteen texts.

I climbed back into my comfy bed and pulled up the flower-sprigged comforter and bit my lip.

The good news: *Text number 1*. Lance had found something that I would find interesting.

Text numbers 2 through 12: Lance wondered why I hadn't responded to his first text, considering all the trouble he went to find out this very interesting bit of information. I had gotten his point, although I would have been happier if he'd said what the interesting "bit of information" was rather than sniping at me for my slowness.

Text number 13: It seemed to have occurred to him that all wasn't well. Was I all right?

Text number 14: What was happening?

Text number 15: Apparently, Lance was getting dressed and coming over to find out what the bleep was going on. Now!

I dialed his number in the hope I could save him a trip.

I blurted before he could even say "hello." "So sorry, Lance. I am alive, but we have been invaded by police today and things were out of my control." I crossed my fingers and fibbed. I couldn't bring myself to say that I'd forgotten about my burner phone.

"I couldn't get near this phone for reasons that I'm sure you will figure out."

"Are you okay? I've been flipping out here. I was just coming over."

"Better to get your beauty sleep. The police are watching us. There's a police car in front of the house, and it's probably better if that officer doesn't see you. You don't want to end up connected to the case."

I thought I heard Lance gulp. "I'm not worried."

"Well, we might need the flexibility of one of us not being considered a suspect or accessory."

"Right. Flexibility, that's good."

"I need to thank you for helping me. How about I meet you at the library tomorrow—if I'm not in jail—and I can take you to dinner to thank you?" I knew he wouldn't be able to resist that.

"I've been looking forward to trying Mr. Grimsby's Bistro," Lance said. "And I have to make a presentation to the library board meeting tomorrow night, so lunch? Small plates are good for lunch."

"Sure thing. Everyone's talking about Mr. Grimsby's." That Lance, so classy. *There you go, Vera*, I thought. *The first of your expenses will go to a stylish new dining spot.* Lunch was better for me because it would get me moving along earlier. Not that I had anywhere to go or anything to do, but I was hopeful. "Now, before we fall asleep, let's hear what you've found out that's so interesting."

I could hear the excitement in his voice. "I recognized an old acquaintance from the photo. I told her I'm doing a bit of research for an article in a library journal on the value of photography in researching social networks."

I laughed out loud. "Brilliant!"

"I know it's a stretch. But she bought it. I sent her the image, cropped out of the group shot, and she told me everything about this woman. Her name is Shelby Church. I'm going to meet my friend for breakfast tomorrow. I'll print the entire group photo and see what else I can turn up."

"But this is already great, Lance. We have a name."

"Maybe not entirely good news."

Lance does love to tease, although sometimes his timing sucks. I sighed. "Why would that be?"

"Shelby's an actress—"

"She's an actress? Really? Why isn't it good news?"

"According to my friend, after a couple of years in off-off-Broadway flops, she's got her first big break in a film and she's finishing up filming a thriller in Europe—Prague, I think. My connection was pretty surprised and insinuated the picture was low-budget and wouldn't ever hit the big screen, probably go straight to DVD or whatever, but my point is I guess Shelby couldn't have been involved."

"It's not hard to be somewhere that you aren't. Or not be somewhere that you are. That's easy peasy, Lance." Or it is in my family, anyway.

"I guess so. I imagine the police will check her flight arrangements and all that."

"Why would they when they're so keen on pinning the whole thing on us? Ah, sorry, Lance. I'm on edge. The cops are getting to me, and we don't know from one minute to the next when we'll be arrested."

"Is there anything I can do to help with that?"

"Thanks. You already have. This could be our first real break. I appreciate it." I figured I could mouse around the Internet chasing this Shelby.

"We'd both better get our beauty sleep. I'll let you know what happens tomorrow."

I could feel fatigue descending, like a big boot from the sky. Seconds after we disconnected, I was sound asleep. So much for chasing Shelby Church across the wasteland of the Internet.

AFTER BREAKFAST, I took a thermos of coffee and some pastries to the latest officer stationed in the driveway.

"I need to go to the library to do some research," I said after handing them over. "If that's not illegal or anything, you could follow me or call for backup. Can you find out if that will be okay? I'm not crazy about having some kind of 'takedown,' so let's do this by the book."

It is possible that I'd been watching too many police procedurals.

He stared at the pastries and then at me. I said, "Take your time and have your breakfast. I have a few things to do in the meantime."

Apparently it was all right. The officer waved me on as I exited Van Alst House to see Lance.

Maybe things were looking up. Or maybe the police were there on the lookout for Kev. I didn't think that would be the best way to catch him, but, hey, I'm not a professional.

CHAPTER THIRTEEN

L ANCE WAS LEANING over the desk, concentrating on a query from one of his omnipresent posse, when I strolled into the reference department. Two more elderly ladies waited impatiently behind the lucky one who had his attention. This was a special crowd for sure, all bewitched by my handsome, flirtatious and very smart friend.

I waited, leaning against a bay of dictionaries, wondering if I would have been better off sending a text. But I was there now, and I loved visiting the library with its combination of historic building and modern technology. Mind you, I'd heard plenty of beefs from Lance about the limits of antiquated and inadequate wiring with contemporary equipment. I was on the side of the old stuff, of course, but then I didn't have to track down information for a demanding clientele five days a week.

I grinned as I watched him. After all, I was also part of that demanding horde. And leave it to Lance; he had turned up something for me with that "borrowed" photo from the Country Club and Spa. Now, here I was with another little angle on that. Therefore, not a good idea to add to Lance's stress.

I made myself comfortable at one of the old pine reading tables and thumbed through some issues of *The New Yorker* and *Architectural Digest*. I kept an eye out for the line to clear.

The minute the crowd thinned, I crossed the room.

Lance grinned. "No genealogy for you, my proud beauty."

"'My proud beauty?' Have you been watching old movies again, Lance?"

"So much better than you with your crime shows." He twirled an imaginary mustache and grinned evilly.

"Actors," I said, meaningfully.

"What about them? Have you been watching *Access Hollywood* again? You used to have a weakness for actors."

"Ancient history. *Although* I was thinking of stage actors," I hissed, making the most of "stage" and "actors" without mentioning any by name.

"Very dramatic. You've missed your calling, Jordan."

"Right now my calling is to clear Vera's name and Uncle Kev's. Mine too. So here's the thing. I've been reading Ngaio Marsh again."

"Love her! All that over-the-top—"

"So you know many of her works deal with theater or plays in some way. I've read seven so far."

"So how's that connected?"

"Everything about our lunch at Summerlea was staged to lure us. No one made a false step. Everyone was perfectly placed, perfectly in character, perfectly calculated. The false Chadwick, the lovely 'Miss Troy,' the formidable Thomas."

"Remind me who Thomas is?"

"The butler we saw at Summerlea."

"Oh right."

"Maybe he wasn't so perfect. I'm not all that familiar with butlers, but he seemed a bit off at the time. He wasn't anything like the ones I'm used to in British fiction and television."

"Different how?"

"He looked kind of rough and burly. His hair was weird, and he had green stains on his hands. I thought he might be picking up shifts in the garden at Summerlea."

"Maybe," Lance said. "You'd think the Kauffmans would have a landscape maintenance service. Of course, I don't move in those circles either."

I nodded. "I think you're right, but he definitely wasn't Chadwick's butler, because as it turns out, there wasn't a butler at Summerlea. We'll have to keep thinking about what his appearance means and digging around, no pun intended, until we find out."

"Maybe they wanted you to feel you were in a *Downton Abbey* knockoff?"

"What do you mean?"

"Thomas is a character in that series. Starts as a footman and never makes it to valet, let alone butler. He's always a wannabe, and one with evil intentions."

I blinked. I hadn't thought that much about the butler and his intentions. I'd been concentrating on "Chadwick" or whoever he was and "Miss Troy," who we now knew was Shelby Church. I hadn't thought about any deeper meaning in the character of Thomas.

Lance said cheerfully, "I believe we agreed all this would be over lunch, Jordan."

"My pleasure."

I could feel the disappointment level rise as we waltzed out of the reference department.

AS WE PULLED away from the parking lot, in the Saab, I couldn't help but notice a dark sedan out of the corner of my eye. I squinted. "Don't look now," I said, "but is that by any chance Tyler Dekker lurking? Lance! What part of 'don't look' isn't clear?"

"Why is he being such a jerk?" Lance muttered.

"You tell me. He broke up with me."

Lance's head snapped. "What?"

"Dumped me when the cops started to investigate us. Didn't I mention it?"

"What a total—"

"Staying with me would be a career impediment."

"And now he's willing to spy on you for the cops? How low can a guy go?"

I shrugged. I'd done my best not to be miserable over Tyler, and I didn't want to wallow. I had lots of stuff to do, and I needed to be coolheaded and tough. "I'm over it."

"Huh. That was speedy. But it's good. You are too special, Jordan, to put up with these losers. You need to learn how to avoid bad boyfriends."

"Wow. And I'd already agreed to pay for lunch," I said.

"Admit that it's true."

"You can hardly call him a bad boyfriend, Lance. Tyler was almost perfect until . . . this thing. Don't roll your eyes."

"Exceptional? I don't think so. Here's a small-town cop with aspirations to be a small-town detective, and the minute you interfere with his plans, there you are."

"Where?"

"Gone."

"I'm right here."

"Don't be obtuse, Jordan. You know what I mean. Dumped. Discarded. Abandoned."

"He broke up with me. He didn't leave me in the middle of the desert without any water."

"You don't need to pretend to be brave with me," Lance said. "You've cried on my shoulder before, you know."

A person could be forgiven for having no idea at all what was being said in our conversation. Lance may be adorable, but he has this weird little way of making oblique yet dramatic allusions.

I slammed on the brakes to avoid going through one of the few red lights in Harrison Falls.

"It's not the first time he's let you down, Jordan."

"I hope you aren't talking about last fall when I needed him and my life might have depended on him and he vanished with no explanation."

Lance opened his mouth.

I continued, "Because *you* were also totally unavailable when I needed you and when, may I repeat, my life might have depended on you."

Lance sputtered, "You know why that was. Tiff and I explained everything. We had an excellent reason. And it was months ago."

"Well, Tyler had an excellent reason too. And—"

"Maybe I'm not talking about him."

"What?"

"You know who I mean."

I glared at him. We had a pact never to speak of my former boyfriend. "We're not going to be talking about Lucas."

All right, from time to time, I might whine about the fact that Lucas maxed out my credit cards, plundered my bank account and left me with my self-respect in shreds and no chance of continuing grad school until I rebuilt my financial side, not to mention my credit rating. He was why I came slinking back to Harrison Falls and my uncles and ended up working for Vera. I do not need to talk about him or think about him.

"You were heartbroken then," Lance said, apparently not remembering our pact.

"And who said I'm heartbroken now?"

He shrugged. "Good if you're not, but I think you are. And these two have lots in common."

"You can't possibly compare them. Tyler is decent and honorable and—"

"And yet he broke up with you when you needed him. What's the difference?"

"The difference is he wasn't a lying, manipulative snake who cleaned me out, and by the way, *I* broke up with Lucas. There's one really big difference. What's more—"

"I'm saying there's a pattern."

Apparently, I used my outside voice. "It's not a pattern."

Lance shook his head. "You can do better."

"But—" I stopped myself. Was Lance right? Was I attracted to men who wanted to take advantage of me? Could I do better?

I thought hard. There was no question that Lucas had been the worst thing that had ever happened to me, except for losing my mother. But Tyler hadn't been. He'd been—if you overlooked the absence last fall—available, supportive. Funny. Kind. A good dog owner. He'd pursued me in spite of my family, um, connections. They couldn't have done his ambitions any good. I might have been furious with him, but I knew he wasn't a "bad boyfriend." Of course, now he wasn't any kind of boyfriend.

I said, "The topic is closed to discussion. We have other fish to fry."

"Good. I'm starving. And we're here."

MR. GRIMSBY'S IS in an old brick house that's been nicely done up. Modern décor, lots of charcoal walls and new muted gold accents. Their lunch specials had been written up by someone with really good handwriting on a chalkboard in a gold-accented frame. I sincerely hoped that this fresh and chic new spot survived in our town.

We were in an intimate corner by the gas fireplace. Our table, like all the others and the bar, was made of weathered barn board, with many layers of high-gloss varnish. No tablecloths. Our spot was very cozy—a good thing, as spring didn't seem to be coming. Our server seemed new and nervous, despite her stylish topknot and sleek black tunic. She handed us menus and stepped back to wait. I think she may have been overcome by Lance.

We settled in, and I managed to smile at her.

"Now, can we talk about the photo?"

Lance leaned toward me and said, "Maybe we should look at the menu and order, and talk while we wait for our food."

I gave a noncommittal nod. I was steamed at my good friend and his attempt to play Dr. Phil with me.

The server—our own one-person studio audience—lurched toward us and slid a basket of sliced bread and a small dish with three flavored butters between us. She recommended that we each choose three small plates for the meal.

It was hard to make that choice. Lance settled on the seared scallops with parsnip puree and a sesame drizzle, and I went with the mini steak frites. What are bistros for if not steak frites, however mini? He picked the cheese plate to start; I went for hot and spicy cauliflower soup.

While we were waiting, Lance produced the print of the photo. Under several of the faces he had placed small white labels. "Shelby Church" was one of them. No surprise there. He also had a thin ribbon of tape on the surface connecting some faces. Shelby had quite a few connections. I figured people in a place like the Country Club and Spa and people who attended charity cotillions would move in the same circles. Not circles that anyone I knew moved in.

I felt my stomach fluttering with excitement.

"What did you find out about Shelby from your friend at breakfast?"

"She's a very pretty girl from a well-to-do but not fabulously wealthy family."

"Not like the Kauffmans," I said, sampling the warm sliced baguette with flavored butter.

She got a solid business degree and apparently was doing well, but in the last couple of years she decided to become an actress."

"What did your friend think of that?"

He shook his head. "She disapproved. She thought that Shelby was not a good actor and would never make it in that world."

I got that. Shelby had let her anxiety show more than once

during our lunch. "So what is this not good actor—a pretty girl from a well-off family—doing, getting involved in a scam that resulted in a murder?"

"I don't know," Lance said with one of his graceful shrugs. "And my friend had no clue. Maybe Shelby's some kind of psychopath."

I thought back to our luncheon and recalled the beautiful, slender and appealing woman who had greeted us. Could she have been a psychopath? "I don't think so. She was a bit nervous, uncomfortable.

"Apparently, Jordan, that's the talent of the psychopath. They make you believe them."

I leaned back and pursed my lips. Shelby could have been a psychopath, but I wasn't buying it. I could certainly believe it of the faux Chadwick with his lizard eyes or even the hulking Thomas with his unmoving face and green-tinged hands. I knew that psychopaths could look like normal people, especially charming and attractive or powerful people. Many people believe you find lots of them heading corporations or in the senior ranks. But Lisa had been genuinely nervous during our meeting and lunch. I would have bet Uncle Mick's shop on it. Yes, you can fake the slight shake in the hands, but she'd gone pale more than once, and there had been the little tic under her eye. Now I wondered if she was nervous about being part of the scam.

"I don't buy it, Lance. I met her. And Lance, if you are thinking about mentioning that my last bad boyfriend— because we're not including Tyler in this—was a psychopath, I agree. He was for sure, and I did a ton of reading about psychopaths after that."

"As your personal librarian, I am aware of that."

The napkins were cloth, so I couldn't doodle on them. I whipped out a notebook, ripped out a piece of paper and wrote:

PSYCHOPATH—Shelby????

Lance said, "Oh good. Here's our lunch. It's hungry work arguing with you."

The server, still with the deer-in-the-headlights expression, placed Lance's cheese plate and my snazzy square soup bowl in front of us and jerked her hand back as if she expected to be bitten.

I gave her a reassuring smile, but I don't think she bought it. Maybe she thought I was the psychopath.

Lance beamed at her. She blushed. Oh, Lance.

"So," I said, with my pen poised, "maybe Shelby Church became involved because of a man. Let's say she had a boyfriend and she was doing it for him. It wouldn't be the first time a woman got involved in a crime because she fell for the wrong man."

He shrugged. "I'm a man. I don't involve women in crime."

"Not every man involves a woman in crime. But let's assume that's the case here."

Lance picked up a piece of artisanal cheddar and beamed at it. "Assume away. So maybe there is a man running the show. Which one of them?"

"I don't know. Maybe neither of them."

"You have got to try this cheese, Jordan."

I kept talking. "The reason I said neither of them is because of how she reacted to Thomas. She wasn't aware of his presence. He wasn't controlling her or influencing her. He wasn't important to her."

Lance gave one of his little shrugs.

I said, "Women know these things. Of course, I had no real evidence, but I did feel confident that Thomas wasn't the man."

"The other guy, then. The one that reminded you of a lizard."

"Now that we're really considering this, I am going to vote 'no' on that."

"What? Why?"

"Because she wasn't in love with him."

"And you know this how? You were only there over lunch."

"You can just tell when someone's got it bad. You can see how they act toward the person they love. Glances, touches, consideration. Everything."

"Okay. I get that."

I almost said, *Take a look at your posse*, but it presented too many conversational distractions. Lance loved his adoring posse right back, although in an entirely platonic way, I was sure.

"I felt that he made her very nervous. She didn't look right at him. She didn't seem comfortable. Now I'm wondering why. He wasn't her boyfriend or her lover or whatever you might want to call him. Don't make that face, Lance. Trust me."

"Did the others notice that too?"

"You mean Vera and Kev? Be serious. They're the two most unobservant people in the world, except when it comes to books in Vera's case and spotting trouble to get into in Kev's. But my point is, why was she there? She was either an employee, which seems unlikely, as this was a scam. Or he had something on her. Thinking back to her behavior, that seems more like it."

"Like what?" Lance said with his mouth full of a creamy artisanal cheese called Humboldt Fog. He offered me a taste while I was waiting. The food at Mr. Grimsby's was so amazing that it could make you forget your manners. We decided to eat first, then talk.

After I finished my own delicious soup, I said, "Maybe she was tricked into it and realized that something was wrong."

"Entirely possible. This is really wonderful food."

"It is. I wish I was here under other circumstances. I'm too keyed up to really enjoy it."

Lance said, "Well, *I'm* enjoying it."

I sighed. "I liked her, even if she was part of this, and if she was tricked into it and things went wrong and that's when the real Chadwick was killed, she's going to be in danger as a witness to a murder, or at the very least, to the person who set it up."

"We know who she is," Lance said. "I guess we'd better find out if she's all right."

"We can and we will. But we should consider some other scenarios."

"Such as?"

"Maybe she's protecting someone. What if that's why she needed to be there? Okay, that's a bit of stretch, but the whole thing is pretty surreal."

Lance said, "Or maybe she was blackmailed into it."

We explored these possibilities until we finished our food, brainstorming and bantering a bit. At the end, we ordered cappuccinos. As our server hurried away with the empty plates, I reached for the photo.

"Now. Let's get back to talking about Shelby and her connections." I took a hard look at the photo. There was still no one who could have been the false Chadwick or Thomas. I was sure of that.

"Talk about the connections, Lance. What are all those tantalizing lines you've put on the photo?"

"Removable tape."

"I can see that, but who are they indicating?"

"They're people that she probably knows and that know her and that I can identify."

The light finally went on over my head. "You mean so that I meet them and try to get—"

Lance said quickly, "I was thinking that I might talk to them."

"Why?"

"Two reasons, Jordan. First, because I have met them and can arrange to bump into them in some social situation."

"That's one."

"And the second reason is because you have been known to go over-the-top."

"Don't be—"

"Yes. Over-the-top! Disguises. False pretenses. You love all that stuff."

"Let's get serious here, Lance. The entire situation we're in is because of false pretenses and disguises, and your friend Shelby—"

"She's not my friend."

"—is in it up to her pretty blond neck."

"But these other people aren't." He pointed to a couple of smiling faces in the photo.

"The people in this photo will know Shelby. That's the biggest lead we have."

"So I'll find a way to connect with them, and I'll bring up Shelby's name in the conversation and—"

"I want to be there."

"Didn't you hear what I said before?"

"I'm the one who's got the problem because of this Shelby and her co-conspirators."

Lance sighed dramatically. It wasn't the first time I'd thought he'd missed a great career as an actor when he went into librarianship. "Chadwick got the shorter end of the stick."

"I'm serious," I said.

"But if you're breathing down their necks, it's harder for me to look natural. First of all, they'll wonder who you are."

"I'm your girlfriend."

"What?"

"Whenever and wherever we meet them, I'm your girl-friend. Why do you have that look on your face?"

"Because I don't need fake girlfriends, thank you very much."

"Your date, then. I'll be your date when we accidentally run into these people. And trust me, they won't recognize me."

"Not the red wig," he said. "We can't have that. I would never date a woman who wore that."

"The red wig is not the only game in town."

"Fine, but I don't want you to take notes or stare obvi-ously at anyone."

"No worries."

"And I don't want Uncle Kev leaping out of the bushes with a camera or something."

"Uncle Kev is in the wind. Don't get me started."

"The less I know, the better."

I said, "So tell me about these people."

Lance pointed to an unsmiling but handsome, preppy-looking guy in the third row. "This is Shelby's ex, Andrew Wilson. He's apparently been brokenhearted since she ditched him around the time this was taken."

"He looks heartbroken."

"They say he was devastated. They were on track to get married as soon as he moved up a rung in his law firm."

"He's staring at her."

"Yup." Lance grinned. "Fixated."

I said, "Good stuff. And do you know him well enough to sit down and talk?"

"I don't know him at all."

"But you have him—"

"I know. I connected him. I know his cousin."

He pointed at a bright, dark-haired woman with million-dollar hair. "Poppy. She'd know most of these people. She's an acquaintance. An artist."

I stared at him. That Lance had his little secrets.

He smiled and answered a question I hadn't asked. "Mixed media. Acrylic and bits of hardware as far as I can tell."

I wasn't in the mood for a discussion of contemporary art techniques. "Can you get to the point?"

"Well, Poppy's having a vernissage tonight. It's in Grand-ville at that little gallery by the river. I saw it on Facebook. A vernissage is a—"

"I know. And I've been to many openings. So we're going to help her celebrate her new show? Oh wait, did you get an invitation?"

"I messaged her to congratulate her and she insisted that I come."

"But did she insist that you have a date?"

"She didn't, but she'll be cool with it, as long as my date doesn't look too much like the person whose face was all over the news or like an escapee from Cirque du Soleil."

"I'll choose my cover with care. So you think the ex-boyfriend will be there?"

"There's a good chance, but if he's not, there will be—"

"Lots of people who know Shelby?"

"Even better, she just got home from shooting her film. Maybe she'll show up. I tried to suggest that."

"You've earned your lunch, Lance."

"We'd better pick up the pace here a bit. Whether I earned it or not, I have to get back to work. Nancy doesn't mind covering for me, but there are limits.

Our server hovered nervously out of reach. Lance gave her what I can only describe as a "come-hither smile," and she darted over and dropped the list of our dessert choices in front of us before fleeing around the corner.

"I predict a career change for that girl," I said, ignoring the menu. "She seems to be very anxious."

"Let's be nice, then." He beckoned to our server and pointed to his choice. "I'd like the trio of crème brûlées."

I laughed. "I think that's for sharing."

"Get your own, m'lady. I found Shelby and Poppy."

"That is worth celebrating. I'll have the Molten White and Dark Chocolate Surprise. We'd better fill up. There's never enough to eat at a vernissage."

CHAPTER FOURTEEN

A FTER OUR LUNCH, I avoided Van Alst House in case the police showed with an arrest warrant. I really needed to get to that art reception and, with luck, the mysterious Shelby.

I called Vera to see if everything was all right and got the usual brusque brush-off. That was good news.

I said, "I'm pursuing information relevant to our current inconveniences."

"Whatever that's supposed to mean, Miss Bingham, I am busy."

If Vera was busy, it was with the crossword or her book collection, so I didn't feel guilty about interrupting. I would have added, "I expect to be back tonight," but I was speaking to the dial tone.

This was not a job for someone who was easily offended.

Instead I popped into Uncle Mick's place, where I keep my surplus wardrobe. I knew I had a little black dress in my closet, and that would probably do for the art opening. I figured I

could scavenge something to update it between my own accessories and the treasures in Uncle Mick's.

It didn't take long to find my little black dress, hanging
in the closet of my pink-and-white room. By some miracle
it still fit, despite the signora's cooking. It may not have
skimmed my figure quite the way it used to, but it would be
fine. I located a pair of dark, sheer hose in my drawer and
found my black stilettos in their shoe box. For some reason,
I'd never found a place to wear them since moving back to
Harrison Falls. They'd been waiting patiently. I would show
them a good time tonight.

Best of all, I located a set of eyelash extensions that I had
bought on ridiculous impulse but never worn. If not now,
when?

I assumed the gathering would include some wealthy and
stylish people and I'd need to blend in. In Uncle Mick's
antique store, in the "Estate Jewelry" section, I found a small
pair of diamond cluster earrings and a tiny vintage clutch
with exquisite black beading, barely big enough for a comb,
a lipstick, my iPhone and, of course, the necessary burner.
My big find was a cut-velvet shawl in a rich garnet. Not the
color of spring, but the night was promising to be nippy, and
the resulting outfit was chic and dramatic. My uncles never
minded if I borrowed things. The items always came back,
and with a bit of adventure attached to them. I cleaned the
earrings with alcohol and steamed the shawl.

As the red wig was off-limits and I wasn't supposed to
look like myself, that left blond. Not the tightly curled blond
wig I used in my short-lived role as Kathryn Risley Rolland,
but an angled bob with long bangs. It was a bit dated, but I
tucked one side behind my ear and twisted a long strand on
the other side and fastened it with a jeweled clip.

I was checking out my look in one of the antique mirrors
in the shop when the proprietor blew through the door from
the kitchen. As everyone knows, we Kellys don't come in

through the front door unless we're up to something, such as throwing the police off our plans.

"Don't you look artsy-fartsy, my girl," he said. With his wiry and faded red hair, bright blue eyes under out-of-control brows, ginger chest hair poking out from the shirt with the three open buttons and a gold chain nestling in it, Uncle Mick looked anything but artsy-fartsy, but I thought he was perfect the way he was.

"That's the plan, Uncle Mick. I figured you wouldn't mind me borrowing a few items."

"Help yourself to anything anytime. That's always been our way."

"I'll bring back the diamond earrings after the event tonight. It's an opening at an art gallery."

"An art gallery, my girl?" He brightened.

"Conceptual art, I think."

"You can keep it."

"No, thanks. So I have to look good but not at all like myself. What do you think?" I examined my reflection in the mirror. I didn't know how I felt about being a blonde. Although I'd always liked the flame-red wig, I was happy with what I saw. There wasn't a glimpse of my dark, curly hair. And my pale skin was fine with the spun pale yellow of the wig. The earrings, small as they were, seemed to make quite a difference. I'd never given a moment's thought to diamonds, but already I could feel their emotional pull.

"You'll be the belle of the ball. But you're looking a bit peaky. How about a bite to eat? I can whip up a pot of Kraft Macaroni and Cheese as quick as you can say 'diamond studs.'"

"No, thanks, Uncle Mick."

"I can fry up some baloney."

"Um, no, I'm good."

"Beans and franks?" This is Uncle Mick's signature dish (secret ingredient: ketchup).

"Thanks so much, but Lance took me to lunch." There was

no point in explaining the dining experience we'd had at Mr. Grimsby's. It would only alarm Uncle Mick.

"Lance? Well, I hope there was something on the plate. That fella's a bit too fancy for my liking."

"The lunch was great. I think I'll head out now."

"Take the new Beamer," he said, magnanimously. "Arrive in style."

A Beamer as well as an Infiniti? Things must be going well. "Don't mind if I do." A BMW would be perfect. I didn't ask where the new cars had come from. Discretion is the better part of valor, as they say. "By the way, any word on legal help for Vera and Kev?"

"That's right, my girl. Talked to a fella named Cory Corrigan for our Kev. He's as good as they come and not too uptight, if you know what I mean. And Laurence Sternberger for the Van Alst woman."

The Van Alst woman? Uncle Mick has relented quite a bit about Vera and her family over the past year, but this sounded like his old attitude resurfacing.

"And is he as good as they come too? Because Vera is absolutely innocent, and if the police come after her or us, she needs to be well taken care of."

"He's good for the job. But he's a bit full of himself and on the pricey side. But I can't say I'm happy about her dragging you into this mess, my girl."

Only in the Kelly family could anyone construe what happened at Summerlea to be a case of Vera dragging me into a mess.

"He'll be in touch," Mick added. "Ready if she needs him."

I was secure in the knowledge that we would all have lawyers who measured up.

Uncle Mick said, "Don't think I've forgotten that the so-called police officer engaged our Sammy for you. If it was anyone but Sammy, I'd think you could trust him as far as I could throw a piano."

"But it was Sammy, and Tyler did call him for me."

"My point, my girl, is that you have family to look after your legal issues. You don't have to rely on the forces of—"

"Don't say 'darkness,' Uncle Mick. Tyler wanted to help, even if he did dump me. And don't even think of any kind of revenge."

He puffed out his substantial chest. "The Kellys do not get dumped."

"It must have been my Bingham side that took the hit, but you know, doing well is the best revenge, and tonight I'm going to this very special event with Lance."

Uncle Mick glowered. "Don't get too involved. I always wonder if he's a bit light in the loafers."

"I assure you his loafers are as heavy as yours, Mick. And who cares anyway?"

"Humph."

"So, do I look okay?"

"You do the Kellys proud. The Binghams too, wherever they might be. You're better with your own dark curls, but you're still gorgeous, my girl."

"Thank you. I'll let you know what happens."

"I think those artsy-fartsy things are known not to serve much food. Couple of Oreos for the road? Make your old uncle happy?"

Who could turn down an offer like that?

LANCE DROVE THE Beamer. It was the least I could do. He was at his most elegant, with that hipster vibe, but without having to resort to a beard. He wore a charcoal double-breasted blazer over a light knit black turtleneck, tailored straight-leg pants and Chelsea boots. I was proud to be at his side and grateful that he would be the focus of attention.

The gallery was in a renovated nineteenth-century bank on the main street of Grandville. The exposed brick and industrial lighting was now fashionable, as was the expanse of pale pine flooring. The white gallery walls were hung with vast aluminum creations. I wasn't entirely sure how the artist had managed to attach feathers and bits of wood to each one.

Six-foot cast iron candelabras with flickering tapers provided a nice contrast to the stark modern atmosphere.

We'd been served Grey Goose martinis, instead of the usual white wine or generic "champagne." The appetizers were entirely unfamiliar except for the little black clumps of caviar with something leafy. "Foraged greens," Lance whispered. "This caterer is the hottest thing north of Brooklyn." This reinforced Lance's view that Poppy's family had more money than the Federal Reserve. I would not mention them to my uncles. They might consider it open season.

Poppy's dark hair was cut no more than a half inch long. Luckily, she had a beautifully shaped head and she was stunning in a simple white silk slip dress and a pair of incredible Christian Louboutins. The trademark red soles flashed every time she shimmered her way through the guests. They echoed her brilliant red gloss lipstick. Girl had style.

I might have looked pretty good back in Uncle Mick's antique shop mirror, but here I was definitely not worth a second glance. Not in a league with the moneyed princessy types and wealthy matrons, but not so down-market I'd rate a curled lip. I was counting on simply blending, and there were plenty of people who must have been old school friends of the artist. I noticed some nervous and uncomfortable glances from people who would have done anything to be home watching *The Real Housewives of New Jersey*.

We were waiting to pounce on the first person who might know Shelby Church. Lance has no trouble pouncing. He's so often on the receiving end of pounces at work that he has developed techniques from the pros.

We found ourselves talking to GiGi and Henry, another couple, our age, looking like they'd rather be anywhere but here. After a few vague comments about the artworks of the "so interesting" and "isn't it?" variety, Lance quickly got to the point. "I thought I'd see Shelby here tonight."

They both shrugged in unison. It seemed obvious that Lance was waiting for an answer.

"No worries," he said. "I know she and Poppy are tight. I was hoping to get her alone to talk about a charity thing I'm planning."

"She has the new guy," I interjected. "Maybe she's off somewhere with him. Not sure if he's the gallery type." I would have suggested somewhere they might be, but I had no idea how people like Shelby Church spent their time.

"What do you think about him, anyway?" Lance said, glancing around. "I wouldn't have thought he was her type."

"I don't think anyone's actually met him. That's kind of weird in itself," GiGi said, "but I haven't seen her *anywhere*. She's supposed to have been in a film in Europe."

"It is weird," I said. "Usually you'd want to show off the new guy." I batted my eyelash extensions at Lance. He looked horrified. I batted a bit more. Lance's horrified glance shifted from my eyes to my martini. Was that black spidery thing what I thought it was?

Lance managed to quickly extricate us from GiGi and Henry once we discovered they had little to contribute. We weren't the greatest company either, so I didn't think they were heartbroken. They might have been relieved not to be grilled. Or possibly scared of the eyelash in my drink.

We circulated around the room. Lance was using his librarian organizing mode to ensure that we didn't miss anyone. I was along for the ride. So many air-kisses. I'd gotten quite good at it by the end. My main worry was that the wig—quite a good quality synthetic—would catch fire from one of the candles on the floor candelabras. The eyelash had shaken my confidence a bit.

A few other people seemed surprised that Shelby hadn't shown up, or else they were willing to fake it when Lance asked. Others didn't know her or didn't care much. Eventually, we were able to get close to the artist, Poppy.

"Wonderful series," Lance gushed when we finally got

our turn. He managed not to introduce me or refer to me by any name. Poppy didn't seem to notice as everything had to be about her and I wasn't. Lance kept it up. "You've really come into your own. The juxtaposition of light and form? Well, I'm at a loss for words."

There was nothing I could say to top that. "Absolutely," I added.

"I feel I'm growing into it," she said.

I still would have liked to know exactly how she attached the feathers and wood, but it seemed gauche to ask.

"So organic," Lance said. "Really." Not for the first time, I wondered if his degree was a BS and not an MLS.

I was tuning out of this vacuous chat when he said, "Shelby's not here?"

"Shelby?" She raised an eyebrow.

"Church?"

"Oh. I guess not yet. She's supposed to come."

"I wanted to approach her about a fund-raiser that I'm starting to think about."

I could tell that when the conversation wasn't about the artist or the party, her interest died quickly. "Oh look, here's someone I need to talk to. Excuse me." She turned her back.

Lance whispered, "Puts me in my place."

"Learn to grovel better," I said.

Lance was saying, "Never mind, I think that girl in the corner was in the photo from the Country Club. We should try our luck with her."

As I turned my gaze toward a young woman who'd backed herself into a far spot where she stood looking wretched, a little buzz swept the crowd as a cluster of glamorous people arrived chattering. They handed their wraps to the coatroom attendants.

"Gotcha," I said, as Shelby appeared right after the group swept into the room.

"Let's head her off at the pass," Lance said.

The gallery was jammed with people by this point. So

very many high-end skinny jeans and ankle boots. So many five-inch stilettos. So much designer scent: Juicy Couture, Yves Saint Laurent and Calvin Klein. We wove our way in between people balancing martini glasses and canapés and headed toward the door where Shelby stood. From the way she glanced behind her, she was waiting for someone to follow her in. Was it the mysterious man in her life? The one who'd enticed her into this very bad situation? As we got closer, I could see she was even paler than she'd been at Summerlea. She'd done a haphazard job of using concealer to cover the dark circles under her eyes and what looked like a minor breakout. But her underlying skin color was gray, and there wasn't a makeup in the world that could hide that. She could have done with a shampoo too. Shelby Church was clearly a woman under stress. And that was about to get worse, if I had my way. Because let's face it, if you're implicated in a murder and you're willing to let other people take the rap for it, whatever bad stuff happens to you, you've got it coming.

Shelby caught Poppy's eye. Poppy lit up and held out her arms. Her face clouded as Shelby worked her unsteady way toward the center of attention.

"Let's position ourselves so she doesn't get past us," I whispered to Lance.

"I'll get over to the front door, in case," he said, sidling smoothly toward the main entrance. "I guess she came alone."

I wiggled my way through the crowd, teetering on my five-inch heels. Now that my days and nights were spent in a small upstate New York town chasing first editions online, I'd gotten out of training in the art of wearing stilettos.

"Excuse me. Excuse me." I kept repeating it as I found myself blocked by men and women who were too fascinated with each other to let another person pass. Finally, I stopped bothering and put my elbows out. In our family, we pride ourselves on our pointy elbows.

When I got close enough to speak, Poppy was holding

Shelby by her arms. "What's wrong with you?" she asked, for a moment forgetting that she was center of attention.

Shelby shook her head and said, "Nothing. Just a migraine. I'm fine. I couldn't stand to miss tonight. I wanted to tell you how wonderful it all is . . ." She took her first look around at the artworks on the wall and turned with a weak smile to Poppy. "Then I'll head home to bed."

No way you will, I said to myself. *Not before I get my hooks into you*. The group between Poppy and Shelby and me simply ignored my elbows and my "excuse mes." Shelby gave Poppy a peck on each cheek and a hug. I could hear their conversation, but I needed to get close enough to speak to Shelby myself.

"I hope you're not driving with that migraine. You look awful."

"Thanks," Shelby said with a crooked grin. "My friend is waiting for me in the car."

"Oh, come, Shelby. Don't tell me you're still involved with that—"

Damn. Why hadn't we asked Poppy about the man in Shelby's life? We'd asked other people.

I pushed my way through two of the chatty types who seemed determined to block anyone from getting past them. As I did, I turned and caught Lance's eye. I made a ridiculously complicated gesture, pointing to Shelby, pointing outside and turning an imaginary steering wheel. I hoped he would understand what I meant.

"Shelby!" I called. She whirled.

Poppy recoiled. "*Sorry*, um," she said, meaning she was not sorry at all, "but Shelby and I are having a private chat. Do you mind waiting?"

Meaning she couldn't have cared less if I minded or not. Face it, this was her party and her friend, and I was nobody and nothing.

But not to Shelby. She whirled and stared at me. She shook her head, frowned, trying to figure where she'd seen me.

"It's Jordan, Shelby," I said.

"Leave us alone," Poppy said.

"I have to go," Shelby said shakily.

"It is a matter of life and death," I interjected loudly.

Shelby flinched. Poppy stared at her and at me. "We have security here," she said, jabbing me with her long red nail. "I said this is a *private* conversation. Spare me the life-and-death crap."

I'd already elbowed so many people out of the way, I felt sure if Poppy raised the alarm, I'd be tackled if not actually lynched.

"When I say life and death, Shelby, or should I call you 'Lisa,' I think you know what I mean."

Shelby swayed.

"Murder is a bad thing to be involved in, Shelby. You'd better come clean, because the longer you don't, the worse it's going to be when the police catch up with you."

Poppy's jawed dropped. "Get out of here! Shelby, what's going on?"

"I'm going to be sick," Shelby bleated. She pushed forward and ran across the gallery, hands over her mouth. People who didn't move in time found their martini glasses flying. Shrieks were added to the din of conversation.

Shelby stumbled but kept going. I was right after her, pushing my way through people and hearing glass crunch under my feet. Shelby hit the emergency exit, pushed it open and vanished.

CHAPTER FIFTEEN

A S SHE RUSHED through the door, the alarm shrieked. I sprinted after her, out the door and into the alley next to the gallery.

"Wait, Shelby!" I screamed as I followed. "You have to speak to me. Please! You are going to get deeper into trouble! Wait for me!"

Please? Was I really pleading with a fleeing murderer?

Shelby reached the sidewalk and turned left. I hobbled after her. The heel on my left shoe snapped off. You can only run so far in stilettos, even when they do have heels. I kicked off both shoes and kept going. I found myself yipping as I stumbled over small bits of gravel and debris. A charcoal Lexus SUV was idling in front of the gallery. Was that Shelby's friend? Apparently, yes. As I limped out of the alley, still shouting, "Wait! Shelby!" she reached the vehicle. The driver reached over and wrenched the door open for her. She tumbled in. The door of the SUV slammed, and the Lexus shot forward and squealed around the corner and out of sight.

All I got was the barest suggestion of a big, squarish head

in a ball cap and large hands in black gloves. And Shelby's backside as she tumbled into the passenger seat without a shred of dignity.

Of course, who was I to talk?

A horn blasted behind me. Lance, my knight in shining Beamer.

As the Beamer glided up, I yanked open the door. Normally, I would have barked at him to watch out for the car. But instead I shouted, "After them!" I'd always wanted a reason to say that.

Lance gunned it, and the Beamer showed its stuff, taking that corner smoothly. Gotta love that powerful engine. In a minute we were almost on top of the SUV with Shelby in it.

I took my lipstick from my tiny clutch and wrote the license plate number on my bare arm. With shaking hands, I pulled out my iPhone and dialed a number I knew by heart.

"Tyler? You have to listen to me. I've seen the woman who was at Summerlea. She's currently fleeing from me—"

A torrent of words swirled from the phone.

"Let me finish! I'm not doing anything illegal. I'm not snooping or interfering. I happened to be Lance's date at an art thingie in Grandville, and there she was. I almost fell off my shoes. I would have thought she'd be in hiding."

Lance and I exchanged glances.

Another torrent. I held the phone away from my blistered ear.

"Well," I said, "that's your opinion, Tyler. But here's the license plate of the Lexus SUV she took off in. Do you want to track it down? . . . Oh, come on, don't be like that . . . Here's something else you should know." I squinted as I got a blast from Tyler. When he took a breath, I shouted, "I am not interfering. I am not messing with the investigation. I happened to come across this information. Perfectly innocent . . . You can check with Lance."

Lance gasped. I glared at him. "Man up," I whispered.

"No, no! That wasn't to you, Tyler. Anyway, I leave it to you and Detectives Castellano and What's-his-name . . .You should pass on the information . . . What? . . . Wait! There's more . . ."

"Get home now. And stop this. I'm serious," Tyler shouted before hanging up.

"That went well," Lance said.

"Better than I expected, actually. At least I can massage my poor, messed-up feet now. I think they're bleeding," I said. "Where are they?"

"Your feet?"

I ignored that. "Shelby and her driver."

"Did you see him?" Lance asked.

I shook my head. "Just got an impression."

"Was the impression like the faux Chadwick?"

"No. It wasn't. That guy had a narrow face, a narrow head and that beaky nose. This guy was more—".

"Big headed?"

"Are you making fun of me, Lance?"

"Never."

"All I saw was a guy with a big, squarish head, wearing a ball cap. I didn't see his face." I chuckled. "Let's hope he's enough of a blockhead not to notice us following him. Oh, and he had big hands too, with long fingers."

"You noticed that in a fraction of a second?"

"I've been reading too much Marsh, I guess. I'm paying close attention to everyone's hands, including yours."

Lance rolled his eyes. "Whatever. Here on the main road, there's lots of traffic, but if we stay on their tail, they're going to notice us. Would Shelby recognize this car?"

"I didn't even know about this Beamer until a couple of hours ago. It's a good thing we didn't take the Saab. She'd have recognized that, for sure."

"Do you think Dekker will follow up on your information about the plate?"

"I do. But I don't think he'll tell me what he finds."

"We'll have to find out on our own, then," Lance said. The Beamer surged faster into the night.

I rubbed my feet and wrote off my hose. There's usually a first aid kit in any car my uncles own, and this one was no different. While Lance focused on the road, I slipped out of the shredded stockings.

He said, "Normally, that would have been sexy."

I used a sterile gauze to get the grit out of my feet and winced when I applied rubbing alcohol. I finished off with bandages and hoped for the best.

As our pursuit continued, I filled Lance in on what happened at the gallery.

"Oh snap," he said, when I told him about pursuing Shelby and the alarm being set off. "Poppy will be out of her mind. Did you see how much they sank into that reception? Caviar? Grey Goose?"

"Yes." It would have been enough to get a good start on a return to grad school, I thought. But I had other things on my mind. Catching up with Shelby, for one.

We managed to get closer to the Lexus and followed as it swerved and shot around corner after corner. I hung on as Lance took the corner on two wheels. I bit my tongue so I didn't say, "Next time, I'm driving." Too late, we realized that the Lexus driver had pulled over to the right and turned off his lights. We shot past. I turned, pointed and squawked. Lance slammed on the brakes, and I gave thanks for my safety belt. Through the window, I spotted Lisa/Shelby's white face and wide eyes. She saw me too. Her hand shot to her mouth.

As we pulled up alongside, the SUV lurched forward, swerved to make a U-turn and sped off in the opposite direction. Lance accelerated and made a tight turn, but those few lost seconds were too many. The taillights of the SUV had vanished. This time for real.

Fifteen tense minutes later, we had to admit defeat.

Lance finally exhaled. "Whoever he is, he's coolheaded. There's nothing we can do now."

That stopped me. "Yes, there is. We can find out where she lives."

"Shelby?"

"Who else. We can drive by there and—"

"She lives in LA now, working on her film career. We'd have to find out where her parents live. And we won't be welcome back at the gallery. I have a feeling that Poppy won't be glad to see me again. Ever."

I thought about that. "Actually, Lance, you'd already left the reception when I confronted Shelby. She saw me, not you. Then she panicked and ran out the emergency exit and set off the alarms. Don't look at me like that."

"Jordan! You told me you shouted at Shelby and you chased her out the door."

"Okay, fine. So I can't go back. But you could go and apologize for me."

"Not the first time."

"Very funny. You could say you need to contact Shelby and say how sorry you are that your psychotic date chased her."

"Sure. I'll make up a story about you."

"I'm sure you'll make it a doozy. I'm counting on it.

"At least with that wig, no one will know who you really are."

"That is one good thing. Drop me off somewhere, so I don't get spotted. I don't really want to spend twenty minutes on the floor of the car. Make sure you get an address for Shelby. Don't get too caught up in the apology thing."

"Give me some credit," Lance sniffed.

LANCE DROPPED ME outside Walmart, as close to the front door as we could get. With my head held high, I limped in. Small clusters of people did notice my bare feet, not the usual style in chilly early April. I sailed by them and found myself some new stockings, more bandages and pair of low-heeled shoes that looked like they'd be good to run in. It had been that kind of day, and it seemed like the right idea to be prepared.

I waited patiently for Lance's return in the evening gloom. We were getting closer to finding the man Shelby had been with. I felt that she'd been an accomplice and not the person behind the killing or even the whole charade at Summerlea. Would the kind of person who could plan a murder panic like that?

Shelby was falling apart.

LANCE SURVIVED THE apology session at the gallery, but barely. He said, "The cuts on my knees from crawling over broken glass groveling to Poppy are much worse than what happened to your feet. Trust me."

"Go ahead, rub it in, Lance."

"I told her that I'd heard what happened and that I'd stepped outside to make a call at the time."

"Did she ask about me?"

"Oh yes. You're toast if you ever see her again. But I told her that I didn't really know you well. Anyway, I don't think anyone noticed us. They're all kind of into themselves. Lots of people walked through the door at about the same time. I said you'd attached yourself to me, and I'd thought that was kind of strange, but not a big deal at the time."

"Good thinking."

"I said that I thought you'd seemed a bit off. She thought so too."

"Mmm."

"I said that's why I went outside to make the call. Just to put some distance."

"Uh-huh."

"I said I really wanted to connect with Shelby because I'd got this weird message from her."

"Very good!"

"Yeah. Poppy's furious with Shelby, as well as with you, whoever you are. Almost ruined the big night. So I said that it looked like everything had been cleaned up really well."

"Had it?"

"Yes. Everyone seemed to have replacement martinis and canapés. I insisted her opening was a triumph. It was painful, but I suggested that it was such a great night it would take more than that to ruin it. I made a big deal about needing to apologize to Shelby too."

"And she believed you?"

"Better. She gave me Shelby's parents' address."

"What are you waiting for? Let's do this thing."

Lance seemed pretty proud of himself as we headed toward this confrontation.

I said, "At least if we find her—"

"Of course we'll find her. We found her at the gallery, didn't we?"

"Yeah. But we also blew our cover there."

"That does make it trickier."

"She's probably terrified by now. She's bound to tell you everything."

I bit my lip. "I wonder. She was looking pretty ragged. And as you said, nervous. Before she had even seen me she was already jumpy. Guilty conscience. Chadwick was murdered."

"Maybe she was also scared of the guy driving the car and the people who set up the murder. She's got something else to be frightened of. She's an accessory."

"Worse, she's a witness. An unstable, terrified witness. She bolted when I called her name. How long do you think she'd hold out in an interrogation room?"

Lance took his eyes off the road to stare at me.

"Watch where you're driving, Lover Boy."

"You think she's in danger?"

"I do, and not only from us."

"So what do you want to do about it?"

"Should we go and confront her? And how do we know she'll be alone? Maybe the real guilty parties will be there. Why not get rid of us if we go nosing around?"

Lance swallowed hard.

NO ONE WAS home at 41 Belleview Crescent, Shelby's parents' address. No car in the driveway. No sign of life. Lance peered through the window of the garage. No car inside that either.

The house was a classic design, updated with a sharp charcoal paint and a new-looking porch in the front. I craned my head and caught a glimpse of a sunroom addition in the back past the three-car garage.

Nice. This was a lovely middle-class home. It was a home to be proud of in a pleasant neighborhood on a tree-lined street where everyone kept their property looking good. But Shelby's family home wasn't in the same league with Summerlea, for sure.

A solitary light glowed from a fixture in the central hallway. That was like a welcome mat for burglars. Come on in. Take everything. We're not home.

I rang the doorbell and knocked loudly for the third time. "She's not here. Maybe she knew we'd find her," I said to Lance as we paced in front of the house, exasperated.

He glanced around and noticed a woman across the street, ambling slowly with a large dog.

I said, "Someone has to come home sometime. I'll sit here all night if I have to."

"I can't stay. I have to work tomorrow. I need to get some sleep. And don't give me a hard time because I have a job."

"When did I ever do that, Lance? Get some sleep. My job is to find Shelby and exonerate myself, Kev and Vera. But I need a car to sit in."

Lance blinked.

I said, "Shelby and her driver know the Beamer now. And I'm sure the neighbors do too. So we need to get another vehicle here for my surveillance until she comes home."

I didn't want to say "if she comes home." I shivered at the thought that I couldn't quite keep out of my mind.

As we chatted and plotted, a silver-haired woman with a matching silver-haired dog strolled along the sidewalk and met up with the first neighbor, whose dog was now sitting patiently. The two women began shooting us glances, not at all subtle.

On the house closest to us, a curtain twitched. That's the trouble with these neighborhoods. They're filled with nosy people.

Lance bleated, "We may need another vehicle, but how can I drive two cars, Jordan? Even I have limitations. Only one body and all that."

"Let's move on before these people call the police on us." I waved to the woman with the matching dog and hopped back in the car.

Five minutes later, Lance and I were parked around the corner on the next block, waiting for Uncle Mick to arrive. We were close enough to see through the trees if anyone arrived at Shelby's place, but no longer in full view of the neighbors. Uncle Mick seemed to have run out of anonymous and untraceable vehicles. Who knew that could happen? He was driving Uncle Lucky's Navigator. That was good news. I love the Navigator. It meant I'd have a comfortable night waiting for Shelby.

I'd left my deep-orange purse with everything I'd really need at Uncle Mick's. I'd asked for that and a change of clothes. He delivered a pair of black Keds, dark jeans and a black hoodie from my old closet. Somewhere he'd turned up a ball cap with a mouse brown ponytail and matching shaggy bangs showing. The things that man had at his disposal . . .

Better yet, it all came with a care package from the Kelly kitchen: Dr Pepper, chock-full of caffeine, a package of

Oreos, a giant bag of Cheetos and a fresh burner phone, because you never know.

He also brought Walter.

"Really, Uncle Mick? Walter? I'm going to be in the car all night. Does that make sense . . . I mean, is that the right thing to do?"

"'Course it is, my girl. Dogs are a good cover. You should know that better than anyone. Everyone trusts you when you have a dog. Especially a little dog like this, not good for protection or anything."

Walter snorted his resentment of this description. In his mind he could take on armed men, Rottweilers, sky's the limit.

"But . . ."

Of course, Uncle Mick was on his way by then. He's quite crazy about Walter, so I could only assume that, although he was back from Manhattan, he still had plenty of places to go, people to see and things to do. The less I knew about any of that, the better.

Lance was supposed to go with Mick in the Beamer, but he wasn't all that keen on leaving me, even with Walter the Fierce snuffling at my side. "What are you going to do if Shelby does show up? You can't go in there yourself. Promise me you won't do that, Jordan."

I yawned, not a good start when there might be a long night ahead. "If I call you, will you come?"

"I'll sleep in my clothes. If the phone rings, I'll head right over."

Uncle Mick leaned on the horn.

I said, "Thank you, Lance."

"It's only about twenty minutes away. Don't get impatient and go inside, Jordan."

"It's a deal. I don't really want to get killed either."

"What if she's with the other guy or guys?"

Uncle Mick actually stepped out of the car and loomed.

Lance leaned away, bravely, and said, "Why don't we call the police?"

There was a sharp intake of breath from Uncle Mick. "What's the matter with you, fella? You call the police over every little hangnail, do ya?"

Lance blinked.

Uncle Mick said, "What did I tell you, my girl?"

Lance said, "What did he tell you?"

"Nothing. It's sort of rhetorical."

"Did he tell you something about me?"

No way was I repeating the "light in the loafers" remark, whatever that stupid phrase even meant. "Focus, Lance. We can't call the police because *they* don't know who Shelby is. They don't believe us that she and the others staged that lunch at Summerlea. We don't know who the others are. We need more."

"But you said yourself that Shelby wouldn't last in an interrogation room."

"She wouldn't, but she won't be in an interrogation room. It's called due process. Cops need a reason to take someone in for questioning—especially someone from an affluent family—and they aren't going to listen to me. I'm one of their prime suspects."

"So what is going to happen?"

"We need to learn more. Then we can find a way to involve the police. Too soon and it blows up in our face."

"Boom," said Uncle Mick. That was his opinion of most police involvement.

"Okay. Keep me posted."

I knew he meant "keep me posted but first let me sleep."

I sat in the Navigator with a view of Shelby's parents' house through the trees. There was no sign of life for the next few hours.

As hours went, they were pretty long. Even the Oreos didn't help much. Or the new Taylor Swift album from my iPhone.

The sky was starting to lighten when I figured I might as well quit. Shelby probably wasn't coming home.

But I still needed to find out what was going on. Where was she? Who knew? If she was living at home, surely her family must have noticed that she was not looking normal. From what I'd seen, she was teetering on the edge of the abyss, as someone might have said in all seriousness in a Ngaio Marsh book.

I wasn't going to be able to sit there all day in the Navigator. People in this neighborhood would notice an unfamiliar vehicle hanging around. I didn't want that.

I made a phone call to Cherie. I already owed her a lot for favors done, including carting Uncle Kev and his moonshine empire away from Van Alst House.

Now I needed something else.

I WAS GROGGY when I called Van Alst House at six a.m. We all know the signora never seems to sleep, but Vera is in the conservatory for breakfast at eight every morning and therefore up some time earlier. I figured they would be worried if I didn't come home. Yes, I was an adult, but I made a habit of mentioning if I'd be away as a rule, and there had been a murder.

"It's about time," Vera blustered as soon as she picked up.

"Sorry—"

"How do you expect to keep any customers if you don't show up when you say you're going to?"

Really? I said nothing.

Vera added, "That furnace won't fix itself, you know. We are good customers, and you are not the only game in town."

Oh.

"Are the cops there?" I said.

"Yes, I do mean it."

"Castellano and Stoddard?"

"What else would I mean?"

"Is it serious?"

"Of course it's serious," Vera bellowed. "The whole thing could blow up in our faces."

"In that case, maybe I won't come home for breakfast."

"You better believe I will," Vera said and hung up.

CHAPTER SIXTEEN

V ERA'S MESSAGE WAS clear: Stay away.
I had no intention of walking into a wasp's nest of
detectives. But I needed help and the right kind of help. The
cable truck pulled up sooner than I could have hoped. Cherie
parked across the street from Shelby's house and exchanged
pleasantries with the two dog-walking women who were once
again parading. I was relieved that they hadn't gotten as far
as my hideout in the Navigator. I'd been lucky that none of
the neighbors, who were busily watching the Church house,
had bothered to come around the corner yet. Cherie was her
unusual self with the high-heeled Timberlands. Her wild
blond curls made a unique statement, although I wasn't sure
what they were saying. The china-blue eyes with that metallic
eye shadow to match and the bubble-gum-pink lipstick were
all so striking, they took your mind off everything else. I
kept my distance. As she got her ladder ready, I called her
on my new burner. I didn't want to be seen talking to her.

"On it," she said cheerfully. "You can go home and get
some sleep."

"Here's the thing," I said. "I can't go home."

"Why not?"

"The cops are at Van Alst House."

"I'm glad that Kevin's not there."

I said, "Absolutely. He'd be putty in their hands, but they'd pay a price for it. They might need to stock up on Xanax to get over the experience."

"So I'll call you at this number then if I have anything?"

"Yes. We really need to figure out what's going on and to try and find someone who might know where Shelby is. A relative. A neighbor."

"Sure thing. I really like this house. I wonder if Kev would like it."

Uh-oh. Was Cherie contemplating a life of wedded bliss with Kev? So many women have gone down the crazy path. I wanted to save her from herself, but, you know, one thing at a time. First she needed to save me.

"It is a nice house, but be careful. Shelby's been involved in a murder, and she is mixed up with some dangerous people."

"Huh. Do you want me to mess with the cable or anything while I'm at it? That could get me inside."

"Maybe not worth the risk, Cherie. Thanks."

"I think her parents must be doing all right. I'd love to live here."

I hoped that Cherie wouldn't lose her edge and start thinking about picket fences. She started up the ladder, and I drove off to Uncle Mick's again.

UNCLE MICK'S DIDN'T work out for me either. As I went to turn onto the street where the shop was, I could see roof lights flashing. A pair of police cars was angled in front of the front door. An officer appeared to be standing where he could see anyone fleeing in the alley. *Good luck with that, Officer,* I thought. We Kellys have rabbit warrens no cop can get into.

Uncle Mick was outside in his shirtsleeves, arms crossed across his ginger chest. He was deep in conversation with the police and kept shaking his head, the picture of aggrieved innocence.

Walter yipped.

The rule in our family is: If you see police, keep moving. I hadn't done anything wrong, and I had been doing my best to rise above my family's rules, but I kept moving all right. Walter was disappointed, however, as I'd learned to say from the Ngaio Marsh books, "needs must."

"Needs must, Walter."

Snuffle.

I found a quiet parking spot at the end of the back row in the Park N Ride. The police had no reason to look for me there, and, in fact, they had no reason to suspect I was in the Navigator. Even though I'd spent the night in Shelby's neighborhood, the plates would have been obscured by dust, and they may have belonged to a totally different vehicle. I checked the storage area and found two neatly folded plaid travel blankets. I let the backseat recline, flipped open one blanket and used the other as a pillow. Walter, who had slept all night, was still game for a nap with me. I was out like a light in a minute.

I WOKE UP, stiff and groggy, longing for my facecloth and my toothbrush. I checked the time.

Nine o'clock.

I ducked into the first Stewart's I found. I bought a toothbrush and toothpaste, some wipes and deodorant. I was still wearing the dregs of last night's makeup. I washed my face in the bathroom sink and brushed my teeth and all that.

On the way out, feeling more—but not completely— human, I bought an Eggwich and an apple fritter, plus two extra-large coffees. One for me and the other for me. I picked up a package of dog treats and some bottled water for Walter.

I polished off the Eggwich, the fritter and the two coffees

in the Navigator, taking care to clean up. Walter enjoyed his breakfast more than I did.

Where could I go? Not to Van Alst House. Not to Uncle Mick's. Tiff had let her apartment go when she sailed away to work on the cruise line. She wasn't one to throw away money on an empty space and we never knew where she'd go next. Most likely not back here to Harrison Falls. My friend Karen Smith—now my aunt—had lost her home in a fire that I still had nightmares about.

That left Lance.

I drove slowly to the library, which was just about to open at nine thirty. Lance would be on duty in the reference department. I figured I'd borrow Lance's key, hide out at his place until I knew what was going on and maybe even sleep on his sleigh bed with the designer linens.

That plan was about to evaporate.

Three police cars were parked in front of the library. I pulled in, parked and called the reference department using the new burner.

Lance sounded breathless and stressed. "Harrison Falls Public Library, Reference Department. May I call you back?"

"Me here. Fake your answers."

"Sorry. We're very busy here."

"Police?"

"That's right, madam."

"Looking for me?"

"Correct. So please call again—"

"Are you in any trouble?"

"I believe so. It will take a few minutes to find out, but it sure looks like it . . . Excuse me . . . Sorry, Officer? What is it? Oh. Yes. I suppose I can come with you. I have to go, madam. You'll have to check your own family history."

Lance? In trouble? For helping me, of course. How was he going to deal with that? Lance has never been in trouble. Lance is the golden boy, the darling of his posse.

The front door of the library opened, and an officer

frog-marched Lance out. Were those handcuffs? I couldn't believe my eyes. The officer put his hand on Lance's head, and the Harrison Falls library legend folded into the backseat of the cruiser.

Kathy, the library director, stood on the steps with her arms folded. But the posse tried to rush the car, several of the members yelling and shaking their fists at the police.

Well, that was something, at least.

Two other officers faced the crowd. I thought I recognized the woman who'd searched my underwear drawer. I also spotted Tyler Dekker. The world had gone crazy.

The posse melted away in the face of armed police. I was a bit disappointed in them. I was hoping at least they'd bang on the hood.

The first cruiser pulled away with Lance, and the two other officers got into their vehicles and followed.

I called Van Alst House from the original burner phone. If it got identified, I'd still have the second, unless, of course, I got all confused about which was which.

Vera picked up and snapped hello.

"Is everything all right?"

"No, it isn't."

"Are the cops still there?"

"I've told you we will be dispensing with your services. The furnace is on its last legs, and you will not be getting our business with the new one."

I figured as that was almost identical to what she'd said the last time that the police were still there and I had better find a place to hide out. But what would that place be?

I was out of places.

The police would be checking out motels and B and Bs and hotels in the area, such as they were. Anyone of my description checking in would get the sirens screaming down the road in minutes. Lance's place was probably off-limits too.

What was going on? I had no idea, but I knew I was in big trouble, and apparently everyone I cared about was too.

I put in a call to Sammy, again on the old burner this time, in case. "Any chance you'd have a colleague who could represent my friend Lance? The cops are taking him in for questioning. He might need someone."

"What for?" Sammy's not big on small talk. Have I mentioned that?

"Don't know. Uncle Mick's got the cops at his door too. And Vera does."

"Really?"

"It's something big, and it must have to do with Chadwick Kauffman's murder. What else could it be?"

"Keep a low profile. I'll try to find out."

"I will find somewhere to lie low."

"Don't check into a hotel. Don't go on the highway in case they have roadblocks."

"Roadblocks?" I may have yelped that. "Really?"

"Don't take a chance."

"Where should I—?"

"Don't tell me."

"Okay. But back to Lance. Uncle Mick got a Cory Corrigan for my Uncle Kevin and a Laurence Sternberger for Vera. Mick's surrounded by cops now too, so I can't rely on him."

"You're my client."

"And Lance is my friend. He's been my friend for a long time. He's a good person. Did I mention he's the reference librarian at the Harrison Falls Public Library? His experience with the police and being questioned is limited."

"And?"

"And he's in trouble!"

"And why would that matter?"

I wailed, "Because I care about him. The cops were all over the library and they marched him away. In handcuffs. That's more than an interview."

Sammy was silent for a bit longer than I would have expected.

I blurted, "It's an arrest. Pretty sure of that."

"Yup."

"And if Lance has been arrested it is because he was helping me. I don't know what's happened, but it's my fault."

"Please don't say that. You're joking, right? Nothing is your fault. Never, never, never say that anything is your fault. 'No comment,' that's what you say."

"But I'm talking to you. You're my lawyer!"

"No 'buts.' Maybe this Lance guy is innocent—"

"Not maybe. Is."

"You are not at fault. Remember that. If he left in handcuffs, then he might be going through a very rough interrogation right now."

I fought back panic. "You mean they'll beat him up?"

"Hey, don't shout. I mean emotionally rough. They'll break him down."

"Oh my God."

"And they'll make him turn on you."

"He won't."

"Don't be surprised."

"This is so awful. But I know Lance isn't going to turn on me. He's—"

"All right, all right. But you'd better prepare yourself, because when they get you in there, they'll try to convince you to turn on him."

"He wasn't even at Summerlea. He had nothing to do with it at all."

Sammy said, "He never knew you were going?"

"What? Yes, he knew. He helped with my research and—"

"So he also knew about the Kauffman guy and the house where they lived?"

I swallowed. "Because I asked him. That's the only reason."

"But he knew. That's what the cops will use to get to you, and then they'll use you to get at him. Then when one of you rolls on the other, bingo."

"We didn't do anything. You are my lawyer. You have to believe me."

"I have to defend you."

I felt tears sting my eyes. I am not a crier. You don't last long in the Kelly family if you're inclined to be weepy. "I'm glad you are going to defend me. Lance is also innocent, and I don't believe he'll ever turn on me, and he needs a lawyer too."

"I'll try. Can he pay?"

"He was always pretty good at saving and he has a professional job and this isn't an expensive area to live in. At least he can pay for the initial representation. After that, I'm sure they'll let him go. Stop sighing, Sammy. It's very unnerving. He won't be going to jail."

"The jails are full of innocent people, Jordan."

"And guilty people too."

"You're right. A guy like Lance isn't going to do well in the prison system."

"I can't let that happen to him. He needs a decent lawyer. I can tell them he had nothing to do with it. Do you think I should turn myself in?"

"Can't hear you. You're breaking up! What? What?"

Fine. I needed to think anyway. But my head felt all fuzzy. This thing with Lance was a big shock. And I'd been behind on my sleep since we found out about Chadwick Kauffman's death. I was starting to shake. I needed to crash for a few hours before I could make a good decision about what to do next.

At the intersection ahead a police cruiser ran the red—roof lights flashing—heading for the on-ramp to the interstate, taking the shortcut to the far side of town. As far as I could tell every cop in town was on the move.

MY BURNER PHONE buzzed. I pulled over. Anyone who had this number was someone I wanted to talk to.

"Cherie? What is it?"

"Bad news."

"If Shelby didn't show up, it's not the end of the world. What's happening there now?"

"Couldn't tell you. I had to move on. There are cops everywhere."

"Cops? At Shelby's?"

"Go figure. I learned some stuff about her, but first the cops. They are talking to everyone on the street. I moved to the next street and, from the pole, I could see quite a bit of action before I figured I'd better disappear."

"Maybe they've figured out that she was involved with the killing."

"Maybe. Whatever. I think it's serious. Uh-oh. Too much heat in the area. Talk later."

There was one place that no one would think to look for me. I stuck my hand in my deep-orange bag and felt around the smallest interior zipped pocket for the key. It fit the front and back doors to the residence of one person who wasn't likely to be home anytime soon. Tyler Dekker.

MY HANDS SHOOK as I eased the Navigator out onto the street and headed for Tyler's small, neat brick bungalow.

"So Walter," I said, "at least we'll look legit, you and me, going back to Tyler's place."

Walter cocked his head.

I assumed Tyler would not have told his neighbors he'd dumped his devoted girlfriend and her dog by text. "That's us, Walter. We've been mistreated."

I pulled the Navigator around the corner, and Walter and I sauntered, bush by bush, to the immaculate front entrance. Tyler was the neatest person I'd ever met.

We were greeted by Cobain, Tyler's shaggy dog. Cobain was so excited he twirled and leapt and licked our faces. He may have accidentally left a small puddle in the entry before he and

Walter raced through every room of the house, yipping with joy. They crashed into the small plant table that Tyler kept near the window. I wiped up the puddle, righted the table and rescued the plant before Cobain ate it. That dog would eat anything. I'd do a bit more sweeping after I slept for twenty minutes. I was so fatigued I could have missed large clumps of earth.

"Glad you're having fun, boys," I said. "Try not to break the furniture." I yawned widely but decided to check what was happening on the news before I hit the mattress. Maybe they'd called off whatever they were doing and Tyler would come home to get a bit of sleep. That would not be good.

Tyler likes the local country station. No comment. And he leaves the radio on loud for Cobain.

> *Police in Harrison Falls are not commenting about the cause of a death that took place last night. The body of a twenty-eight-year-old woman was found in a patch of woods on the outskirts of Harrison Falls early this morning. Police received an anonymous tip about the body, which was discovered off Durham Road. The victim's name has not been released, pending notification of next of kin.*

I sat there openmouthed.

Was that woman Shelby? Dead?

That would account for the police presence that Cherie had spotted in front of Shelby's parents' house. Durham Road was less than half a mile from Van Alst House. That explained what Vera was trying to convey. Detectives must have put two and two together and gone to Van Alst House. Now I assumed they were looking for me. Was there evidence that tied me to Shelby? I had chased her from the gallery, but no one knew it was me. Or did they?

> *Police are holding twenty-eight-year-old Lance DeWitt, an employee of the Harrison Falls Public Library, as a suspect in the case.*

Oh no. Poor Lance. He'd done nothing but try to help me. Even if the truth came out, could things ever be the same for him in the job he loved?

Aside from making sure that Sammy actually delivered and found someone good to represent Lance, there wasn't much I could do at that moment that wouldn't make things worse.

Sometimes I look to the characters in the mysteries I'm reading for insights into the situations I'm dealing with. I'd found Lord Peter Wimsey very helpful, and Harriet Vane, as well. Archie Goodwin could walk the walk and talk the talk, but none of them were of any help to me. I was up to my ears in Chief Inspector Roderick Alleyn, and if he'd been real and walked into Tyler's house at that moment, he'd have had no choice but to arrest me.

My head was spinning. The prospect of life in prison after a night of little sleep can do that to a person. "Come on, dogs," I said. "Let's hit the hay."

Ping! Another random text from Tiff came through.

I am on a floating boat to hell.

You and me both, sister. I didn't bother replying. The cops would probably be able to locate me if I did. Instead, I let the idea of sleep set in. Cobain and Walter were more than delighted to leap onto Tyler's immaculately made bed. I had a random thought about creases, but then darkness descended. Too bad it brought nightmares.

THE *SNICK* OF the lock turning woke me with a shock. Or maybe it was Cobain shooting off the bed with that massive leap. I sat up, and Walter snorted at me in irritation. He wasn't finished napping.

Cobain galloped.

"Hey, boy." My blood ran cold when I heard Tyler's voice.

Goldilocks must have felt it too when she was grilled about the porridge, chairs and beds.

"What you been doin', Cobain? Looks like you tried to trash the place. I'm sorry I haven't been home much, but I've been up against it. Big problems. I don't even want to tell you what they are, because I know you won't side with me."

I assumed the thumping noise was Cobain's tail.

There was no way I could escape through the small window in the bedroom. Ducking into the hallway would have been even riskier. La Casa Dekker was tiny.

Without a thing to lose, I rolled off the bed and took Walter with me. There wasn't much headroom under Tyler's bed, but if I'd been looking for an upside, it would have been that Tyler Dekker was an immaculate housekeeper and there wasn't a single dust bunny to scare up a sneeze.

"Bear with me, boy," he said, plunking himself on the bed.

Walter was making his snuffling noises. He's very fond of Tyler Dekker, not having fully grasped what a total traitor and jerk he'd turned into.

Lucky for us fugitive felons, Cobain was making quite a racket whining and barking. It was enough to drown out Walter's snuffling and my pounding heart.

Of course, Cobain was trying to tell Tyler that we were under the bed, but, smart as he was, Smiley didn't speak dog as well as I did.

"Be a good guy and settle down, boy. I've got a call to make."

Cobain did not settle, but we did. Turned out Smiley was checking in with Castellano. She had news for him.

He said, "So the girl has been identified as Shelby Church? . . . For sure? . . . Oh. The parents . . . Right. That's that, then . . . I did follow up on that tip as you requested, and it seems that Shelby Church was last seen at an art installation thing in Grandville, last night. According to a witness, the artist whose work was on display, Poppy Lockwood-Jones, the victim was accosted by a weirdly attractive blond woman who chased her out the fire exit. No one saw much after that because the alarms went off and that caused some chaos. Martinis were spilt and some caviar was lost. There were quite a few critical remarks about the blonde's outfit . . . No, ma'am, I'm not trying to be funny. I'm reporting back.

"We confirmed that the librarian, Lance DeWitt, was also there, asking about Shelby. He left before she did. That's right. Shelby was spotted running from the gallery and jumping into a Lexus SUV and leaving the scene. Lance DeWitt and the blonde were seen pursuing the Lexus in a BMW . . . No one got a plate from either vehicle. They were both muddy, apparently.

"Yes, we were able to collect CCTV footage from the area.

"It appears that the same BMW, with DeWitt and the blonde, was seen in the vicinity of Shelby Church's parents' house at 41 Belleville Crescent in Grandville at around eleven last night. We're canvassing door-to-door in the neighborhood, and we've learned that the BMW was joined by a Lincoln Navigator driven by a burly redheaded man in his fifties.

"At seven this morning, I went by with a photo of Michael Kelly, and at least one witness is certain it was him. Sorry? . . . No, it was definitely not Kevin Kelly, ma'am. I had pictures of both of them. Then the librarian and the large guy left with the Beamer and the blonde drove away in the Navigator. She may have had a small dog with her. The neighbors notice things like that, but they didn't get any license plate numbers.

"The Navigator was observed by an avid birdwatcher living on the next street over. It was parked there all night. There is no reliable description of the woman in it. But several robins were seen, and there was talk of an early scarlet tanager.

"Sorry, ma'am, I do know this is a serious business . . . Yes, I realize that you are taking a chance on me as an investigator . . . No, I won't screw up. So to continue, we're not sure how Michael Kelly was involved with Shelby, but he seemed to be aiding DeWitt and the blonde. As far as the timing goes, they had left Belleview Crescent in plenty of time to have killed Shelby Church. But if you don't mind me saying so, ma'am, I find it hard to believe that either of—Sorry, ma'am . . . Right, I'll keep an open mind.

"Both Michael Kelly and Lance DeWitt are in custody. Kelly's asked for his lawyer. We're letting them cool their heels.

"I'll be back at the station in a half hour. Yes, ma'am. I do realize this is a murder case.

"To finish up, I was able to use the warrant to get the information you wanted from the library. We did turn up extensive searches for"—and here he paused a bit—"Jordan Bingham on the Kauffmans and their country home, Summerlea. We turned up evidence of a search on Shelby Church, and also we found a digital image of a group at the Country Club and Spa. Shelby is in that. The librarian has labeled her and made connections with other people in the photo. You'll be interested to note that Chadwick Kauffman is also in the photo. Also labeled . . . Yes, ma'am. I brought it all in. It's on your desk."

I could hear Castellano squawking on the phone. Some phones make you sound like a deranged chicken when you're on speaker.

"Ma'am? There could be a way to explain that. And there's something I wanted to mention. You remember that Jordan Bingham and Vera Van Alst insisted that the people they met at Summerlea were not Chadwick Kauffman and his assistant, Lisa? . . . Yeah, I know that Kevin Kelly is in the wind and we 'like' him for the killing of Kauffman, but if you'll hear me out, please. The dead woman, Shelby Church, fits the description of the woman they described at Summerlea . . . No, I'm not saying they killed her. I'm suggesting they would have wanted to talk to her. They would need her alive. Alive, she could confirm that they didn't kill Chadwick. Dead, she's—"

Another nail in our coffin, I thought. How's that for a tired cliché? It had been a night of clichés, right down to hiding under a bed with someone sitting on top of it, like something out of *I Love Lucy*. Really, it might have been funny if I hadn't been so close to getting arrested for something I hadn't done.

CHAPTER SEVENTEEN

"NO, MA'AM." TYLER'S voice rose. "No. I don't think the blonde was Jordan Bingham. Jordan has beaut— . . . long dark hair to her shoulders . . .Yes, I have heard of wigs . . . Someone recognized her? Was she caught on camera? . . . A tip? Just to clarify, was it an anonymous tip? . . . It was. I was wondering who is calling in these anonymous tips. What are they getting out of it? . . . No. No, ma'am, I'm not taking Jordan's side . . . We aren't together anymore . . . Yes, I did have some understanding that her uncles were, um, somewhat unorthodox, but, I checked, and Michael and Lucky Kelly have never been arrested, although we've been interested in them more than once. The word is that they don't run any operations in our area. It's all down South. Anyway, for your information, Jordan and I broke up. I haven't had any contact with her at all . . . No, ma'am. I haven't spoken to her except when I was on duty at Van Alst House . . . Yes, I'm sure. I have seen her from a distance, but that's it. If you're worried about it, you can always move me off the case. There's always lots to d— . . . No, ma'am,

I'm not trying to tell you how to do your job. I'm fine with whatever you— . . . Right. I understand that my opinion is of no importance at all . . . Yes, ma'am. You can believe me. I have not been in contact with her.

"Where am I? Well, um, I'm at home, getting changed. A couple of angry older women were waiting outside the station, and they took me by surprise and one of them threw coffee at me.

"Seems they were protesting outside the station in support of the librarian and they recognized me.

"They claimed that they didn't throw the coffee. It spilled.

"The woman who actually *did* throw the coffee says that she's eighty-two years old and her hands shake and try to arrest her and watch the sh—

"Seems like extortion to me too, but the crowd backed her up. I decided we have better things to do than lock up a crowd of senior citizens when we don't have much chance of a conviction and we're in the middle of a murder investigation.

"Well, she was standing on a step and I walked past her. She could have tripped, although I know she didn't.

"I'll be back at the station shortly. Thought I'd use my lunch to get respectable."

The rest of the conversation was all on her end. Chicken squawks that meant nothing.

In the end, Tyler said, "Yes, ma'am. We'll get them."

And that was the end of that.

I listened as Tyler padded off toward the bathroom. As soon as I heard him turn on the shower, I slipped out from under the bed with a very good plan to race along the hallway and out the back door off the kitchen. I wanted to check his cell to see who else he might have been talking to besides Castellano, but I figured I'd better get out of there.

I picked up Walter and began to tiptoe out. Tyler's cell phone rang on the side table. He always turned on the ring and raised the volume when he was out of the room. In that tiny bathroom there was nowhere to put a phone.

Why had I forgotten that?

I heard Tyler thundering toward the room. Too late to get back under the bed. I hugged the wall in the faint hope that he wouldn't notice a woman and an extra dog standing there, trapped.

"Hello?" Tyler clutched the oversized blue-and-white-striped bath sheet around himself as he fumbled with the phone. "Yeah, Stoddard, I'll be there as soon as I get cleaned up, and yes, I'll be wearing plain clothes. And no, they won't be coffee-colored."

He clicked the phone closed and turned. I held my breath. Maybe he wouldn't notice. But that would have been too good to be true.

Walter yipped happily. He'd been missing his friend, Smiley. Cobain barked in agreement.

I wiggled the fingers of my free hand to say "hey" and sidled closer to the door.

Tyler's blue eyes popped. His familiar blush rose, this time from his chest to the roots of his hair. I should add the hair had a nice lather of shampoo on it.

"Wha—?"

"Good to see you too," I said.

"I just assured my commanding officer that we're not in touch."

"Well, that's a fact. You said that you hadn't spoken to me, and it was true at the time."

"It's not true anymore."

"But it was true then."

"Really, Jordan? Do you think that would matter to Castellano? We can't be together."

"I didn't want to be together. I needed somewhere to sleep and I didn't think you'd be goofing off from work to take a shower. I still had my key and—Do you really think I murdered that woman?"

He blinked. "Well, of course not."

"And what about Chadwick Kauffman? Look me in the eye and tell me you think I did that."

He swallowed.

I had the advantage over him, being fully dressed and with a lot to lose. Plus I'd learned from the expression on his face that he didn't believe I'd killed Chadwick. I also knew that he was going to pursue that case under orders.

He said, "When this is over, we can—"

"That's not going to happen."

"Jordan—"

I felt a buzz of emotions. Fear of getting arrested didn't even make the list. How could he? How could he suggest that we would ever even talk again?

"Never. Not in my lifetime. I don't ever want to see you again. I am only hiding out here because I had no choice. And I had the key."

"I realize that, but since we're face-to-face, let me explain—" By now, Tyler was flushed from his hairline to his feet. Usually I find his blushing endearing, but not this time.

I sputtered, "Explain? Explain? What's to explain? I can't believe you said that. You broke up with me by text. You didn't have the courage to do it to my face. And that was after I forgave you for everything that happened last fall. Now this? No explanation possible except that you are a colossal jerk."

"I'm not. I mean, I may be a jerk, but that's not why. I had to."

"Stop wasting my time. I'm out of here."

"I had no choice. They were watching you."

"What?"

"They were watching you."

"Who was watching me?"

"The police. Us. We were."

"What are you talking about?"

"We got a tip about you."

"A tip about me? From who?"

"Anonymous."

"Oh great. So some anonymous crackpot calls in a tip about me and you accept it without question and break—"

"Not me. I didn't believe it. But Castellano and Stoddard were informed about it."

"Informed?"

"The information about the tip came down from one of the higher-ups. I don't know who passed it on. But Castellano and Stoddard were told to keep an eye. And then when Chadwick Kauffman was found murdered and the circumstances were similar to the tip—"

"What?" I knew I had to stop shouting "what?" but every step of this conversation made me want to bellow it. I also knew I was hyperventilating.

"Sit on the bed," Tyler said. "Put your head down between your knees. I'll find a paper bag for you to blow into."

"Oh no," I rasped, "don't you leave this room so you can call for backup."

"I don't need backup for you, Jordan. I'm trying to tell you what's going on and you're freaking out."

"Who wouldn't freak out? Are you telling me that the tip came in before the murder?"

He nodded. "The tip specified the three of you—Vera, Kevin and you—were planning a theft of books and other valuables. It didn't specify Summerlea."

"But that means—" I had a bit of trouble with my breathing.

Tyler said, "Please, Jordan, sit down. Get it under control and we'll talk."

"It means that whoever sent that tip planned it."

"Yes."

"They planned the killing too."

"I believe so."

"That explains why Vera was told to bring Kev and me to Summerlea. They set it all up. And they planned to implicate us."

"That's what it means. I'm sure of it."

"But why?"

"That's the part we don't know."

"We? You and Castellano and Stoddard?"

"You and I are we. And *we* don't know *why*."

"Did they try to trace the tip or find out about the tipster?"

"Of course. They're very good investigators. Especially Castellano. She's going places. She'll be chief here or somewhere else before too long."

"Solving the Chadwick Kauffman case will make her get there faster."

"You got that right."

"Let's not get sidetracked. Did they find out anything?"

"They didn't confide fully in me, as I was still your boyfriend at the time. That's why I—"

"Move on from that."

"As far as I can figure, they've worked it out that it came from someone at the Country Club and Spa."

"But I didn't even know anyone there before—" I stopped myself from saying "before I dressed up as the auditor and swanned in and stole the photo." After all, Tyler didn't know about that escapade, even though I thought he may have spotted me. And I still wasn't one hundred percent sure I could trust him. I didn't plan on handing over details that might add to charges against me. "It doesn't make sense. Someone was clearly setting us up to take the fall for their crime. Wouldn't they have to check that out?"

"Castellano and Stoddard are convinced that one of you did it. They don't care about the motive of the tipster."

"They didn't find the phone-in tip odd? Before the fact?"

He shrugged and blushed a much deeper shade of red.

"They think it's a falling-out among, um, criminals."

"Criminals?"

"Sorry. That's what they believe."

"But, I'm . . . I'm not a criminal."

"I know that."

"I've always gone straight. I don't break the law." I didn't give a minute's thought to any incidents with lock picks and trespassing or impersonation. They were always with good cause."

"I know you've been framed. I knew that you were being set up as soon as that tip came in."

"Did you talk to them about it?"

"Jordan. You're a very intelligent woman. I was seriously involved with you. Do you think they would have trusted me?"

"Oh. No. But then I don't trust you either."

"Well, you have to. I broke up with you in a dramatic and—"

"Cruel—"

"Not cruel. It was crass, and I know it seemed uncaring, but I needed them to think that we were done and it didn't matter all that much to me, but you were furious."

"Couldn't you have stood up for me?"

"Not if I wanted to stay in the loop in the investigation." I snorted.

He said, "I miss that snort. I've already let you know about the tip. The tip could be useful ammunition for your lawyer. I figure you have Sammy Vincovic."

"Yes." I couldn't let on that I knew he'd arranged that. I'd tricked that information out of Sammy, in a surprisingly unguarded moment. Sammy would be very unhappy, and we all like a happy lawyer in a capital case.

"Well, he's the best, isn't he? He'll work that angle, and if it turns out they didn't investigate when they should have, he'll take them apart on the stand. I mean, if it comes to trial."

I gulped.

He reached out and squeezed my hand. "He'll dig around to find out who the tip might have come from and to find someone else who'll be a credible suspect but wasn't investigated. That will count. Believe me, I wanted to let you know what was really happening."

I gave a sharp bark of laughter. "Uh, things are bad now. Really bad, and, by the way, you kept me in the dark."

"I just told you about the tip! To be fair—"

"I don't care about being fair. You let me down in the worst way."

"I admit it. I thought it would help to work the case, and I was sure I could let you know why I broke it off, but I couldn't reach you."

"What do you mean?"

"Every time I need to speak to you, Castellano or Stoddard is around. They have taps on your phone."

"I have a burner."

"But I don't know the number."

True. I hadn't given it to him. He was on the other side.

"And anyway, I think they're tracking my calls too. The best thing was not to contact you, to pick up more facts and to make sure that nothing really bad happened to you."

"Bad like being suspected of murder? Like being treated as the lowest type of criminal?"

"Jordan. This is how I can help you."

"You only care about your job. That's what it is."

"If that was all, do you think I would have fallen in love with a member of Kelly family? Well-known—"

"Local entrepreneurs." Did he say "in love with"? I wasn't sure I believed it. And if I did believe it, then this was one really unromantic situation in which to unfurl that declaration.

"Whatever. They are what they are, but they're not your responsibility."

"I'm responsible for keeping them safe," I said, Kev's silly and much-loved face flashing in my brain.

"Maybe, but *you* are not responsible for any of the things they do."

"They're my family."

"Sure, they make their choices and you are loyal. I get that."

"Too bad it's a stumbling block, career-wise."

"I can find a way to live with that. But right now, I need my colleagues, especially Castellano and Stoddard, to think that I've washed my hands of you. And I need you to know that I trust you and I believe in you."

"Well, I'm not sure that I can say the same about you."

"Fair enough. But do you think—deep down—that one of the reasons you came here was because of us? Maybe you wanted—"

"Don't push your luck. I'm leaving now."

"I can't let you leave, and I'm going to have to arrest you."

I sputtered. "Really, Tyler? Really? It's one thing for you to dump me without any feelings the way you did—"

"I explained all that. Don't you think my neighbors will have seen you come in here? Your face has been all over the TV."

"What?"

"Everyone's looking for you. It's serious. For all I know Castellano has someone watching the place. Who knows what could happen if some trigger-happy type shows up?"

I kept going as if I hadn't heard him. "But it's horrible for you to arrest me, especially when we both know I didn't do it." All right, so I was stalling. I know what cops have to do. If I was a police officer, I would have arrested me. There was no question that Tyler was conscientious, but I believed he didn't want anything bad to happen to me. Being arrested would be included in the category of something bad happening. What choice did he have?

"Horrible of me? You broke into my house!"

"You gave me a key. You didn't ask for it back. In a court of law, that could be construed to mean—" Okay, so I was babbling to stall.

"Come on, Jordan. That's just plain stupid."

"Who are you calling stupid?" Walter yipped when I yelled. "Here! Take your nasty little key." I flung the key to the far side of the bed where it hit the wall with a *plink* and fell behind the mattress. Cobain leapt onto the bed, and Walter yipped wildly and spun around in circles.

Tyler stared in the direction of the key and at his own dog. Cobain was doing his best to retrieve that key. Yes, Cobain, who will eat anything.

Tyler shouted, "Don't eat that key, Cobain. Leave it!"

I used that diversion to race for the back door and outside. I scampered down the stairs and ran like the devil was chasing me. I let Walter run ahead of me. I smiled and called to him. He yipped and skipped. What fun! Nosy neighbors would see a woman having a fun time with her adorable pug. Nothing suspicious about that. I headed in the opposite direction to where the Navigator was parked, planning to approach it from the other side. I glanced back and saw Tyler framed in the doorway, still clutching his blue-and-white-striped bath sheet. Good. Tyler Dekker was not likely to chase me down his street clad only in that towel.

I made the international sign for "sorry, I had no choice." I hoped that shrugging-and-grimace combination wasn't misinterpreted. Tyler Dekker might have had his doubts about my guilt, but he'd probably never be able to forgive me for humiliating him.

I figured by now he'd be calling the police to intercept me.

I was out of breath by the time I reached the Navigator. Panting, with Walter yipping by my ear, I tried to think where I could go next. I didn't hear the sound of sirens, so that was good. I tumbled into the car panting. Walter matched me pant for pant.

How had all this happened?

One week earlier my life had been rosy. Beyond rosy. Perfect job, perfect living arrangements, perfect relationship with Tyler, all things considered. I had been secure and happy. And now? It seemed like I was the victim of a cosmic joke. Everything was falling apart. And the worst was yet to come.

I looked out the rearview mirror. The joke apparently was continuing. Tyler, still wearing the large striped towel, was thudding along the sidewalk in his bare feet. Those large white feet were rapidly approaching the Navigator. My first thought was horror that Tyler was going to wreck his soles. Were they bleeding? I knew what that was like. My second thought was to get out of there.

My hands shook as I put the key in the ignition.

Tyler thudded closer.

The Navigator purred and leapt forward. Tyler bent over, hands on his knees, probably gasping for breath.

I suppose if I hadn't been looking out the rearview mirror, I might have noticed the dark van pull up beside me. But of course, I was staring back at Tyler, realizing what I had lost.

It would have been better if I'd spotted the van before it cut me off.

"WHA?" I SAID like a fool.

But there was no time to articulate a better query.

The door to the Navigator was yanked open. I yelped as a man in a balaclava dropped a bag over my head.

The safety belt loosened, and I was dragged from the vehicle. My ankle banged on metal as I was pushed, shoved and finally lifted off my feet. I struggled. I hit out and reached nothing. Soon I found my hands bound. Duct tape? I tumbled to a floor. Hard. Cold. Was I in the back of the van?

My captor mumbled something, but I couldn't make out what it was.

The van screeched away. Was that Walter yipping? What if he got hit by a car? OMG.

Now there was only the whir of the tires and highway noises. How many times had I been told, "Never let them take you to a second location"? It was one of the many tenets of my unorthodox childhood. Well, I would have wanted to stop them—whoever they were—but what chance did I have with a bag over my head? My uncles had never mentioned that possibility.

It seemed unfair. I mean, Inspector Alleyn never had to put up with anything like that. Not that he'd never been attacked, but always with dignity. Even Fox managed to escape.

Well, back to the here and now, I told myself. Use what you know, and don't go mooning over your bad luck. My uncles had of course explained how to undo duct tape. I hoped that's what I was bound with. Its holding powers are overrated. Plastic ties are much, much worse. Maybe these kidnappers didn't keep up with the latest trends. My plan was to free my hands first. They were duct-taped in front of me and not too tightly. This didn't seem to be the work of an experienced kidnapper, I decided. Was that good or bad? Time would tell.

I brought my hands down as far as I could and snapped the tape open.

Unlike heroines in the movies, my hands shook, quite violently, and I was breathing loudly. There are probably quieter freight trains. *Think of something soothing*, I told myself. With an image of the signora's lasagna in mind, I managed to collect myself enough to reach up and test the bonds on the bag over my head. It felt like burlap, and, oddly, there were no bonds. I yanked it off to find myself in a dark interior of a van that was rattling along. The ride was so uncontrolled that I wondered if anyone was actually driving it. I edged toward the back of the van and tried to figure out where the rear lights were. My captor hadn't secured my feet, so I had some options. Everyone knows that if you kick out the back lights of a vehicle, then people will spot you and call 911. I did my best to listen, for a train, traffic, voices, familiar noises. Anything to identify where I was being taken and the route. I never did figure out where the lights in the van were. Maybe that's easier in a car trunk.

I willed myself to be calm. I would need my wits about me when we stopped and I came face-to-face with whoever was behind this.

Be logical, I said to my quivering, terrified self.

The police were looking better by the minute. As much as we distrust them in our family, they don't kidnap people and put bags over their heads. Not in this country, anyway.

I was not wealthy. So most likely not a kidnap for ransom. Could it have been a random attack? Unlikely. I was close to—inadvertently, but still involved in—two murders. I was nosing around about those murders. Therefore, this was almost certainly connected to them.

I really didn't want to meet this dude face-to-face.

I didn't know if he worked alone. Chadwick Kauffman was dead. There had been a gang of three at Summerlea, and now one of them was dead too. That left two. I might have been terrified, but I could still do simple arithmetic.

Time to get a plan.

Now we were bumping and bouncing along some very uneven terrain. Whatever we were driving on, it could not possibly be a road. Therefore, there probably wouldn't be many people to see my efforts even if I did get the lights kicked out. Plus my captors might hear the noise. Better to see if I could get out of the van.

Find the windows. What was covering them? I stood up, woozily, and promptly fell down again as the van bounced in another direction. I tried again, gripping a piece of metal and easing myself up. Maybe I could pull off whatever was blocking the windows. I felt . . . curtains?

Curtains? Really?

The van lurched to a stop. My heart almost did too. I had to get out of there—wherever "there" was—before my captor arrived. I needed to see.

I yanked open the curtains and screamed.

CHAPTER EIGHTEEN

"UNCLE KEV?" I slumped to the floor of the van and sobbed.

"Jordie!"

I gathered enough strength to stand up and shout. "Are you insane?"

The familiar look of hurt crossed his handsome Irish face. "That's not nice."

"Demented? Crazed? Delusional? Mad? Off your rocker? Just plain nuts?"

"Why are you screaming, Jordie? It all went according to plan. Ouch, that hurts."

I got to my feet so that I could hop around with rage and frustration.

"What plan? What plan is that, Kev?" I may have augmented my point by beating my shaking fists against his handsome Kelly chest.

"The plan to pretend to kidnap you so the police would lose interest in you as a suspect."

I resisted the urge to bang my head on the side of the van.

The only thing that stopped me was that I already had so many bruises from that metal. Plus I had a message for Uncle Kev.

"The police, as you may not be aware, Kev, do not actually *lose* interest in people who are kidnapped."

"Okay, okay, but you have to admit it worked. You should see the clips online."

I rubbed my temples. "Clips of what? The police?"

"Your kidnapping!"

"There are clips online?"

"YouTube and everything. It's big news."

"Well, that's terrific. But I was scared to death. What if I'd had a heart attack?"

"Jordie! You're only, what, twenty-seven? Why would you have a heart attack?"

"Oh, I don't know. Maybe because I thought I was being kidnapped by the person who killed Chadwick and Shelby, you . . ." Words failed.

"But it was *me*."

"I know that now, but I didn't know it when you put that bag over my head."

"Of course you knew. It was part of the plan."

"Maybe it was, but I—the person with the bag over her head in the speeding vehicle—didn't know about the plan."

Kev shook his handsome ginger head. "Why didn't you?"

I thought for a second that my eyes would pop right out of my head. "Good question, Kev. Why didn't you tell me?"

"I did!"

"You did not. I would have noticed if you had mentioned it." Kev shrugged.

I resisted the urge to slug him.

He said, "I did tell you."

"When? When did you tell me?"

"I left a message on your burner."

"How did you get the number?"

"Cherie gave it to me."

"That makes sense. And you left a . . . ?"

"Yeah. Left a message. Burner to burner, no problem there."

"There was a problem, Kev, in that I never got that message."

"You didn't? But you called me back."

I scratched my head. "I did?"

"Yes."

"Um, what did I say?"

"You said, 'I don't know what you're talking about, Uncle Kev.'"

It actually hurt when I scratched my head. "Okay, I did call about a particularly obtuse message and said I didn't understand it."

"Told ya," Uncle Kev said with a grin.

"But the thing is that you left me a message saying, 'All systems are go and the eagle will be landing and we will have liftoff, Houston.'"

"Exactly."

"But that didn't come across like you were going to stage a faux kidnapping, Uncle Kev." I tried to speak gently, although I actually felt like . . . Well, never mind.

"Oh."

"Next time, a bit of detail."

"I thought I'd be careful in case the cops or someone got hold of the message even though it was burner to burner."

"But I had Walter with me. What happened to him? He could have been hit by a car or something. He won't know what's—"

As my voice rose, Kev cut in. "Don't worry about the little doggie. Your cop friend picked him up when he tried to chase the van."

All I could utter was a strangled gasp.

Kev added, "He had a hard time hanging on to the pooch without dropping his towel or his cell phone. It's all good news. I hope someone got a video of it."

I stared at Kev as I imagined that scene. Smiley would have been reporting my kidnapping. The neighborhood would be swarming with police in minutes. He probably would have had to admit that I'd used a key to get into his house. No doubt some helpful person on the street would have spotted me coming or going as well as Smiley in his towel.

"It was pretty funny, Jordie."

Sure it was. I'd been rolling around on the floor of the van, terrified. Smiley would have been better off, but not much. Walter would be hungry and peevish.

"Let's not talk about it anymore. Let's get out of here." I glanced around. Kev had tucked the van into a small clearing in the woods.

"Great. Come on in."

For the first time I focused on something other than woods and van. "In where?"

He puffed up with pride. "Our cabin."

"We don't have a cabin."

"Hey, we do now. Wait till you see it."

I followed him into a larger clearing. There was no question that I was looking at a quite lovely log cabin in the middle of nowhere. If you like log cabins in the middle of nowhere. I was pretty sure I didn't. I'm more of a library and art gallery and vintage shop and formal dining room kind of girl.

"What if someone sees the van, Uncle Kev?"

I hated that van, yet now I needed to protect it.

"No one's going to see it. They don't even park there. They park by the house."

I just had to let that go. There wasn't much I could do about it. Driving off in a van that was all over the news seemed like it would just make a bad situation worse.

Uncle Kev strode ahead and opened the door. I followed, but only after giving a longing look back to civilization, assuming that it was in the same direction. I had no real reason to assume that. Mainly, I stared at trees, thick, dark, impenetrable, as far as the eye could see, except for the dirt track I assumed we had lurched in on.

Kev disappeared into the cabin, and I followed. What else could I have done?

Inside, there were more surprises. Mainly, food. It looked like the signora had catered for our hideout. There was a huge dish of stuffed manicotti, a mountain of rolls that smelled freshly baked, green beans and salad. I glanced around, worried that the signora and Vera had also been 'napped, but it was only me.

It felt wrong eating, but I was ravenous. I suppose being faux-kidnapped can do that to a person. When I'd wolfed down the last bite, I felt calm and soothed enough to ask, "When did you rent this cabin, Uncle Kev?"

Kev chortled. "I didn't rent it, Jordie. Do you think I'm an idiot?"

I chose not to answer that. Not that Uncle Kev takes offense that easily, but I was marooned here—wherever "here" was— with him, and he's hard to take when his feelings are hurt.

"How, then? Exactly how did you borrow it?"

He wagged his finger under my nose. I felt like biting it off, but I put that down to recent stress. "Don't want to leave any kind of trail."

I sighed. If you didn't want to leave a trail, maybe kidnapping someone in broad daylight in sight of a serving police officer wasn't the way to go.

"It was empty. No one here."

I glanced around. The inside was definitely rustic. It was made of logs inside and out. Some beautiful old quilts covered the furniture, which had a handcrafted look to it. Other quilts were hung on the log walls. They looked handmade by someone's grandmother. I stepped forward to examine the tiny stitches. Lovely. I couldn't imagine Grandmother Kelly making a quilt, although she drove a getaway car like an artist.

There was so much to look at. The wide plank flooring, the spectacular stone fireplace that must have taken someone an eternity to complete. At the back of the cabin, overlooking what I thought was a ravine, was a sunroom with a sloping glass roof and three sides of windows. A pair of battered recliners, with a small table between them, pretty well filled the room. This was no abandoned cabin. Someone loved this place. A lot of work had gone into making it a serene escape. And then along came Kev.

"Was there anything in the fridge, Uncle Kev?"

"Oh yeah. Lots of stuff. Beer, cheese, bacon, eggs, bread, a cake. Some wine. I brought our food from the signora, but we coulda been all right anyway."

"Uh-huh. But you know that kind of food spoils quickly."

Uncle Kev nodded, waiting for me to make my point.

I made it. "That means that whoever owns the place either comes often or is planning to come back soon."

"That's not good."

"No, Kev, it isn't."

"But they won't because—" A loud clap of thunder drowned out whatever else he was going to say. The thunder was followed soon by a flash of lightning and then the slash of rain. We glanced out the window. Soon the view was obscured by heavy rains.

"That'll wash out that track," Kev said with enthusiasm. "At least once every spring it gets washed out. They'll have to regrade it."

"Mmmm. And how will we get out then?"

"The old van will probably make it."

Personally, I bet the owner would have an all-terrain vehicle or at least a pickup.

"They'd never drive out here midweek in this anyway," he said, happily. "I'll make a fire."

"Please don't. Someone may see the smoke."

"No one's going to see it, Jordie. We're in the middle of nowhere."

I experienced a pang in my heart. Uncle Kev was so kind, cheerful and well-meaning. He was also so hopeless and innocent and unable to make the right decisions. How would he ever survive in prison? The way we were going, Kev and I would definitely be behind bars within a day, for crimes we hadn't committed, compounded by a few crimes Kev had committed and, um, mistakes I had made. Even Vera might be arrested and detained, possibly convicted.

I knew that near heroic action would be required to save us, and it would be up to me to take that action. Unfortunately, I was swaying with fatigue and what was probably a reaction to my apparent kidnapping. My head swam, and my knees started to buckle.

"Uncle Kev, you need to put the van out of sight and then we need to be ready to get out quickly if anyone comes. I'll leave it to you to stand guard. I only need a short nap. No fires, please. Promise. It would just take one hiker to—"

"There's a storm, Jordie. No hikers are out there now." He chuckled fondly, as if I was a slow but beloved child. "Oh yeah, that reminds me."

"Something about hikers, Kev?"

"Huh? No. No hikers."

"What then? The storm?"

"No. Why?"

I sighed deeply. This was the man who had kidnapped me in front of a police officer. Why would I expect his conversation to follow logically?

"What did it remind you of, Kev?"

"Cherie called."

"Okay."

"She had something really important to tell you."

"Did she?" I tried not to think about throttling Uncle Kev and to focus on Cherie. She had wanted to tell me something about Shelby. Cherie might be outrageous, but at least you could count on her to make sense in her own unique way.

"Yeah."

"I'll reach her as soon as we get to a place where we have cell phone reception. I wonder if I wander around outside when it stops raining if I could find a high spot with a signal."

"Nah. I tried that. Even stood on the van. But I've got her on the line for you."

With horror, I saw that he was holding the receiver of the landline in the cabin.

Two things became apparent. One, we couldn't have been in the middle of nowhere, as Kev claimed, if there was phone service. And two, if the police discovered we'd been in this cabin, they could make a link to Cherie by checking the phone records. Well, maybe that was an unlikely scenario, what with the storm and all. I hoped she had a burner and that was the number Kev had called.

"Cherie?"

"You're all over the news."

"Let's not, um, go there. What did you discover about our mutual friend when you visited her home?"

"Oh. Right. Our mutual friend. Yeah, really interesting, and I think it explains why the neighbors were so fascinated by you."

"Okay."

"Guess who showed up?"

"Can't guess. Not a good time for games. Could you just tell me?"

"Repo!"

"What?"

"*Ree*-po."

I hadn't seen that coming. I thought back to the pleasant home on the leafy street in Grandville. "But what was being repossessed?"

"Her car. You know you're having a real bad day when they try to repossess your car and then you get—"

"Don't say it. Are you sure?"

"Yup. Talked to the guys. Wasn't too hard to get into a conversation."

It never is for Cherie. That's what comes of looking like a modern-day Marilyn Monroe with a side order of Wonder Woman and a dash of the Cable Guy. "And?"

"They'd been trying to get that Lexus for quite a while. She was pretty slippery, the guy said. She'd moved back home with her parents and didn't leave a forwarding address to any of her creditors. Threw them off."

"I guess it would." I thought back to Shelby Church, whom I still thought of as Lisa Troy. She'd been a woman with a lot going for her. How had all this happened?

"Yeah," Cherie said. "Why do you suppose she'd leave a job and a life and come back here? No offense."

"None taken. I came back because I was broke and needed a place to live." I didn't mention a place to heal. "And I needed to save some money and rebuild."

"That explains it, then. I got a chance to talk to one of the neighbors. I guess the repo guys weren't the first. Everyone at the Church place was going crazy. Lots of bill collectors."

"Coming to the door? Really?"

"On the phone. One of the neighbors has a part-time cleaner who also does the Churches' house. The stories she could tell, apparently. No one could figure out how this girl, who wasn't doing well as an actress, could afford that car."

"So were the parents drowning in debt? Or was only the daughter?"

"As far as I can tell, it was just the girl. The parents are salt of the earth, if you listen to the neighbors. Boy, were they keen to talk. I guess the daughter was in a bad way. Crying all the time. There was no way she could pay off her debt. Guess it was more than credit cards and car loan. She had personal loans, line of credit, everything."

"Student loans too, I guess?"

"No, her parents had put her through. They had a college fund for her from the time she was born. They wanted her to have a great education. And in the end, after she got a good, solid degree, she got herself in this mess. She was trying to make it as an actress, and roles had dried up lately. And then she met this guy. The parents were afraid of what she might do to herself. Everyone says they were trying to help her. They were going to take out a second mortgage. And now . . ."

"Yeah. And now look."

"What do you think it all means?"

"It's a pretty good motive." I could see how separating Vera from ten thousand for an afternoon's work would be very appealing. You'd have a few out-of-pocket expenses: mostly food and alcohol. You'd take the money, hand over the collection you had no right to in the first place and then make a clean getaway. Maybe you'd take some other stuff too. Uncle Mick had known a lot about the value of stuff on the walls. When the theft was discovered, there would be fingerprints of the obvious thieves, namely us, all over the place. And with our dingbat story about being invited. We'd driven up to Summerlea without a care in the world, in full view of the local walkers and snoops, even as the police had been receiving a tip.

But I worried that ten thousand dollars didn't seem like enough to deal with Shelby's terrible problem, especially if she had to share the take with the other conspirators. I knew from my own sad experience how credit card debt could mushroom, even if in my case someone else had done the spending without my knowledge. And Cherie had mentioned a big line of credit. So what else would they have taken?

My mind flashed to Uncle Mick, outside his shop. Had just enough of the Summerlea valuables found their way to Michael Kelly's Fine Antiques to get him arrested? Had the police received a convenient tip for that too?

That would explain why the cops had been at Uncle Mick's antique shop. And once again, it told me that my friends and family had been purposely targeted.

On the bright side, whoever brought in those items would have been caught on camera. And Uncle Mick's cameras weren't necessarily where anyone would expect they'd be. There were no polite signs warning about their presence and suggesting that your privacy might be violated. Uncle Mick didn't give a flying fig about your privacy.

So that could be good.

But how could I get my hands on any of those images? Our visit to Summerlea was now four days past. The setup had been earlier. It was possible that any clues planted at Uncle Mick's would have been there even earlier.

Cherie said, "Are you still on the line?"

"Sorry! My mind wandered. I'm afraid I'm going to have to ask you for another favor."

"That's what I'm here for. Wherever I am!" She laughed cheerfully.

I took a chance. No one knew we were here. The police probably didn't know much about Cherie yet, although Tyler had met her before all this happened. But right now, he most likely still thought I'd been kidnapped, so he'd be focusing on that. I wondered if not letting him know I hadn't been was so much worse than breaking up by text.

"Okay. We need some security camera footage from my uncle's place." I didn't want to name names over the phone. "That's the same uncle who gave you the big, sloppy kiss on St. Patrick's Day. The device will be in the building across from his workplace. It's upstairs over the vacant shop in a storage space. There's an entry keypad. The code is our dog's name. Take the whole laptop and keep it somewhere— What's that noise? Cherie?"

"Sirens," she said. "I'm moving on. I'll be in touch. I'll get your stuff."

My eyes were heavy. I needed a bit of sleep, even half an hour. There was a funky old alarm clock on the wobbly side table. I set it for thirty minutes. That would be enough to keep me going.

Then, yawning and swaying, I checked the window and left it open so that I could get out quickly if I needed to. Tired as I was, the old Kelly training kicked in. Survival of the fittest and all that.

I set up a small tower of pots and pans where it would be knocked over if the door opened and before the light could be turned on. Like I said, training.

I cornered Kev. "I have a getaway plan. If someone comes in, you get yourself out by the main bedroom window. I'll leave by the other one."

"I know all that stuff, Jordie."

"Promise?"

Silence.

I said, "Because if we're caught here, I don't want to have to worry about you. I'll meet you at the van."

"Guess you're right."

With that I fell onto the bed and into a deep sleep, even though Uncle Kev was building a spectacular blaze in the huge stone fireplace.

CHAPTER NINETEEN

I DIDN'T WANT it to be a dream, because I was so happy to meet Roderick Alleyn. He was every bit as charming as I'd imagined him on the page without any of the elitist characteristics I'd ascribed to him.

I offered him everything I could think of from the fridge in the cabin. He declined, citing legal reasons. Oh well. Before he faded from my mind, he did take the time to offer me what he called a word in my ear. "Look to the stage."

"You would say that," I answered.

Alleyn was smiling enigmatically and twiddling his silk tie when my eyes popped open. I lay in the dark, listening to Kev's gentle rhythmic snore from the next room. All the Kellys snored. I'd always liked the sound; it made me feel safe and happy. Of course, I was far from happy and not in the least bit safe. And there was a lot to think about. There would be a bonanza of Kelly DNA in this cabin after we left, but the police wouldn't be doing much DNA work even if they did show up. Smiley had always said that forensic resources were tight in the Harrison Falls police budget, and I figured cabin break-ins weren't top priority.

The fire was glowing nicely. The rain had stopped. The sky was clear. The funky old alarm clock must have been for decoration. It had failed to ring. It was now the middle of the night, We'd need to get going soon. Not that I expected any owners to arrive before dawn but I had the idea that people who loved cabins in the woods also loved arriving at them as the sun was coming up. Even so, I knew better than to wake up Kev too early. He's bad enough with a full night's sleep.

I made myself a cup of cranberry-orange tea, picked up the two quilts from "my" bedroom and headed for one of the recliners I'd spotted in the sunroom earlier. Right at that moment, it should have been called the moon room. With its sloped glass roof and glassed sides, it was a magical place, reflecting a black but twinkling universe.

This quiet, deserted and illegal hideout had to be good for something besides keeping the rain off our heads and giving us a place to sleep.

Without the buzz of phones and the presence of real police, I could actually think.

As my life and the lives of people around me were spinning out of control, I needed to be calm and to reflect. Job one: Figure out what was happening to us and why.

The million twinkling stars reminded me of my tiny role in this universe. I don't know how long I sat there, watching. The night sky reminded me that life goes on, and sometimes we need a little distance to make sense of things.

For the first time since we'd heard of Chadwick's death, I felt a bit of pleasure. The stars can give you perspective. Perspective was something I'd totally lost. It had been replaced by fear, anxiety and panic. Yet here, I could feel peaceful.

From the time I was a little girl I'd adored the Big Dipper and the Little Dipper too. I'd particularly loved how the stars made such vivid pictures in the sky.

Uncle Mick always said when you saw the Dippers to make sure someone wasn't dipping into your pocket to steal your wallet. I chuckled to myself remembering that, even as I unconsciously checked my pocket, as I'd done when I was five years old.

Uncle Lucky had gone even further and introduced me to the constellations when I was six. He'd taught me that my beloved Dippers were part of the Ursa Major constellation. He promised that the Great Bear was something I could count on. It would always be there. I smiled. I could also always count on Uncle Lucky, who was a great bearlike figure himself. It was good to remember that. Uncle Mick might be out of commission, but Uncle Lucky was out there, and tomorrow I would find a way to reach him.

I scanned the sky, and sure enough, there were the three stars marking Orion's Belt. I had to admire a constellation with great accessories. But Orion, the hunter, always had to watch his celestial back. Behind the scenes—and unseen in April—was Scorpius. I knew there was some kind of Scorpius behind our scenes too, lurking out of sight, malicious and dangerous. Who was my Scorpius? Why was he or she targeting us?

I hoped that, like the outlines of the constellations, all would be revealed if I could just see the patterns. That was something else Uncle Lucky had taught me. Look for the patterns; your eye will fill in the connecting lines.

All my uncles were fascinated with the night skies, maybe because so much of their business took place under cover of darkness. I shared the fascination, if not the business.

It felt good to sit there, covered in the quilts, thinking, reviewing everything that had happened without distraction. By distraction, I meant Uncle Kev and the police. But no matter how I looked at the stars, we were in a mess of some magnitude.

Would Inspector Alleyn have seen the connections between the seen and unseen players in our drama? He sure had a knack for finding links and noticing small, discordant elements. Would he have spotted our Scorpius?

Of course, unlike me—a fleeing felon on the run and in the woods—he'd be well-groomed, calm and aristocratic, and he'd never find himself hiding under a bed. He'd take his time and look at each aspect of the case. Mull over the small things that stuck out and nagged at the back of the mind. I hadn't done that. I'd been too busy dashing around and panicking. Not that I didn't have good reason to panic. I had people to worry about. Uncle Kev wouldn't last ten minutes in prison. Vera might, but that was an awful thought. I wasn't so crazy about hearing the doors clang behind me either. Orange didn't suit me at all, as I've mentioned.

It looked grim for all of us. Were the police still holding Mick and Lance? I couldn't check with Smiley. Kev was a disaster. I was working alone.

Not only were we headed for the slammer, but two people were dead, two people who didn't deserve that fate. What had Chadwick Kauffman ever done to be bashed with a sculpture and pushed down the staircase at Summerlea? Nothing, as far as I could see. His employees seemed distraught. He had no heirs. There didn't appear to be anyone with a motive.

But, like the constellations, things were starting to take shape. I just couldn't make out what that shape was.

"Look to the stage," Inspector Alleyn had said in my dream. What did he mean by that?

WELL BEFORE DAWN, we met Cherie at the edge of the road. For once she was not in the cable van, but in an unmemorable older Ford Focus. She followed us to the most isolated spot we knew of, a quarry twenty miles north of Harrison Falls. There Kev drove the van into the lake. He'd wanted to torch it, but saner voices prevailed.

It is said there are more cars at the bottom of that quarry

than at any car dealer in the region. I chose not to think about that as we drove back.

Cherie had the laptop from Uncle Mick's secret location. "That's a cool space across the street from Mick's antique shop. You ever think of opening a boutique in the vacant shop downstairs, Jordan? It might be less dangerous that working for a book collector."

Kev said, "But we love working for Vera."

Cherie said, "It takes all kinds, I guess. Well, you two can stay at my place until this blows over."

Kev brightened. I hated to tell him that there wouldn't be much romance.

I said, "I'll need you to help me some more, Cherie."

"I'll help you too, Jordie."

As with so many of Uncle Kev's comments, I let it slide. Cherie said, "Whatever it takes. This has been fun so far."

Fun? Maybe I was getting old. Aside from lunch at Summerlea, nothing about it had been fun.

Kev and Cherie flirted happily in the front of the car. In the backseat, I left a message for Uncle Lucky from my burner phone.

Then I sat back to focus on our situation and all the unknowns we faced. How had our players gotten into Summerlea? I had nothing to lose by speculating. The housekeeper was a possibility, but she'd lost a good job when Chadwick died and she had nothing to gain from his death.

My intuition told me that the answer lay at the Country Club and Spa, now known as a source of at least one false tip for the police. The Country Club was the connection. But who was the weak link? Was it Lisa Hatton? Infatuated with Chadwick? Would she have betrayed him out of revenge? Was it anger over unrequited love?

Or had Shelby been the person who managed to get that key? She went to events there. I assumed her family were members. She could have called in a tip. She'd been involved in the trickery at Summerlea. Would she have been able to get the key and the codes from Chadwick? How?

Was the Country Club where I should be spending my energy? Or should I look back to the stage? Whatever that meant.

I felt a shiver down my spine.

But I had an idea.

CHERIE LIVED OUTSIDE Maple Ridge, two towns past Grandville, just over the county line and yet far away enough from Harrison Falls to mean we wouldn't be dodging police. She was down a long driveway off a road with few houses. I was happy. Uncle Kev was in heaven. Cherie had every channel in the universe and more movies than you could ever imagine. I was glad to know Kev was sitting safely on her leather reclining sofa, with a couple of bags of Cheetos and a cluster of remotes.

I sat with the laptop and began the tedious job of checking out everything that had happened in Michael Kelly's Fine Antiques for the week prior to our adventure at Summerlea. Luckily, at most times nothing was happening at the shop. I was able to skim, but even skimming took time. I may have eaten a few Cheetos too.

Uncle Mick came and went. Walter enjoyed a lot of walks. I popped in to say "hi" more than once. There I was, showing off my raspberry dress to Uncle Mick and Walter. Uncle Danny and Uncle Billy paid a social call. I paused when the occasional customers came in. I captured their images and moved the individual images to a memory stick. Most people were buying things. I was pretty sure the culprits weren't going to be middle-aged ladies on the hunt for estate jewelry, but you have to keep an open mind.

I found myself yawning, but there was no stopping now. An elderly man tried to interest Uncle Mick in a stack of

National Geographic. Uncle Mick turned him down gently, but did offer a glass of Jameson whiskey as a consolation prize.

Click. Click. Click.

There. A pretty young woman with a cloud of curly hair was taking a great interest in the estate jewelry. I couldn't see the color in the grainy gray footage, but I knew that hair was strawberry-blond. Mick took a great interest in her too. She had him taking out earrings, rings and necklaces. Helping her to put them on, leaning forward so clasps could be fastened on her neck. Holding out her hand for Mick to assist as she tried on ring after ring, diamonds from the forties, a garnet dinner ring I'd noticed, a square sapphire.

Oh, Mick. How could you let yourself be so deluded? I shook my head.

Behind her other customers browsed around the shop. Most were regulars and waved cheerfully to Mick as they left. One man seemed to be killing time. He shrugged to indicate he was also in no hurry. Mick didn't pay much attention.

The camera was not so foolish.

He was tall, with a square, well-shaped head hidden by a baseball cap. He kept his face turned away from the security cameras on each wall. Of course, those cameras weren't hooked up to anything, so that was a waste of time. The camera in the cuckoo clock and the one in the shabby teddy bear were a different story. They even captured his hands, large and covered with black leather gloves. I was surprised Uncle Mick didn't notice him, but he had other things on his mind. I'd seen that ball cap and those gloves recently in the Lexus SUV that scooped up Shelby the night she was killed.

The girl who was busy wrapping Uncle Mick around her little finger wasn't Shelby. But she did answer one of my big questions. Miranda, the pretty, young receptionist from the Country Club and Spa, could have been a pro at the distraction game. Uncle Mick was otherwise engaged when the man in the ball cap had planted a few selected items from

Summerlea here and there in the dustier regions of the shop. When Uncle Mick left the shop to get some extra stock from the mysterious regions of the rooms behind it, the camera caught the visitor running his hand down Miranda's back, a sensuous, intimate gesture.

I knew who he was.

I recognized that gesture.

At last, I was starting to understand what had happened and why.

LOOK TO THE theater, Alleyn had said in my dream. That was what I needed to do. And I had an idea how to. I borrowed Cherie's nondescript car and dressed down in a dark hoodie I found in her hall closet. No sparkles, so she had no problem.

Larraine Gorman seemed genuinely pleased to see me when I showed up at her house while she was in the final phases of packing. I was glad to find her still there, and even happier that I'd never given her my name. I wasn't too worried that she would realize I was either a suspect or a kidnapping victim. The Gormans were focused on their moving madness, and Doug had already taken the radios and TVs to their new condo on my last visit. Anyway, as I couldn't get to Lance, she was likely to be a good source of information.

"Sorry to disturb you when you're right in the middle of all this."

"Bad timing," Doug hollered from some unseen corner.

"I enjoyed your company and talking about the books the other day. I don't have your new address and I wanted to stay in touch." I added for the unseen Doug, "I won't stay long."

I heard a grunt of approval.

"I'm so glad to see you again. I forgot to ask your name and phone number in the confusion the other day," she said, pointing a finger in what I assumed was the direction of Doug. "We don't have that many friends in this area, and it's been a tough week."

"Tell me about it," I said, with a weak grin.

She blinked when I told her about Shelby Church, a young actress found dead this week.

She pushed back her auburn hair. "That's so sad. Was she a close friend?"

"More of an acquaintance, but I need to try to find some of her colleagues to let them know about a memorial we're planning."

She shook her head, puzzled. "I'm not sure what I can do."

"If I remember correctly, you go to a lot of live theater and you keep your playbills. Or did they get thrown out the other day?"

"They did not!"

"If I could go through them, I'm sure I could find the names of some people she'd acted with and track them down. That would help a lot." I felt bad not telling Larraine the whole truth, but I couldn't risk complicating things any more. There'd be time later if we got out of this in one piece.

She didn't question it. "They're upstairs and they're organized by year. I'll bring the box with the last couple of years' playbills."

Doug thundered past her on the stairs. He was carrying some electronic equipment. He stopped and said, "Some of us are busy getting the job done. I'll be over at the condo hooking things up."

She smiled and waved, and I thought I heard her say, "Good, I need a break from the grumbling." But he was already out the side door with a slam.

Three minutes later she came downstairs with a banker's box.

I called after her, "I don't want to keep you from anything. I can certainly do this myself."

"That's probably a good idea," she said, carting the box

to the dining room and thumping it on the table. "Call me if you need another box or have a question. Good luck."

Under normal circumstances I would have loved going through those playbills. But now the stakes were too high. If I didn't find what I was looking for, I'd be in a tough spot.

A half hour later, I got my first break. I read each cast list carefully, in case Shelby was calling herself something different. I also scanned for familiar names, but no luck.

Last year's production of something called *Dirty Monkey Blues*, off-off Broadway, listed Shelby Church among the actors on a cheaply reproduced playbill. I put it aside.

I continued back in time. Larraine had seen a lot of plays. Some sounded better than others.

Shelby turned up again in the cast for something called *Beware the Treehouse*. I chuckled. I hadn't heard of any of these. I checked dozens more before I found Shelby's name again. This time the production was called *Morgue: The Musical.*

With three playbills, I started to look at the other cast members. Sure enough, two names—Brent Derringer and Tom Kovacs—showed up on *Dirty Monkey* and *Beware the Treehouse.*

Only one name was on all three. Ward Lucasky.

Larraine came puffing down the stairs. "Any luck?"

I kept my voice even. "I think so. I'll try to track them down now."

Larraine said, "If they're Equity, you should be able to find them. I can help."

"Thanks. First, I'll try to see if these are the people I'm looking for. I'll search for their images online and then circulate them to some other friends of Shelby's. I'll get in touch if I need more help."

I worried that Larraine might question my very odd story, but she was happy to help. "Too bad Doug took our printer over to the new place. I could have printed them out for you. You're taking my mind off this move."

"No problem. I can get it done. Mind if I borrow these playbills?"

I COULD NOT relax at all until I got back to Cherie's. Cherie was out, apparently on a call. Maybe she did have a real job. Once I was in the house, I went to work to find what I could about Brent Derringer, Tom Kovacs and Ward Lucasky. Google Images paid off quickly.

Brent Derringer surfaced in a number of casual and promo stills. He was big and beefy. Kev leaned over my shoulder and whistled. "Yowza, Jordie. You found Thomas, the butler."

I tried Tom Kovacs next. "Whoa," Kev said. "That's Chadwick, only not the real one. So these guys killed Chadwick and then killed Shelby to keep her quiet, right?"

I pulled up Ward Lucasky's photos.

Kev glowered. "I don't know that guy, Jordie. Go back to the others. They're the guilty ones."

I pointed at Ward Lucasky. "This is the guy who's behind it."

Kev stared at me. "What are we going to do about him?"

"We are going to fix him, but good."

Kev nodded.

I said, "He's the reason you're on the run. He set you up."

"But I don't even know him."

"It's okay. I know him. Let's get the printer going."

THE MEMORY STICK with the images from the security tapes was fingerprint free and wrapped up. In the same print-free package were copies of the playbills with Shelby and Ward Lucasky's name on them. I'd used highlighter to mark their names and the names of the other two. I'd printed out images of the three actors and added the name to each.

I addressed the package:

OFFICER TYLER DEKKER
Harrison Falls Police Dept.
1 Center Street
Harrison Falls, N.Y.
<u>**URGENT**</u>

Now, on to the next step.

On our way to that, we stopped the cable van and I took the package to a local delivery company. The dispatcher didn't give me so much as a look as she took the package. Within the hour that evidence would be at the Harrison Falls Police Station.

CHERIE WAS MAGIC. There was no doubt about that. She also had the security staff of the Country Club and Spa wrapped around her sparkly blue fingernails as she engaged their help to find her adorable mini dachshund, Starlight, who had apparently wandered onto the property. The security staff followed Cherie like puppies themselves after she waved the photo of the alleged dachshund and batted her eyelashes. Braydon looked like he'd been hypnotized. A few of the club members prepared to join in the search.

I was close enough to watch and marvel.

"She needs her meds too," Cherie said, ramping up the dramatic impetus. "And she's terribly susceptible to hypothermia. It could kill her in less than an hour." As much as I wanted to see how long she could keep them distracted, I ducked into the club. I was pretty sure that the cops would have given security my picture, as I was still a suspect—even with my "kidnapping." But with Cherie at her finest, nobody noticed me slip by and hurry down to the admin offices. Kev had done a decent job of confirming that the admin staff was in the office before we started our little act.

Miranda's eyes widened as I pushed my way into the

office. Even though I was wearing the plain, dark hoodie and sunglasses, she knew who I was, all right. She grabbed for her phone. I said, "I need to speak to Lisa Hatton. The police are closing in on Chadwick's killer, and she'll want to know who it is. There's good news."

In her office, Lisa got to her feet. Miranda left her phone and followed.

I said, "Lisa, I am Jordan Bingham. You may have been led to believe that I am responsible for Chadwick's murder, but I'm innocent. I need you to believe that. I feel so terrible about his death."

Lisa's face crumpled. "What do you want? Everyone's looking for you."

"That's just a ploy to lure the real killer. I'm here, you'll notice, walking around. Free as a bird."

"How did you get past security?"

I smiled reassuringly. "It's all going to be okay. I've just heard from my boyfriend, who is a cop in Harrison Falls, that they will be bringing a new forensics team tomorrow to go over the upstairs rooms at Summerlea again. They're looking for DNA in one of the bedrooms. There's something else. He wouldn't say what, but it was found on the scene and they believe it will link to the real murderer."

Lisa's forehead creased. "But they must have checked everything already."

"This is a pretty small place. We don't have the top teams here, but this new detective Castellano—did you meet her?"

Lisa nodded.

Miranda stared.

I said, "Lieutenant Castellano is very thorough. She called in a crack forensic team. She'll get this guy. Trust me."

Lisa sank back into her chair. "I hope they do."

Miranda gripped her desk. Her knuckles were white. "This guy?"

"Yes. Apparently there's a suspect they've been looking at for fraud and some other financial crimes, and his DNA showed up on stolen items that were planted on innocent people and also at the site where they found Shelby Church's body. The cops have reason to think they'll be able to wrap things up after they do this analysis."

In a tight voice, Miranda said, "What did they say about the suspect?"

"He didn't tell me much. He's not supposed to be in touch, but he knew I'd be happy. That's it, Lisa. I just wanted to let you know. I know how awful this has been for you."

I left her sitting there staring. Of course, I'd been weird, but, as long as the plan worked.

As I headed through the door, Miranda was already back at her desk, hand on the phone. Looking good.

I hurried out of the building and over to the vehicle. At the sign, Kev burst from car and went racing toward Cherie and the search party with the happy news that little Starlight had been found and was ready to be picked up. I could see him gesture in the direction of Starlight's unseen rescuers.

All was right with the world.

CHAPTER TWENTY

S UMMERLEA WAS DARK.
  Not only dark, but quite dangerous. I knew how per-
ilous it was going to be and gave a shiver as I thought of
Chadwick Kauffman's tragic end at the top of the wide
mahogany stairs. *Never mind,* I told myself. *We're here because
we set this up.* There was definitely more than one way to
manage a bit of theater. We entered the stage from the back
door, and only after we'd hoofed it through the wooded ravine
on the far side of the property. The center stage was intended
to be empty for the most important player. In this case, one
who thought he was in a one-man show. And the one who
was probably keeping an eye on the front entrance, in case
it was a trap.

  I knew our cast was larger. One person had gone ahead,
and two more would be creeping after me. We had to assume
that we might be observed if we arrived from the front or
used flashlights in our approach from the back. I imagined
muffled curses as they stumbled over some unexpected rocks
and picked their way up the steep, wooded bank. I always

worry when Kev's involved. After the rain, last night's sky had been bright and clear with sparkling constellations and a crisp moon. Even though the moon was full tonight, the sky was murky and overcast. The few breaks in the cloud cover were welcome, though, and possibly kept some of us from plunging into the ravine. We'd wanted that overcast sky as we ran, one at a time, bending low so we wouldn't be spotted, even though our clothes were dark and we wore balaclavas.

I wished I'd thought ahead about how to manage the squeak of some of the old doors in Summerlea as I tiptoed into the back of the building. Already, after a few days, you could feel the property decline. The dark and the chill air combined with Chadwick's death all played a part in the desolate mood. I left the door slightly ajar so that the others could enter. When the alarm didn't sound, I knew that Cherie had been successful in the first of her tasks. The alarm system would be rearmed as soon as we were in.

As long as they could keep it quiet. When he arrived it was essential for our star player to believe he was alone and unobserved. He needed to be convinced that he had a job to do and that time was not on his side.

If the scene at the Country Club and Spa had played out properly, he would indeed believe that. If it hadn't, I was going to be in more trouble than I'd ever been in before.

"Ouch." Someone didn't catch themselves in time, and the sound escaped. Behind me I heard a sharp gasp. Not Kev, though. I'd suspected it would be a mistake to bring Kev along and therefore he had a task of his own. Outside and alone, but essential.

I figured I knew who the gasper was, but this wasn't the time to lay blame on one's relatives. No one wore scent. We wore soft soles that wouldn't squish. Any light bits on the soles had been blackened with marker. It had been essential to do this right. No one had a device that would beep, emit light or otherwise give us away. With Kev, there would have always been that risk.

Our challenge was the number of possible exits. Summerlea was awash in French doors, sliding partitions, cleverly hidden staircases for servants, closets and so much more. I needed my watchers to make sure our key player didn't vanish into the night if he spotted us. We needed to have every eventuality covered. Apparently, we also should have been able to see in the dark. Or at least count steps accurately.

Seconds later, we were all feeling our way along walls, counting steps and in some cases praying. There was no way to know if everyone was in the right place. All we had to do was wait.

When it's important to keep quiet and not twitch, itch, squirm, moan, yawn or otherwise betray your presence, your body will do its best to blow your cover. The damp sent chills through my spine. I felt a sneeze coming on. I was pretty sure the others were fighting burps, flatulence and sudden spasms. Life's like that.

What felt like a week later, our play began. Well, it was probably half an hour.

The front door rattled. We heard what sounded like a lock turning. The door squeaked a bit too. Good, if anyone had dozed off, that should have jolted them awake.

The soft pad of footsteps was next, getting closer. My heart was racing. If our plan was successful, we'd be face-to-face with a murderer.

As the footsteps stopped by the security console and someone presumably keyed in the secret code, I switched on the grand chandelier.

The hallway flooded with light. Frozen in front of us, was our target. "Jackpot," as the uncles would say.

"Hello, Lucas," I said. "Or should I say Ward Lucasky?"

His jaw dropped. That gave me a lot of satisfaction, but I knew better than to let down my guard. The glow from the chandelier highlighted the face that could break a heart and empty a bank account before you could blink. A handsome and dangerous face.

"Fancy meeting you here," I added jauntily. I leaned against the mahogany paneled wall. I was hoping to convey an air of insouciance, but really my legs were about to buckle. Lucas could always have that effect on me. Okay, maybe some of it was because he had a gun in his hand. Guns and legs are a bad combo.

He found his voice. "I hear the police are about to catch up with you."

"I have the best lawyer anywhere," I gloated. "Too bad he's mine, because you're going to need someone exceptional when they get through charging you."

He snorted. "Charging me with what?"

"Where to start?"

"Why not start with what are you doing here?"

"Nice one. I like the arrogant touch, as if you owned the place. The real question is what are *you* doing here?"

"I followed you. You had no business coming to Summerlea. I wanted to warn you off. There was a time when we were very fond of each other. I would hate to see you rot in prison."

"Nice attempt at a save," I shot back. "But I will now be able to inform the police that you are here, as I told them you would be." I lifted my iPhone and started to key in 911.

He shook his head. With the slightest of sneers, he said, "I don't think so. Unless you want me to shoot you."

I let the hand with the phone drop to my side, dramatically.

"It's a shame," he said, "really. You're beautiful but you're a real pain in the—"

"Lucas, I don't believe you would really shoot me."

"I'm afraid I have to. You know too much, and, as you said, you'll lead the cops to me. I can't have that."

I said with a calm I did not feel, "You brought it on yourself. Why did you drag me into this in the first place? What was the purpose of the whole elaborate setup with the luncheon and the books and all that?"

"Well, it *was* April Fool's Day, and you know I love a good joke."

"Right. You love any joke at someone else's expense."

"What's the point of a practical joke if it's not at someone else's expense? Sometimes you're a bit dim, Jordan."

"No doubt, but why pick on me?"

"You really shouldn't have tried to turn me in after that misunderstanding about your bank account."

"You mean when you cleaned out my savings?"

"You know what happened when the college found out? That was it for me. Out the door. You've ruined my career. You put an end to my education. The cops spoke to my parents. No one in my family will speak to me now. Are you happy? You really twisted the knife. You did everything you could to ruin my life. I'm going to make absolutely sure you never try anything like that again."

I stood there, openmouthed and astonished. How could he twist my actions that way? How could he ignore his role in what happened? How was I the bad guy?

I sputtered, "But you were the one who stole from me!"

"We were in a relationship. What happened to sharing?"

"All the sharing was one-way. And what about my credit cards? You maxed them out. My credit rating ended up in the toilet."

He shrugged. That was not the response I wanted. I added, "That was just nasty and . . . unsporting."

"Oh, grow up. These things happen."

"I was in love with you."

The beautiful lips smiled. Not a nice smile. "Whatever. What's yours is mine and what's mine is yours. Don't you remember saying that?"

"It doesn't sound like me." In fact, it didn't sound like anything a Kelly would say except for the "what's yours is mine" part. "I never told you to help yourself to the money I needed for grad school. You forged my signature. That was a crime."

"Well, you had your bit of revenge, didn't you?"

"Sort of. But it was two years ago this month, and you

haven't been prosecuted. There's been more than enough time to move on." I'd dropped the charges at my uncles' urging. No point in drawing any attention to our family, they'd said. A good defense lawyer could turn up the odd embarrassment. At the time I'd wondered if some of my educational savings might have had suspect origins. Not that it mattered, because Lucas had made sure they vanished into his pocket.

I glared at him as he said, "There would never be enough time for me to forget what you did to me. And now I will get my revenge. No one messes with Lucas Warden."

It was time to pick up the pace if the unfolding drama was to have its denouement and if our final big scene was not to involve me in a bleeding heap on the floor.

"Fine. I regret reporting it to the police in the first place. I cared about you. I guess I still do."

He actually sniffed. What an ego.

I piled it on. "But why was it necessary to involve Vera Van Alst and Uncle Kev in your scheme? You could have pulled the stunt with just me. I could have carried Vera's money."

"Where would be the fun in that?" he chuckled.

"I don't get it," I said.

He grinned. "It wasn't enough to get the money. I wanted your life turned upside down. Like mine was. This was the perfect setup. Chadwick would discover the books missing. Then the police would be called. There would be plenty of evidence that you were at Summerlea. The police would come calling. You would spin this ridiculous story of an invitation for Vera, you, the lowly researcher, and your uncle with the criminal record. Chadwick would recover his property from Vera Van Alst. She would hold you responsible for the loss of her ten thousand dollars. Being the witch she is, you'd lose your job. Your uncle would be immediately under suspicion for theft."

"That explains the loot from Summerlea you tucked behind the bush by the driveway at Van Alst House. I guess you wanted to make sure that Uncle Kev was charged no matter what."

"It's your own fault. You never should have told me all your family secrets and that you were the first one to go straight."

"Explains a lot." I wondered for a second if it explained why I'd fallen for this monster.

He laughed. "Your new life, which, face it, is not that great, living in an attic and taking orders from that ratty old harridan—"

"I love what I do."

"And all that would be gone. And you asked for it, didn't you?"

I hadn't asked for anything, but I needed to keep playing along. "What made you think of me, Lucas, after all this time?"

"I saw your name in the local paper when Shelby dragged me to this area to meet her stupid parents. There you were. Little Miss Hero. Solved a murder, saved her boss. Full of herself. It gave me a great idea for making you pay."

"I'm beginning to understand. And that bouquet of dead roses? Was that just a finger in my eye?" I wondered how much of his connection to Harrison Falls was a coincidence. He'd obviously burned with anger at what he saw as my betrayal. Had he picked Shelby because of that?

"Got to you, did they? That was the idea."

"I see you went to quite a bit of trouble to make it creepy. What happened to you, Lucas? What changed you from a charming scoundrel to a murderer?"

He narrowed his eyes at me.

"That's right. I did say 'murderer.' Did Chadwick show up unexpectedly?"

His nostrils flared.

I needed him to talk, not nod, shrug, smirk or flare his nostrils. "Did Miranda let you down? She had it bad for you, didn't she?"

He smirked.

"She had access to Chadwick's keys. It was easy for her to get a copy made. She could find out the code. Of course, she knew when he'd be away."

"Stupid girl. She told me he'd gone to Manhattan for a meeting. She claimed the house was empty."

"But she lied. Why did she do that? Had she found out about Shelby? Did she realize you were just using her?"

"Yes, she lied, and it's on her that he died."

"And Chadwick died because he found you on his property?"

His mouth twisted.

"Oh," I said, "let me think how that could have happened. You had to be there, of course, watching your production. You wouldn't have been able to resist being at Summerlea during the luncheon. Must have been fun. Did Brent Derringer and Tom Kovacs—your old acting buddies—depart the minute their parts were played? Did you pay them? Are they a couple of scam artists too? Or did you have something on them?"

"You always did think you were smarter than everyone."

I kept talking. "When they took off, did that leave you with the new woman in your life here in this grand house to celebrate your windfall? Were you 'celebrating' with Shelby in one of those luxurious bedrooms upstairs?"

He actually blinked. "How did you know that?"

"It wasn't hard to figure out. Chadwick must have been attacked upstairs. Not many people would be strong enough to have carried his body up that staircase. Therefore you must have been upstairs first to attack him. If he'd felt he needed help, he'd have picked up the phone and called the police."

"He came charging like a lunatic, waving that statue at me."

"Oh really? Chadwick never waved that statue. His prints would have been on it if he had, and there was only one set of prints: Uncle Kev's. And we both know that Kev didn't kill Chadwick. You did."

"Clever girl."

"That's right. Thomas—or should I say Tom Kovacs—spotted Kev fondling it and told you before you left. My guess is that, for some reason, you took that statue, wearing gloves, of course. Maybe you were thinking of planting that somewhere too. Then what happened? Did Chadwick show up?"

"I liked that little statue. I thought I'd keep it as a souvenir of our afternoon. But then, that old fool went for me. I was just defending myself."

"Oh please. Self-defense? But Chadwick was killed while you were committing a felony, so naturally that won't be worth anything to you during your trial. Did he find things a bit off and go looking to see if someone was in the house?"

"I won't be on trial, and I'm starting to get bored," Lucas said with a yawn.

You're going to keep talking, I thought.

"So what happened? Did Shelby scream? Did poor Chadwick think he was saving a woman from an attack? No one's going to buy that."

"I don't know what he thought, but he came at me."

"So let's see, a forty-three-year-old man, pudgy and out of shape, not used to violence, rushes up the stairs to confront an intruder, barges into the bedroom and attacks you."

"Yeah, that was a bad break for him. I did what I had to."

"Except you'd left those gloves on—or put them on again—and hit him on the back of the head. Was he running away at that point? You made sure there weren't any of your fingerprints, because you were known to the police as a result of my complaint and maybe others. And then, once you'd killed Chadwick, you hurled him down the stairs."

"The situation got away from me—"

"And of course, Chadwick recognized Shelby when he discovered her upstairs in the bedroom. She must have freaked."

"She was a silly, nervous thing, not nearly as intelligent as she looked. She started screaming when she saw him. How stupid was that? She should have just laughed it off, explained and apologized for our romantic interlude in his 'country house.'"

I wasn't sure that Chadwick or anyone would have bought that. Not with keys and codes involved. "But silly and nervous or not, she was the person who brought you into contact with Summerlea. She was your entrée into that kind of society. Lots of wealthy young women to plunder, trust accounts to play with once Shelby was stripped clean. And you managed that, didn't you? Her car was being repossessed. She was being hounded for debts that you'd actually incurred."

He practically spat. "Spoiled brats. You think they deserve their privilege, these rich bitches? Who cares what happens to them?"

"I'm guessing she wanted out even before Chadwick was killed. She was jumpy and nervous during the whole luncheon scene. But I'm sure you had a hold over her. Did she steal from her parents? Was that what you were holding over her head? Then with Chadwick's murder, she started to fall apart. She became hysterical when I saw her at the gallery. Now she was in too deep to walk away. Did you decide then to get rid of her?"

He shrugged. "It's all water under the bridge now. But you have to admit, it's worked out according to plan in the end."

"You mean with me, Vera and Kev accused of murder rather than breaking, entering and theft?"

"Exactly."

"Thank you for calling the police with those tips. That brought us a lot of grief. And then planting stuff on my uncle Mick beforehand. He didn't have anything to do with this."

"That was the idea. I thought it was a laugh. And it got to you, didn't it? As I said, you brought it on yourself."

The best plan was to play to his massive, twisted ego and give the psychopath in front of me a few ego strokes. "I see you've been very clever with all this. I have to admire your entire plan. It was brilliant. You get even, I get blamed. My friends and family get damaged."

"You don't have to tell me it was brilliant. I thought it up."

"Tell you what, Lucas. Because of what we used to have together and because I can't help but admire your ingenuity with this whole production, I'll just head out and that's the last any of us will hear of this. Not a word from me."

"Get real. Do you think I'm falling for that? With the police crawling all over the county looking for you? You'd blab everything you know about me before the door shuts behind you."

"But that's not going to happen. You have some stuff on my family, and that's enough for me to keep my mouth closed."

"Right. It's not going to happen because you are going to be dead."

I injected a little shake into my voice. "Come on, Lucas. We were in love once."

"Don't think so."

"That would make three people you'll have killed, Lucas. Is it getting easier?"

I heard a small rustle in the darkness. I only prayed he hadn't heard it too. Apparently not. He was too focused on me. And not in a good way.

"You know what? It is getting easier. And you don't know the half of it."

A cold shiver ran over my body.

Lucas kept talking. "And don't bother trying to trick me. The conversation's over. It doesn't matter what you say. You're too much of a risk to keep around. And I have so many reasons for my revenge."

"You don't mean that!" I was hoping against hope that everything was in place as it should have been.

"I do. But feel free to beg. I think I'm entitled to that after all the trouble that you brought me."

"Trouble that I—? Wait a minute. Please think about this. You don't want to hurt me. I could even help you. And if they find another body here, it's just a matter of time before someone breaks down and fingers you."

"They won't be finding another body here. And they'll never find your body where you're going."

"What are you talking about? They found Shelby where you dumped her corpse."

"That was different. I didn't plan that. I had to do what I had to do to shut her up. But at least I was able to point the finger at you."

"You phoned in another police tip, I suppose?"

He smirked again. "You really shouldn't have chased her out of that gallery and then followed us. You and your pet librarian were the obvious suspects. You make it too easy for me. You forgot that I'd seen you in every imaginable wig when you were onstage. I know the way you move, the way you walk. You couldn't fool me with that getup."

Time to manipulate his vanity. It was the only tool I had left. "You're a despicable human being, a psychopath. You've caused a lot of misery to many people. You've murdered two, and you've just threatened to murder me. Furthermore, you're not as good-looking as you used to be. You're getting a little jowly. Put on a bit of weight. I see that your hairline is receding. You won't be able to play the leading man for much longer the way you're going. But the other inmates may still find you attractive in prison when you get there."

I needed him off balance, emotional. I guess I succeeded. "But I'm not going to prison, Jordan." This time he raised the gun.

I shouted "NOW!" and dove to the side, rolling toward the open mahogany pocket doors that led to the parlor. When I stuck my head out a minute later, Uncle Kev had Lucas in a headlock. Uncle Lucky was sitting on his back. Soon, they moved out of view, and Officer Tyler Dekker fastened handcuffs on Lucas while doing a great job of reading him his rights. Quite a multitasker, our Smiley.

Lucas wasn't planning to go without a fight. He kicked out hard at Smiley's knee and connected hard. Smiley gave a grunt of pain but got those handcuffs on. Lucas tried to arch his back without success. Uncle Lucky is no lightweight. I knew I could count on him.

Lucas swore and bellowed, "I'll kill you! You're dead, every one of you."

"Sheesh," said Smiley, standing and rubbing his knee. "Assaulting an officer of the law? And then a death threat? Make my day."

"Hey," I said, with a wobble in my voice. "And threatening me isn't bad enough?"

"With all due respect," he shouted over Lucas's raving, "this was a crazy idea for you to meet a killer here, Miss Bingham. It was just lucky for you that I got an anonymous call on my cell phone while I was off duty not too far away."

"But who could have called you? No one else knew I was coming here." Unlike Smiley, I had been very good on the stage.

He shrugged. "I'm sure they'll trace the call."

They wouldn't, because the burner Kev used would have already been tossed into the lake. Even if they brought it to the surface, it wouldn't tell them a thing.

"A tip? And what did the tip say?"

"The caller told me if I came in through the back door, I'd find Chadwick's killer and maybe save another life. From the look of things, I got here just in time."

Kev was flushed with pride. He'd managed to make that prearranged call to Tyler without screwing up. Of course, Kev hadn't been able to resist coming into the house instead of remaining outside as agreed. Good thing that Tyler Dekker had been in on the sting. I was glad he wasn't the kind of guy who let his mail pile up and he'd opened the envelope I'd sent him. And he'd trusted me.

I hoped Smiley's career in the police took off, because he sure wouldn't make it as an actor. But he didn't need to. While Smiley called for backup, I skipped around the corner and found Cherie with a huge candy-pink grin splitting her face.

"Did you get everything?" I said.

"I got it all right. And it's beautiful. Even better than beautiful. You know, I think a person could enjoy doing this for a living. I edited out the bit that shows Kev and Lucky. No point in complicating things. And even if the cops might notice the video's been edited, it's not likely they'll be able to get it back."

"Good thinking. You sure have the gift for taping evidence. I'm not sure how many opportunities there will be for business, but my money's on you," I said. She was truly a perfect fit for my family. Perhaps we should make her an honorary Kelly.

As the adrenaline in my system faded, I wanted the night to be over and Lucas Warden to be safely behind bars. I needed to know he wouldn't outwit the police, because he was capable of it. I wanted to be free to go home and to tell Vera and the signora that we were no longer suspects in a murder case. I wanted to tell Mick he didn't have to worry anymore about being charged with possession of stolen goods and Lance that his job and freedom wouldn't be threatened.

But of course, there were hours of interviews to get through first. It was just as well that Uncle Lucky, Kev and Cherie were able to melt like ice cubes into the dark night. They wouldn't have been at their best under those circumstances. Good thing they'd all worn gloves too.

For once I was happy to hear sirens in the driveway.

CHAPTER TWENTY-ONE

WHEN THE DUST settles, there's no place like home. Not that Van Alst House had been my home for long or would be home forever, but I was back again, and it sure felt like home to me. I had barely stopped myself from kissing the floor when I finally returned at two thirty in the morning after our great adventure.

Vera met me at the back door, in her tartan dressing gown. If it wasn't totally out of character, I might have thought she'd been nervously hanging around for my arrival. I couldn't help noticing that she'd brought a book to read while she waited for me.

Walter scampered merrily to me.

"Your police officer friend dropped him off earlier today. He said you'd be missing him."

"Hmm. Well, the big news tonight is that they've got the person who killed Chadwick, and Shelby Church. In case you don't know, Shelby was the woman pretending to be Lisa Troy. We have good recorded evidence—audio and video—

against him. It adds up to a confession, really. And more to the point, we are all off the hook."

"About time," Vera sniffed.

"Agreed. I'll fill you in with the details in the morning if that's okay." I wasn't looking forward to telling Vera that my former boyfriend was the reason we'd all been dragged through this hellish week. More to the point, that relationship was why Vera had been of interest to the police. My head would be clearer in the morning. Vera was always in a bad mood at breakfast, and maybe I would think of a decent spin to put on it.

Vera said, "Mr. Kelly gave us quite a play-by-play before he left to visit a friend. He's staying over at the friend's place tonight."

"Oh, is he?" And what had he told Vera? Accuracy isn't Kev's best thing. He probably came out as a hero.

"Yes. You were lucky to have him with you when you did."

"Indeed," I said and left it at that.

All the time we were talking, the signora was beckoning me to the dining room. I was dead beat after the days we'd had and the relief of Lucas's capture. My black clothes were muddy from the ravine. My hair was a mess from the bala-clava. And I was pretty fried from the encounter with Lucas and his gun.

"Stop fussing, Fiammetta. Let her take a breath. We are not going to the dining room. Have a bath, Miss Bingham," Vera said. "Relax. Fiammetta will bring your meal to your room. This once we can dispense with protocol and, please, don't feel you must eat anything."

The signora crossed herself.

Vera added, "But I should warn you: Fiammetta will not rest until you do."

"Thank you, Vera." I was proud that I didn't make a single remark about the fact it was three in the morning. Not a time to eat, you might think, but then you might not have quite the same delivery service.

She added, "I don't think it will be necessary for you to arrive for breakfast at eight. Whenever you're ready will be fine."

I managed not to fall over at that. But it was good. I decided that Uncle Kev hadn't filled Vera in on the particulars of my connection to the killer. Just as well. I'd have to own up soon enough, once I'd had some sleep. At that moment, all I could do was grin like a fool.

"And Miss Bingham."

"Yes, Vera?"

"You know, I really do believe that this all calls for a party. Fiammetta has enough to feed the multitudes between one freezer and the other."

Maybe I was already dreaming.

THE EVENING MOOD was festive, in the way that the dropping of criminal charges and getting a murderer locked up can lift the spirits. I'd had a happy week to recover, catching up on my sleep with Walter, Good Cat and—although that may have been a dream—even Bad Cat.

Although we usually dine at eight (and not one minute later, Miss Bingham), tonight we were in a formal mood. Our dinner would take place at nine, and we were enjoying what Vera referred to as preprandial libation in the rarely used parlor next to the dining room. The evening light added a glow to the proceedings, as did the blaze in the fireplace. Tonight Vera had pulled out all the stops. As a rule, on a cool April evening, we'd be bundled up in Van Alst House, but you'd never have known it on this occasion.

Vera seemed marginally less grumpy than usual, which is her way of showing euphoria. It seemed that the executor of the estate had agreed to let Vera have the Marsh books once they were no longer required as evidence. The executor felt this would be an appropriate expression of gratitude for our part in catching Chadwick's killer and his accomplices. Vera had on the blue silk blouse I had purchased for her to celebrate an earlier narrow escape. I think she was wearing it to send a message to me. The message was received with pleasure. The fact our troubles had been caused by a person from my past was not a problem.

"Let us not forget Muriel Delgado, Miss Bingham," she had said by way of absolution.

I was not likely to forget our nemesis from last fall.

Kev was buzzing about like a demented wasp. He'd just finished showing Cherie every nook and cranny of the house. I was pretty sure she already knew the place, but why rain on his parade? I hoped she'd enjoyed the dumbwaiter and the spiders in the attics.

The signora pirouetted into and out of the parlor, beaming and apparently speaking in tongues. I peered through the crack in the oak pocket doors that separated us from the dining room. Every time she returned that way, she fiddled with the place settings and adjusted the crystal glasses to the point where I wondered if she'd been binge-watching *Downton Abbey.*

As for the guests, we were all standing somewhat stiffly, sharing cocktails that Cherie had prepared. She'd found some interesting recipes. I was pretty sure that the "grappa" that was billed as an ingredient in my favorite of the cocktails— the one called I Have No Fear of Death—was actually a product of Uncle Kev's dismantled still. A more timid person might refuse a moonshine cocktail with a name like that, but I'd been through the wars and felt some residual bravery.

Everyone in the room seemed to believe that they were personally responsible for solving the mystery that had led to Chadwick Kauffman's murder.

Drea Castellano wore a simple scarlet silk shift dress. Under normal conditions, she would already have hypothermia, but tonight, near the fireplace, it was perfect. She looked so good that I feared Uncle Mick would have a coronary. His face was the color of that dress. His gold chains glinted at her from the luxurious bed of ginger chest hair that all the Kelly men are so proud of. He gazed up at her with something like awe. She tilted her head and watched him much as a scientist might watch a lab rat, with silent but worrisome interest.

I wasn't thrilled that Vera had decided to include Castellano and Stoddard in our grand celebration dinner. They were well aware of my family connections, and who knew what they'd try to ferret out about the Kelly clan while they were with us. Another worry was what might turn up about Cherie. Cherie was a treasure, practically my favorite person in the world lately. I would have hated to see this party bring her trouble. Never mind. I shook my head. We were all adults, it was a great night and we had plenty to be happy about.

Meanwhile, Uncle Mick had clamped his hairy Kelly paw onto Castellano's toned arm. I tried to telegraph a warning to him. She was probably capable of flipping him across the room where he'd crack his hard Kelly head on the marble fireplace surround and that would be the end of him. But she seemed to be having a good time. I only hoped Uncle Mick wasn't so besotted that he dropped hints as to the nature of his current enterprise, whatever it was. However, on balance, his fascination with her was a good thing, as it took the pressure off me and my relationship with Smiley.

Speaking of Smiley, he was still working on getting that smile back after his first glug of the moonshine cocktail. Maybe he did have a fear of death. Oh well. I was sure he'd get his grin and his voice back eventually.

"Don't say I didn't warn you," was my only comment.

Vera might have gotten dressed up and even clipped on one of her Art Deco diamond brooches, but I noticed she was still working on a crossword in the corner. Uncle Lucky was standing next to her, and that would have suited both of them just fine. I shook my head at Uncle Lucky just in case he'd thought the clasp on that brooch was a bit loose.

Near the bow window, Lance had struck up a conversation

with Cherie. They had a certain theatricality in common, and I shouldn't have been surprised. Both were talking with their hands and sharing. I did my best not to be jealous. After all, what would I do without either one of them?

Kev was busy attempting to refill drinks. Most of us managed to cover our glass with our palms before he descended with the cocktail pitcher. Stoddard was the exception. With one hand he held his cocktail, and with the other Stoddard managed to snag the *prosciutto crudo* canapés that the signora was currently circulating with. He also eyed our special guest, Larraine Gorman, who was looking glamorous with her wild and wavy auburn hair and a deep-purple dress with a low neck. Without her playbills, we never would have found Lucas and his accomplices. Larraine didn't seem to notice, but Doug, suddenly possessive, gave the detective a dirty look.

Our last guest to arrive was Sammy Vincovic, who blew into the room like a tropical storm. Even before dinner, his suit was straining at the seams. He seemed to be in great spirits, considering the amount of money he might have made from a trial.

"Don't worry about me," he said, generously. "Things have a way of workin' out. You're looking good, by the way."

"Thank you," I said with pleasure. I was wearing my raspberry dress again.

Sammy glanced down to see that Walter and both the Siamese were advancing toward him. Good Cat sidled up and managed a silky caress against one leg. Bad Cat headed for the other.

I gasped. "Look out!" But it appeared that Sammy was invincible, a nice trait in defense counsel.

By the time we all sat down at the long Sheraton table, set with gleaming silver and glittering crystal, more than one truce seemed to have been struck. I was seated between Smiley and Sammy. Everyone watched with interest as Uncle Kev poured the wine. Vera had produced several bottles that had been aging expensively in the Van Alst wine cellar since her father placed them there, back in the day.

Sammy broke the silence that settled over our odd little group. He nodded at Castellano and Stoddard. "So, Detectives, I understand you've both received commendations for your work on the Chadwick Kauffman case."

Castellano nodded gravely, although she did narrow her eyes a bit. Probably wondering what Sammy was up to. Stoddard just showed most of his teeth in a grin. I attributed much of that grin to the moonshine cocktail.

Castellano added, "As did Officer Dekker."

Vera said, "Good for Officer Dekker. Perhaps he'll become Detective Dekker after this."

Stoddard merely slouched a bit more. You could tell he didn't care for that idea.

Castellano said after an embarrassingly long minute, "Unfortunately, we have no openings for detectives for the foreseeable future.

Naturally, the telltale pink blush transformed Smiley's face.

Sammy helped deflect our attention by leaning back in his seat and saying, "So everything's cleared up now?"

Castellano said, "Pretty much. We've turned up the delivery driver who saw Miss Van Alst, Kevin Kelly and Jordan Bingham leave Summerlea. He confirms that there were still people in the house after you left."

I blurted, "I told you he was real. But after Lucas admitted on tape what he'd done, why do you need to keep checking with witnesses?"

Stoddard said, "We have to dot every i and cross every t. We even found the caterer who delivered the food for the luncheon, and we can connect her to Shelby Church, not that we can charge the caterer with anything. She appears to be above board."

I knew that it was Smiley who'd done that footwork, even though there was no way he'd be breaking in as a detective.

Castellano gave Stoddard a poisonous look. "More important, Miranda Schneider broke down under questioning and admitted her roles in the crimes, including planting stolen goods in Michael Kelly's Fine Antiques."

"You had evidence of that."

"Everything matters. Lawyers can make everything look different in court. We needed to nail down her testimony. Lucas Warden had dumped her once he got what he wanted. After Chadwick Kauffman died, he convinced her that she'd been an accessory to murder for providing the key and the security code. She was trapped, but now she'll testify against him in return for a deal. She is terrified."

"Rightly so," said Lance.

I wondered about Miranda. How different were we? We'd both been deceived by a psychopath. I was the lucky one. He only got my money and he gave me a few scary days. He hadn't involved me in someone else's murder.

Vera raised her crystal wineglass. "To our detectives, for a job well done."

Castellano and Stoddard were a bit more respectful when it came to Vera. After all, they had been involved in a concerted attempt to prove that she'd been complicit in Chadwick's death, based on phony tips from a killer. That sort of thing can mess with a career. I believed that what are known as the "higher-ups" may have whispered in their ears about making nice. Now, apparently, all was forgiven, and this meeting of the mutual admiration society was proof.

We all raised our glasses dutifully. I managed not to shout that if they'd had their way, Vera, Kev and I would be awaiting trial now. But I knew—and they knew I knew—that they'd been set up and manipulated by a pro. Only Smiley got full marks on this one, and I was the one person who really appreciated the full story there. I felt two other unseen guests, Inspector Roderick Alleyn and his lovely wife, Agatha Troy. I raised my glass to Alleyn for his advice: Look to the theater.

After the soup course—while the signora was serving her superb homemade spinach fettuccine with a light tomato sauce and a dusting of fresh Parmesan—Castellano said, "I know we agreed not to talk about the case tonight, but I would like everyone to know that through some excellent work by Officer Dekker we were able to track down Brent Derringer and Tom Kovacs. They've been arrested for their part in the scam at Summerlea and, not surprisingly, they've also rolled over on Lucas, whom they knew as Ward Lucasky. Looks like they all met in New York, off-off Broadway, unless we need another "off" or two. All of them were less-than-successful actors, willing to take a chance to make a few bucks. Now they're accessories to murder. I call that a happy ending."

Everyone either chuckled or applauded at this.

Across the table I made eye contact with Larraine. A small smile played around her lips. I winked at her, and she raised her wineglass and gave me a wonderful, mysterious smile. I planned to do something nice for her. She seemed to be enjoying her dinner here at Van Alst House. She'd earned it, as she'd been the key to finding the bad guys. I'd always be grateful, and I was glad to have her as a friend. I looked forward to some theater excursions with her in the future. Doug was mercifully silent, a tribute to those cocktails.

The dinner was a triumph for the signora. Everyone ate with enthusiasm. She does love that. After the pasta, the turkey scaloppine was a masterpiece with that perfect lemon and parsley sauce. How she'd managed to make risotto while pulling off the rest of it was beyond me. She refused help, no matter how many offers she got. We're used to that.

I felt a rush of happiness, and not just because I knew there was tiramisu for dessert.

I STOOD ON the broad front porch of Van Alst House, enjoying a peek at the new moon. Smiley stood beside me. Walter danced around us happily.

We watched the twinkling taillights as Lance and Sammy Vincovic, Uncle Mick, Uncle Lucky and Karen, the Gormans, Castellano and Stoddard left.

"Nice detective work, Officer Dekker."

Even in the dim light, I knew he flushed. He squeezed my hand. "Next time, I'll do better."

"With luck, there won't be a next time with a murder involved," I said, squeezing back.

"I have something to tell you."

I turned to him.

"We can't go on like this."

My happiness evaporated. I yanked my hand back.

He kept talking. "Hear me out. I'm not breaking up with you. But we have to face it, my job and your family connections are always going to be an issue here in Harrison Falls."

I wasn't planning on leaving. Did that mean he was?

He said, "I've been offered a position as a detective in Cabot. Just got the offer tonight."

"You'll be a detective? That's what you've wanted. But when did you apply?"

"About a month ago. Before all this started. I was waiting until I heard to tell you, and then all hell broke loose. I want us to be able to be together without worrying about conflict of interest and pretending to break up with you whenever you or one of your relatives . . ."

I knew what he meant.

"I don't know anyone in Cabot. It's what . . . a half hour from here?"

"About that. It's in the next county and an easy drive in either direction."

"That could work."

He grinned. "Maybe. You have any uncles there?"

"No connection with the town of Cabot at all."

"That should seal the deal."

I felt a thrill of hope. "Castellano is going to be—"

"Yup. She's got plans for me, and tomorrow will not be a good day. But I only need to give two weeks' notice, and she did say there would be no detective position for me here."

"When do you start?"

"A month from today. I need to put my house on the market, and I have some vacation to use up."

He pulled some papers from his pocket.

"What's this?" I said.

"Tickets."

"Tickets for what? A play?"

"A trip together. Our first vacation."

"But where?"

"Somewhere I know you'd love to visit with me."

"Somewhere romantic?"

"You bet." The man was becoming a tease.

"Let me see."

Laughing, I reached for the tickets, just as Vera opened the door.

RECITES

TIRAMISU ALLA SIGNORA

Tiramisu means "pick-me-up" in Italian, and it sure does the trick. As she adapts or invents many of her recipes, Signora Panetone's tiramisu doesn't contain ladyfingers or custard, or eggs. Instead, chocolate cake and lots of mascarpone cheese form the base. Tiramisu sure does pick up the mood around Van Alst House. There's never any left, so you will have to make your own.

8 ounces plain chocolate cake (homemade or purchased)
¼ cup very strong, fresh, hot coffee
¼ cup good-quality DARK rum
1 cup whipping cream
½ cup sugar
1 tsp real vanilla extract
1 cup mascarpone cheese, room temperature
Grated zest of ½ orange (optional)
½ cup coarsely grated bittersweet chocolate

Cut cake into slices. Place the slices in a shallow dish—only one layer. Combine coffee and rum. Sprinkle over the cake.

Whip cream, sugar and vanilla until stiff peaks form.

In a separate bowl beat mascarpone until softened. Fold in the whipped cream, gently. Do not overbeat.

Arrange ⅓ of the cake slices in an attractive, shallow bowl. Layer over ⅓ of the cream mixture and ⅓ of the orange zest (if using). Sprinkle ⅓ of the grated chocolate evenly over the layer.

Repeat for two more layers, ending with a lovely dusting of chocolate on top.

Cover with plastic wrap. This dessert is best the next day, but make sure you chill for at least four hours.

CRISPY ROSEMARY CROSTINI

The signora never wastes anything, even bread. That's a good thing, because slices of baguette (or slices of leftover ciabatta bread) turn into these crispy snack breads.

4 rosemary sprigs
½ cup good olive oil
Slices of baguette or ciabatta bread (about a half loaf)
Sea salt

Add the rosemary sprigs to the olive oil well in advance. The day before is better. Of course, the signora has oil with herbs in her cupboard all the time. You might consider this too as it amps up many dishes and salad dressings.

Preheat oven to 350°F.

Place sliced bread on a metal baking sheet and brush both sides of bread with rosemary oil. Bake for about 10 minutes until brown.

Turn slices over. Sprinkle sea salt lightly on top.

Bake for another 10 minutes.

Cool and enjoy. You can top with salsa, white bean dip, cheese or whatever your favorite topping or dip is. Jordan likes to eat the crostini as is, and Uncle Kev steals them right out of the oven. We do not recommend that.

SCALOPPINE AL LIMONE

Everyone loves it when the signora serves these tender and delicious chicken cutlets.

6 small boneless chicken breasts (or turkey)
3 tablespoons flour
1½ tablespoons olive oil
3 tablespoons finely chopped fresh parsley
Juice and grated zest of one large lemon
2–3 tablespoons dry white wine
Sea salt and freshly ground peppers
Extra parsley, lemon wedges or zest for garnish

If chicken pieces are large, cut in half. If they are thick, slice them in half. It is very important to make sure they are thin enough. Cover each piece of poultry with a sheet of plastic wrap. Pound the scaloppine with a mallet or a cup or a rolling pin until they are ¼ inch thick. This is pretty easy but also essential.

Coat with flour and shake off excess.

Heat two tablespoons of oil in the pan. Sear the chicken quickly on both sides, and then sprinkle with parsley, lemon juice and zest and white wine. Add remaining oil if needed.

Lower the heat and cook for about five minutes. Turn chicken over again. Season with S & P and cook for about five minutes until just cooked through.

Serve at once with lemon and parsley as garnish. They are great with rice, potatoes or pasta.